Prologue

Pontassieve, Italy

The Past

In a vineyard in the Tuscan countryside surrounded by the gentle hills of Santa Brigida a boy sat amongst rich green vines shaded from a hot sun. He drew angry circles in the soil with a twig as he listened to the shrieks of his brother being chased by their father along the tracks between them. He might have joined the game, but he couldn't dismiss the feeling that his presence would rob it of something. He longed for the cool of the farmhouse's terracotta floors and the noisy comfort of his mother's kitchen, but he did not move. He remained, as he always did, watching them until they grew tired and he was able to trail behind them as they headed home.

Francesco had turned eleven three weeks before, an event that served to remind his father his brother would soon turn ten. He didn't understand why he was overlooked and his father, believing he was ignorant of it, never bothered to explain. For the longest time he would go on hoping things might change, but they never did.

Vito Militello had survived the war and later the economic fallout that followed the Treaty of Peace in Paris. He resisted the migration to the north in search of better paid work and returned to the untroubled oasis, which had sustained him in the mud and terror of the trenches. After a short courtship he married a local girl Rosa believing, in that peculiar way, a family might mitigate the waste of the years before. Death, however, had pursued him from the battlefields and personal tragedy became a punishment for crimes unarticulated.

When Francesco clawed his way into the world he was the sole survivor of four sons Rosa had brought to term and the miracle of countless wretched prayers. But it was not without cost. Indeed, his very name told of a battle fought and lost.

In the peasant fields of Italy it was an eldest son's privilege to carry the name of his grandfather and as each of Vito's sons perished the honour fell to the next. The passing of his third child changed all of that. The doctors gave their explanations to Rosa, but she was a superstitious woman, unable to accept banal medical truths when there were greater ones she might turn to. It took months to wear her husband down, but her dogged resistance won out in the end. Her swollen belly, should it be a boy, was to be named Francesco after Francesco Saverino Castiglione, Pope Pius VIII. If goodness lay in a name then surely it would protect him. He had agreed to her demands, expecting in his heart for his son to die, but Francesco didn't die. He flourished.

For a time his infant son's tenacious grip on life insulated him against the effects of what he'd done, but as his anxiety receded he realised he resented being given what he wanted in the way he had. Misfortune did not lie in a name, only respect, and he could not have a son without honouring his father. He vowed if God blessed them again he would not be dissuaded.

When his wife became pregnant once more he fought her hard, holding steadfast even as the proof of her reasoning crawled at his feet. The new born, despite everything she threatened, defiantly bore the name Giovanni and the rest was left to fate. To everyone's surprise he survived, just as Francesco had. It would be the last time Rosa would conceive, but his arrival finally gave Vito the peace he'd hoped for.

His refusal to bend to Rosa's exactions had moved his father and the unspoken wedge that had been driven between them was lifted. As their relationship became like that of old he couldn't help but love his baby son for it. He didn't think the little differences in the way he treated them amounted to very much. He could not see that Francesco craved not affection but equality. To have treated both of them badly would have been better than the pain of being loved less.

Chapter One
The Conclave

The Vatican City

Present Day

The piazza of St Peter's Basilica was alive with movement as thousands of the faithful swarmed about it like a colony of ants around its queen. Bernini's immense semi-circular colonnades reached out to embrace them as stony saints, perched as ravens on top of the columns, observed them from above. The crowd had briefly thinned on the fifth day as voting was suspended for twenty-four hours of reflection and prayer, but it had swollen by the next morning in expectation that an announcement would soon follow.

In the dim light of the Sistine Chapel eyes looked on solemnly as the Cardinal Dean knelt before the altar. Rising slowly against the tremendous fresco of Christ

Coming in Judgement he held aloft a folded slip of paper and spoke the words,

"I call as my witness, Christ the Lord, who will be my judge, that my vote is given to the one who before God I think should be elected."

He placed it on the paten and tipped it into the chalice. Heads stirred into life, many of them tilting upwards in quiet contemplation toward Michelangelo's Creation, which had been witness to their gathering for centuries.

The sixth day of deliberations had begun.

\#

Twenty-four days earlier the Cardinal Carmelengo had stood by the papal bed struggling with his grief as he discharged his final duties for the still figure lying beneath the white veil.

As the papal apartments were sealed the bells of St Peter's rang out their lament and the churches of Rome joined them in a mournful clanging chorus. Across the globe the cardinals removed their mantillas, a distinguishing feature of their rank, and began to converge on the Vatican, descending like bats into a belfry from all the continents of the earth.

For eighteen days the world had waited, first as the Novendialis, the nine days of mourning, took hold and then the period of stagnation before the deliberations could begin. Papal law decreed elections could not start any sooner than fifteen days after death and no later than twenty.

The burial had taken place on the fifth day and the body, clothed in red vestments and a gold mitre, was removed from where it had lain in state in the Basilica to a marble crypt in the grottoes below. There it took its rightful position with the others who had come before him.

On the nineteenth day the cardinals were ready to begin. They would not emerge again until they had chosen one among them.

\#

The last cardinal approached the altar and placed his ballot in the chalice. Those seated betrayed no emotion as the votes were poured out. The first of the scrutineers unfolded a slip and read the name below the printed words, *Eligio in Summum Pontificem*, before passing it to the second for confirmation. The third scrutineer did the same and then pushed a needle and thread through the word *Eligio*. With each pass the chain grew longer until attention shifted to one chair in particular. A murmur of approval ran around the room like falling dominoes.

The shouts outside turned to a roar as a wisp of smoke became a puff and then a billowing stream. The thin pipe to the left of Michael Angelo's mammoth dome spat white. A Holy Roman Pontiff had been elected. The souls that filled the square and the Via de la Conciliazione roared in delight as the eleven-ton Kanchenone of the Basilica began to sing out.

Inside, the assent to the nomination was given and the chosen papal name recorded by the Master of Pontifical Liturgical Ceremonies. The new pontiff looked around self-consciously. Things were different to how he had imagined. He hadn't expected to feel quite so visible, at least not right away. He tried to organise his thoughts, but it was difficult with the din of bells and the multitude beyond. He moved slowly, allowing himself to be guided to the Room of Tears where the papal vestments were prepared. He barely registered the movement of his body as they helped him into the white soutane and then the stockings and red slippers embroidered with the golden cross of the papacy. He could see them fussing around him, but felt oddly disembodied as though he were looking down at them from above. Here he was, he thought. It was done. He stared ahead with a smile as the cardinals descended on him one by one, each pledging their obedience with a kiss of his hand.

The main balcony of the Vatican opened and the senior cardinal deacon was met by a wall of sound that made him step back. Looking at the people below him he was overcome by a rush of feelings that mixed jubilation with excitement and pride. Taking a deep breath he cried out:

'Annuntio vobis gaudium magnum: Habemus Papam.' The crowd roared again, the force of it unified and powerful.

He waited for a hush to fall. Some sank to their knees, but every one of them was fixed on the balcony above waiting for a glimpse of the white robe.

The Vatican radio station received the electronic signal and began to churn out the news in dozens of languages. Millions of Catholics across the planet sat keenly in front of their television sets. The speculation and predictions would be answered. In a few seconds the whole world would know.

Chapter Two

Lazy days and bad dreams

Shenyang, North East China

Five weeks earlier

A fat man in a brown tattered armchair stared at a powdery cream wall. On his face was a strained expression that lay somewhere between rigor mortis and a kick to the groin. To a casual observer it might have looked like he was simply sitting, but they would have been mistaken. He was, in fact, silently waging war. Without warning he pitched himself forward, his features bulging with bug-eyed determination, and willed the caterwauling behind it to stop.

George Kent fell back deflated. The situation clearly required more substantial measures than a fanciful hope in telekinesis. He guillotined his tongue between his tea stained teeth, the prelude to any kind of serious thinking, and considered his next move. Some time passed before he stirred again, but with a quiet rage that caused his temple to pulsate like an alien life form he nodded decisively. He knew what he had to do. It was what he always did.

He levered himself out of the chair with greater effort, more gravity and less grace than any one might have reasonably expected and he drew the black and red striped bathrobe he was wearing tightly around his pendulous breasts.

'I'm coming for you, boy,' he hollered as he lurched down the hall. Ten elephantine steps later he found his neighbour's door and some of his breath.

'Open up, boy. I know you can hear me,' he barked, pounding against it with his fists.

It hadn't escaped the fat man that such an epithet in the wrong ears might sound a tad colonial, but in lieu of a name and a language impediment that stood between them like a nightclub bouncer he was content to take the risk.

'Shei?' a muffled voice inquired from its bowels.

'Don't shei me, you indecipherable inbred tone-deaf throwback.'

'Shei?'

'Don't make me repeat myself, boy,' he warned.

'Shei ya?'

Kent glared at the cheap wood in front of him, the beleaguered representative of the many unclaimed voices that unwittingly sheltered under its protection. The fat man's wrath had damaged its varnished surface on more than one occasion.

'You shei me one more time and...' Unable to think of anything to finish the sentence he kicked out the toe of his boot and elicited a dull thud.

'Shei ya?'

There was an incredulous intake of breath. Was he being deliberately obtuse?

'I know you don't know who it is, but if you open up you might find out. Christ, if you can be bothered to squat while you defecate surely you can muster the energy to walk a few steps?'

A humiliating slow motion replay of the first time he tried to imitate the feat in a Shenyang public loo swam into his mind, specifically the moment his thighs had given way as he hovered precariously over the hole that moonlighted as a toilet. Sadly, he had lacked the strength, skill or constitution of a hummingbird that might have enabled him to suspend gravity in such a manner. Foreign excrement was unfortunately every bit as bad as one might imagine and it appalled him how often he thought about the incident, particularly what might have been had his hands not been fatefully engaged in safeguarding his nose.

'Shei ya?'

Kent thought he detected an anxious note, but the Chinese language had made a fool of him more than once. If he had a pound for every time he saw two people screaming at one another only to discover they were chatting quite amiably about who had the longer chopstick he'd make Bill Gates look like a tramp. Conceding defeat he returned down the hall and slammed his door.

He slumped back into his chair and cajoled it with a shimmy of feet and a rocking of flesh away from the wall and back to the video, which had been rudely interrupted. The singing had stopped, but it would soon start again. The Chinese loved to sing. In China a carpenter didn't fix wood or die on a cross. She was a deceased hippie, kept alive by the collective will of one and a half billion followers. She had them all yearning for *yesterday once more*, which was ironic when he considered in historical terms this meant either famine or a good kicking by Mao's Red Guard.

He picked at the leather of the chair arm thoughtfully until a piece came away. At least, he supposed, his pal on the other side of the wall wasn't hacking up phlegm, which was what usually filled in the gaps between the disharmonies.

The Chinese did most things they liked with remorseless enthusiasm which included the spitting that went on day and night. The sudden inclination to disgorge the contents of a lung on anything with the misfortune to be nearby was a real threat when venturing outside. A hellish discord of throaty snorts and growls accompanied him everywhere.

Kent reached for a bag of prawn-flavoured flakes amongst a carpet of discarded chocolate wrappers on the floor and opened them with a pop. The crackling brought out his roommate who had been until that moment snoring lightly under the bed. He felt for the warm fur nestling against his shin and obliged it with a sprinkle that fell like snow between his legs. She greeted it with a smacking of lips.

'Hey you,' he said, scooping her up in his lap. 'How's the sleeping coming on?' She cocked her head at him, which he took as an indication that it was going quite well.

'You fancy a game of go prawn?' he asked. Her ears perked up at the last two words.

Her intelligent expression followed him as he tucked a couple of flakes into a tear in the chair arm. He gave her the signal to begin and watched her scratch frantically to get at the bounty inside. It amazed him how utterly complete her life was. She had three decent meals a day, sixteen hours sleep, regular bestial exertions with a Pekingese floozy down the road and no pesky self-awareness to pick over the bones of experience. Her existence was a philosophical master class in how to be happy.

The decision to re-home her had not been an easy one, but Daisy had demonstrated on many occasions that defecating indoors was not an issue she felt she could negotiate on, dropping her indiscretions in all but the most inaccessible places like some demonic Feng Shui expert. He saw her dilemma. Trying to crap in a snowstorm nineteen degrees below was unlikely to be an agreeable experience.

His attempts to find her a new home had met with complete failure. She had come back four times to date without apology or explanation and he had come to think of her as a casserole dish people borrowed and then felt obliged to return. He would keep on trying, he owed her that. She was a good friend and a tolerant creature. She never mocked his patchy beard or his pointy bald dome. She never commented on his emotional night-time eating or his predilection for high-end Hungarian porn and she harboured no grudge when he almost killed her with his colossal behind as he sat down. But it was more than that. Finding attractive women to sleep with a four hundred and twenty-five pound man was a problem. Daisy, combined with a generous dollop of existential crisis, had delivered the only real success he had ever known. To wake up without the smell of shit in the morning carried a heavy price indeed.

Kent had been an English teacher in China for almost six years, an arbitrary decision taken after university and cemented by indolence. The adulation he received for getting Mother Tongue to do her tired dance made living an easy affair. In exchange for the ten hours he taught each week he was given bed, board and enough money for the odd act of immorality which he excused on the grounds it was legal in Holland. In the classroom he exuded confidence like a cheap aftershave and tried to avoid giving tiresome explanations to dull questions.

For the most part things continued at a pace just below sedate, which was faster than he liked, but everyone had to make sacrifices. The truth was no one really cared what he did. His face alone, bar the inevitable ridicule elicited by its size, bought him for modest exertion the time he coveted to do nothing.

In stories and in life men in tattered armchairs tended to be of a certain kind and Kent was such a man. He resided in a provincial backwater hotel room in the arse end of a country that modernised like an outbreak of e-coli, teaching English to a gaggle of kids that didn't want to learn it, for one simple reason; He couldn't be bothered to do anything else. He wasn't a tin man searching for a heart or a fat man looking to be thin. His goals were uncomplicated and achievable - female affection, alcohol and culinary excess. In different degrees he'd achieved them all, paid for by the good and benevolent central government. China was his Eden and he its overweight Adam.
#

14

Half way across the world a terrified arm swung out of the darkness and knocked a glass off a table. It landed with a clink as fingers scrabbled for the light above, fearful the night might give their terror a more concrete form. A bulb flickered on, stilling them as flared nostrils sucked greedily at the air.

David Trimble blinked uncomfortably, letting its glow nourish the onset of consciousness. As his breathing slowed he sat up and turned the light sideward. He took a cigarette from the packet by his bed, lit it and walked to the window. In a runway of orange set down by the streetlights two men and three women swayed from too many drinks and a happiness that indulged it. As they started to laugh he turned away and returned to his bed. Kneeling, he slid out a cardboard box from beneath it and opened the flaps. He stared at the envelope lying on top of a stack of papers, shivering at the touch of the cold sweat soaking the back of his T-shirt. How had everything changed so quickly, he thought?

He took a long drag and listened to his flatmate snore in the other room. The sound repelled him. He would need the morning to remind him why he had brought him here. The adrenaline that woke him from his dream was ebbing away. In a little while the dread would start to dissipate, losing definition over the hours until it was no longer strong enough to occupy him. He stubbed out the cigarette in an overflowing ashtray by his knee, a grim reminder of the many nights he had been there, and slid the box back.

He left the bedroom and walked down a narrow corridor to the living room. The light in the kitchenette had been left on and it seemed even smaller floating in the dark. The memory of looking around the flat with his father came back to him. They had joked about it being more like a Swiss Army knife than a place to live, but he insisted it was the best they had seen, secretly convinced, Trimble suspected, that the rise in price was proportionate to an increase in security. Safety had been his father's illusion. He rubbed the scar on his forehead. He'd buried his life in three boxes and they told him he was lucky.

The reasons for buying the place were gone. The PhD at LSE had been abandoned along with everything else. But he was stuck. His father's approval of the flat was a cause to stay, but this paled to the other memories that abided there. This was where he found her now. Here she would be forever twenty-six; Sitting up in their bed with her laptop, hair pinned back with a grip; Screaming at him to shut the bathroom door after he walked in on her and left it open; Laughing at some idiotic thing he had done to amuse her as they watched trash on TV. Her memory lived in the objects and the space around him. He could not give up the affection however hopeless.

When she died he fell inside himself, unable to accept she was gone. His being had been so completely tied up in hers that without it there was no meaning. He felt sick with emptiness and consumed by anger for those around him who were unable to see the awfulness beneath it all. Eternity did not recognise bonds of love. There was no transcendence. The infinite would make her a stranger and it would be as if they'd never known each other.

Scared of what he might do he'd exiled himself from the world. But the letter had given him an unwanted interest in it again, even if he hadn't allowed himself to admit that yet.

Chapter Three

Ghosts from the past

Wiltshire, England

On a bench under a group of oak trees an old woman stared down at her feet, which were planted firmly on the hard mud that made an island in the grass around them. She sighed gently, sad the meeting was over and pulled the brown shawl tightly around her shoulders before returning her gaze to the rolling fields beyond. The day she had longed and feared for so many years had come and gone.

She had not noticed the figure approaching from the manor house behind and it was almost upon her, casting a shadow like a gravestone, before she spun around to meet it. An elderly man returned her startled look with an embarrassed smile. The sight of him almost stopped her heart. It was *him*. His hair was white, the strength of his body pared down by the years, but the glass hard green eyes had not changed. She kept his stare for a few seconds longer and calmly turned back to the fields, her insides churning.

'Hello, Bee,' he said.

She opened her mouth to speak but closed it again, allowing her silence to hang like a barrier between them.

'It's been a long time,' he said.

Her shoulders stiffened.

'Do you know who I am?' he asked, realising immediately the question was a foolish one. Her reaction had left him in no doubt of that.

'I'm old, Frank, not senile,' she said, pronouncing the last word with a hiss. She instantly regretted it. Anger was such an inadequate emotion.

The man frowned. 'Frank?'

'You always looked like a Frank to me,' she said. 'Perhaps you're the one who doesn't remember.' Too ordinary, she thought.

A smile crept over his face.

'Yes, that's right, isn't it?' he said, shaking his head. 'I can't believe you still remember that after all this time...Amazing,' he chuckled, moving a couple more steps so he could see her properly.

'I remember a lot of things, Frank.'

His casual manner infuriated her. A lifetime had passed since they'd last spoken and circumstances had not been good to her. The presumption that he could come and resume their acquaintance with such perfunctoriness made her feel worthless.

'Do you mind if I sit down?' he asked.

'Do you know how many times I thought about this? You coming here?' she said.

He didn't say anything.

'Too many,' she answered. 'In the end I learned to stop thinking. How dare you resurface like this.'

Truthfully, a part of her had been expecting him. The past had been awoken and although she resented it, having him here seemed appropriate.

'I know you're mad at him.'

'Him.' Her voiced trembled. 'So you're blameless in all of this?'

'That's not what I meant?'

'Mad doesn't even come close to the way I feel,' she said angrily.

He took a seat next to her. 'It would never have worked between us, Bee. Not with the baby.'

'Don't you mean *responsibility*?'

'That's not fair,' he said.

'Why? You were happy to share other things.'

'What could I have done, Bee?'

The conversation was happening too quickly, she thought. She hadn't seen him in thirty years and here he was leaping between past and present like it was nothing. He did it because he hadn't suffered in between and it made her feel old and used up. The weight of those years demanded more. She imagined the two points in time transposed; an embrace between the old man before her, loose flaps of skin hanging off his neck like chicken clinging to bone, and the taut luminous glow of her former self.

'You were always so damned scared of him. What were you frightened of? That he would leave me? He did that anyway.'

'If I stayed he would have destroyed us.'

'Like he destroyed me?' She heard the bitterness in her voice and hated it. He was the one that should feel like this.

He ran his fingers through his hair in frustration.

'I didn't mean that-'

'So you keep saying. What do you mean?'

'You can despise me if you want, but I didn't come here for myself.'

She looked at him. 'So why are you here, Frank?'

'I came for my brother.'

'I have nothing to say about him.'

She stood up and began to walk away.

'Please, Bee, let me explain,' he called.

'No,' she shouted, waving an arm behind her as though trying to obliterate his words from the air.

'Believe me I understand, Bee.'

She turned around. 'Why now?'

'He's dying,' he said quietly.

She laughed hollowly. 'Why does that not surprise me?'

'I know you have no reason to care.'

'You're right, I don't.'

'Please,' he said, gesturing to the bench. 'Just hear me out.'

She took a step forward and then back before turning to face him. He seemed smaller than she remembered and it made his desperation appear all the more pitiful. She told herself she didn't care and yet she couldn't bring herself to leave.

'You have five minutes,' she said, walking back to him.

He waited until she sat down before he spoke.

21

'Everyone wants one last chance to do something right. Surely death entitles us to be a little selfish?'

'One last chance?' A magpie flew off from the bough above her. 'When did he try before?'

'I know raising a child on your own is tough, but that wasn't his fault. He never knew about it...I didn't tell him.' He rubbed his face tiredly. She wasn't going to make this easy.

'I don't care that he ran away,' she said softly. 'It's not that.'

'Then tell me.'

She folded her arms defensively. 'It's too late, Frank. I needed someone to listen three decades ago.'

He watched her as she spoke to the distance. Age had given her a dignity she lacked back then.

'It's cancer, Bee....pancreatic. He's got a few months, if he's lucky.'

'And what do you want me to do?'

'I'm not asking for forgiveness, just a bit of pity.'

'Pity? Christ, you have a nerve.'

'He hasn't got long.'

'Why should that mean something to me? Let him die. What do I care? I won't give him a version of events that makes a lie of what he's done.'

'I told you, Bee, he didn't know about the baby.'

'You knew though, didn't you?' she said, acrimony dripping from her mouth.

'Yes. So if you want to blame someone, blame me.'

'You really think he would have come if he'd known?' She laughed. 'Anyway, like I said, it's not about that.'

'Then what is it about?'

22

'I doubt even he fully understands what he did.'

He waited for her to elaborate, but she didn't. He was getting tired of guessing.

'Maybe you're right,' he said. 'I shouldn't have come. Perhaps when he dies you won't be able to hate him anymore. I hope I've given you that peace at least.'

'Oh, I'm sure I will.'

He rubbed his brow irritably. 'Do you want to carry this around for the next thirty years?'

'Don't insult me with platitudes, Frank. You haven't earned the right to talk to me like that. Besides, I'm seventy years old. I think I can live with it.'

'I should go,' he said, putting his hands on his knees in preparation but stopping short of getting up.

'He doesn't know you're here, does he?' she asked.

He shook his head.

'Does he know about us?'

'He has no idea I even know about you.' He shrugged. 'We don't share stories, Bee.'

'Just women.'

The man looked away self-consciously. She had become harder, he thought.

'Are you going to help me?' he said.

'Why should I put aside what he's done?'

'I'm not asking you to.' He sighed. 'But tell me, what exactly has he done? As far as he is concerned you were a fortnight fling a lifetime ago. The truth is he probably hasn't thought about you since.'

The comment knocked the wind from her. Had her suffering made such a small impact on those responsible for it?

'Well, that's not exactly endearing him to me, Frank.'

'That's not what I mean. The point is he was ungracious and perhaps unkind but-'

'I can't forgive him,' she said.

'For what?'

'For taking my son away.' Her jaw muscles quivered as she battled to stay in control of her feelings.

'I don't understand,' he said, confused.

'Do you remember phoning me after he was born?' she asked.

'Yes.' He'd broken off contact shortly after that.

'I wanted to say something to you then, but I was in a strange place. I was struggling to understand things...events. It was only later I realised what he'd done.'

'I don't understand. How could he take something he didn't know about?' His brow was creased in deep ridges. 'Are you telling me he knew? When did he find out?'

She smiled at his baffled expression. 'He didn't.'

He started to say something, but the words died on his lips.

'He was taken before,' she said.

He studied her for a moment. Was she being evasive or was it something else? She certainly looked well, but that was no guarantee of anything. He had seen some of his contemporaries emerge from illness outwardly unchanged but shaken like a snow globe inside. Why had he found her in a care home? Was she too affected in some way?

The old woman looked back at the house and suddenly felt homesick. They would be serving dinner soon. Her friend Mrs Knight would be setting up two television dinner trays so they could watch Coronation Street while they ate.

'Why did you phone that night?'

'I don't know...I suppose I wanted to make sure you and the baby were doing well.'

'You know, I thought you would come. It's always the way, isn't it? Things unexpected, I mean.'

'Bee, please? Make me understand.'

'You have no business understanding,' she snapped. He had no idea what his brother had done, she thought. How could he?

'I think you should go,' she said.

'I can't do that.'

'You can sit there until he dies, but I'll not go to him and hold his hand as if I meant something.'

'I never expected you would.'

'Then what?'

He shrugged. 'A letter, a photograph?'

'What good would that do?'

'It would give him a son.'

'Why should I do that?'

'It's different now,' he said.

'Because he's dying?'

'The news will give him some peace,' he said.

'What about my peace?'

'Why do you hate him so much?'

Where could she begin?

'I'm sorry for whatever he's done, but he is terrified. We get one go at this life, Bee, and his is over. If I was able to tell him something...give him proof he'd continue in some way...it might...'

Was it possible for a monster to be sorry, she thought? She too found herself longing for the reckless indifference of her youth, unburdened of the past and unafraid of the future. It was time that made you guilty of the things you did and it was a cruel trick when it took away your power to make amends.

'I don't know,' she said.

'He would still have his guilt, Bee.'

'I suppose it doesn't matter now, does it?' she said, softening.

'Then you'll do it?'

She gave an almost imperceptible nod. 'But I'll not absolve him.'

'Thank you, Bee.'

He exhaled heavily, tired by the negotiations. He leant back and stifled a yawn, knowing he would not return again.

'Bee?'

'What?' she said gently. The altercation seemed to have purged the worst of her anger.

'What did you mean before?'

Chapter Four

The call

Shenyang, China

Kent rolled over in his bed cocooned in three duvets like a nightmarish silk worm the size of a hippo. He winced at the sharp ringing beside him and fumbled groggily to silence it. Finding it on the second pass he placed the mouthpiece on the pillow beside him.

'Why?' he asked sleepily.

'Am I speaking to George Kent?' asked a tinny voice that sounded long distance.

'I'm nobody for anybody at this time.'

'You don't know me, Mr Kent, but I must talk to you.'

'Are you aware it's the middle of the night?'

'I'm sorry, I thought it was morning over there?'

It had gone seven thirty am, but Kent had a somewhat vampirish relationship to the day.

'Never you mind what it is.'

'I have some information you might be interested in.'

'Who is this?'

'A friend.'

'Then you'll forgive me for what I'm about to do.'

Kent yanked the phone out of the wall and swept it off his saliva stained pillow.

'Idiot,' he muttered.

Turning over like a gigantic hog on a spit he tried to re-join his dream where he had left it.

#

London, England

Trimble silenced the television with a click of the remote and stared at the phone ringing noisily on the coffee table in front of him. Who could be ringing at such a late hour, he wondered? He picked it up nervously. Calls at this time were seldom good.

'Hello?' he said, watching the silent mouths on the television screen.

'Is this Mr Trimble?' asked a male voice with a light accent.

'Yes,' he said, surprised it was for him and not his flatmate. He hadn't spoken to anyone in months.

'Mr David Trimble?' he said.

What other Trimble could it be? He tightened as he answered his own question. There was only one left now. He thought everyone knew that.

'What can I do for you?' he asked, trying to conceal his anxiety.

'Well, it's really what I can do for you.'

The statement was left floating like a temptation.

'Do for me? I don't understand. Who is this?'

'I'm a friend of your fathers.' Trimble flinched. He hadn't talked about him with anyone since the funeral.

'Hello?' the voice said searchingly.

'Yes, I'm here,'

'Is there something wrong?'

He had the feeling it already knew the answer to that.

'My father's dead,' Trimble said, delivering the words without sentiment.

'Oh, I'm sorry, I didn't know.'

That was a lie, he thought. He didn't say anything else, hoping his disinclination to speak would encourage the man to finish his enquiries. After a moment Trimble realised it was waiting for him.

'Look, it's late, what do you want?' he said bluntly. He was in no mood for games.

'Yes, of course...I need to talk to you about your father.'

'Why are you forcing me to repeat myself? I told you, he's dead.'

'I think we both know that's not true, Mr Trimble.'

His stomach somersaulted.

'Who is this?'

'I think you might be interested in what I have to say.'

'Who is this?' he repeated, resisting a powerful urge to put down the phone. He needed to hear more. He'd spend the rest of the night worrying otherwise.

'Somebody who can provide information about your parents...about your father.'

'I have no idea what kind of sick joke you're playing, but you'd better stop,' he said, trembling.

'Are you not looking for your father?' The question was arrogant and assured in a way that scared him.

'I'm hanging up the phone. If you call again I'm ringing the police.' The image of flashing blue lights, broken glass and blood came back to him. It was an empty threat. He didn't want to deal with them ever again.

'Are you sure you want to do that?'

'My parents are dead! Do you understand? They are dead!' He started to wonder if this might be one of his dreams. It was hard to tell sometimes.

'I'm sorry, you'll have to excuse my English, Mr Trimble. I am not familiar with the proper terms. What would you be more comfortable with?'

'This is over. I'm hanging up.'

'You met with your mother the other day, Mr Trimble. You must remember?'

He gripped the phone tightly. Had someone been following him?

'How did you-?'

'That's not important,' he interrupted.

'What do you want?' He was terrified of another revelation, but he had to find out more.

'Why don't we stop playing games? We both know you're looking for him.'

'My father is dead you fuck.' He hit the disconnect button and threw it on the sofa, his hands bunched into fists. He hadn't told anyone about the letter. Who was this man and why was he watching him?

The phone sprang into life and sent his heart cantering across his chest. He wanted to throw it against the wall, but after more than a minute he picked it up and placed it to his ear.

'Do you want to find him?' the voice asked.

Trimble looked behind him. His flatmate had come into the room looking concern.

'Are you okay?' he mouthed.

He nodded, feeling simultaneously embarrassed and relieved. His friend's presence helped negate the otherworldliness of what was happening.

'The man who was my father is gone.'

'That is a distinction for you, Mr Trimble. It's not one I am interested in. The only thing that concerns me is whether you want to know?'

Tears of frustration ran down his cheeks. 'Why are you doing this?'

'Do you want to know?' he repeated, his tone flat and unyielding.

'Yes,' he said finally. 'I want to know.'

'Then we should meet. Are you willing to do that?' he asked.

'Yes,' he said, his reply almost inaudible. How did this stranger see so much, he thought? How could he know he would betray them?

'Where?'

'I'll call again.'

A click changed to a dial tone and Trimble let the phone drop to his side. Looking up at his flatmate he shook his head and began to weep.

Chapter Five

A ticket home

Shenyang, China

Kent glanced up at the worried faces and groaned. The strain of being on his feet was taking its toll, which was evident from the sound of creaking emanating from the lectern on which he was leaning. The flesh of his gut had settled around the wood, forming an enormous pair of fleshy lips that clamped down on it like a giant catfish. He looked at the pad of paper on which he had been doodling for the last hour and the words *I hate every single one of you* came into focus amongst the illegible scrawl. He nodded sagely at its truth and then repeated it several times in green Biro.

It was the oral examination preceding the summer break, a bleak period in which Mother Tongue took a horrific beating and a sadistic Old Man Time just loved to watch. He had tried humming to deflect the nonsense spewing tonelessly from the head in front of him, but it was difficult without drawing attention to himself. He had not foreseen that a harmless hypothetical question about time travel would yield such mind meltingly dull flights of fantasy.

The first seven students had given near identical speeches extolling the virtues of the Tang Dynasty. Cherry, a bovine brained irritant much less attractive than her name suggested, was the only one of the group to deviate from the script. She had drawn parallels to the present and remarked, without any apparent irony, that she thought it unfair girls were free to sew all day and not shackled to compulsory education. Kent marked her down for lack of aspiration. He also felt obliged to point out in red pen that *ambition* wasn't a small town in Texas.

The next five had voiced a desire to return to the *ancient time,* which wasn't terribly specific. The subsequent lecture on steel production did nothing to clear up the ambiguity. Ten inevitable 1949 references to New China followed after that, which caused considerable pain to his anus as he tried to stifle his lack of interest.

'Mr George, I'm finish,' said a tiny girl with bunches in her hair. At twenty-two she would've had trouble posing as a centrefold in any one of the gentleman's magazines he had stashed in a cupboard under the sink in his room. Kent nodded gravely and scribbled the word *fish* before motioning for her to leave with an elaborate swish of his hand. He counted the remaining bodies. To his dismay a sizeable number remained.

Nine students followed like a rotten run of cards, each choosing some trivial childhood transgression they wished to expunge from their histories. The last had been marginally more industrious, pilfering from a story of terminal illness to stoke up his sympathy. She'd evidently forgotten he had seen her burning joss paper in veneration of her dead grandmother during the ghost festival earlier in the year. It seemed unlikely she had risen from the dead, contracted ovarian cancer and died again, unless she was incredibly unlucky.

'Apple,' he said loudly, hoping to cause some anxiety to a stumpy fellow with a black leather bomber jacket and shoulder length hair. Such a getup signified a bit of a maverick in a Chinese classroom. To Kent it denoted a bit of a tit. He taught many others that were bearable, but this one and his gang were little bastards. Their adolescent posturing was particularly grating when he considered they were in their early twenties and he'd reminded them on numerous occasions the class was voluntary. But each week they continued to come, sometimes five minutes late, acting out the role of dissident to the only person that would tolerate it.

In reality the university made insufferable demands each student happily endured. The day commenced at the crack of Wally's ass, except Mondays when it began even earlier to raise the flag and sing the national anthem. Dressed in bad tracksuits and accompanied by a music track that made depression sound exciting they would count and march their way through thirty compulsory minutes of morning exercise. This was the physical component of a two pronged approach to student health. Complimenting it like a fork in the eye were hour long social lessons that were peppered throughout the week like buckshot in the back end of a deer.

By six o'clock breakfast was over and a morsel of time was thrown at them for private study before they were assaulted by a cannery packed day of lectures. The whole experience was sound tracked by a never-ending musical score piped throughout the campus like some God forgotten prisoner of war camp.

In the beginning Kent had quelled his murderous impulses toward the boys with ridicule, but their lack of comprehension made it an empty victory. Only his American pal appreciated his acerbic put-downs as he re-enacted them in Sophie's world, a small expatriate's bar, over the weekend. He persevered, nevertheless, hoping time and his reluctant role as teacher would yield a glimmer of understanding.

'Good morning, sir,' Apple said, giggling and peering over his shoulder at Shadow and David Beckham who were dressed in the familiar ensemble of black Chino's and a dull blue wafer thin polyester jacket. They high- fived each other. He could only guess what that meant.

Kent had grown accustomed to the pick of odd names over the years. They were intended to make his job easier and for them to enter the spirit of their endeavour. Most were plucked indiscriminately from a dictionary, but a few had succumbed to inspiration. The name David Beckham was an obvious choice. English football was spoken about with unreserved affection and something which he had to tiresomely explain he didn't give a gnat's shit about. Most of his transactions with the male of the species were littered with the aborted remains of such conversations.

'You're not a gangster rapper. You're a twenty-two year old pubescent with the mental age of an eleven year old girl,' Kent said.

'Rapper, yes.'

'Oh, for God's sake,' he said, annoyed at the pretence of understanding.

'Teacher, I begin,' Apple replied confidently, which irked him even more.

'If you must, but I have to tell you, bearing in mind our mutual animosity, a passing grade is unlikely. Even if you perform adequately, which is improbable, the record will not reflect the achievement. You have to be prevented from advancing wherever possible. It is my ardent wish that you fail to obtain a good job on graduation. Your lack of prospects combined with your unsightly appearance will hopefully deter any potential mate. It is imperative we stop you breeding.'

He paused for this to be digested. A blank stare indicated it hadn't been.

'Perform, yes,' he said.

'One tip, Mr Granny Smith, swallow the dog.' Kent ignored the look of bewilderment and instructed him to continue with a regal flourish of his index and middle finger. The boy disregarded the instruction and continued to speak as if a four-legged mammal had climbed into his mouth and prevented him from closing it properly. Unable to recreate the required syllables the outcome was similar to listening to a chimpanzee under anaesthetic.

After he had finished Kent wrote the word *country* and then crossed out the *o* and two letters at the end before sending him back to his seat. He pointed at the last girl to begin. After a mercifully short period she concluded.

'Tell me, Mr George,' she said with a furtive look behind her. 'Can I pass this exam?'

He wasn't sure whether the action was conspiratorial or if she had forgotten what the classroom looked like. He suspected she was checking if it was empty. Most Chinese girls got the warning about the foreigners' voracious libido. To be alone with one was practically a guarantee of a nasty sexual assault.

The month before a pygmy sized female student with black teeth and a weeping complexion had approached him for help in translating her doctoral thesis into English. He didn't know much about pesticides and increased tomato yields, but he did his best to faithfully render what she was telling him. After five days she had stopped coming to see him. What should have been a reason for celebration, however, was marred by learning the cause for it. A third party had expressed concerns regarding their arrangement and in the process induced quite giddy heights of paranoia regarding his intentions. This affronted him as the only conceivable way he might pounce on her was if the room was on fire and he needed to step on her back to reach the window ledge.

'It's Mr Kent my dear, and yes, I don't see why not. The girl smiled her incomprehension and scurried out the door.

He gathered up the papers and stuffed them into the pocket of his trench coat. Draping it over his shoulders Mafia style he followed her out. He sauntered down the bare concrete corridor to the double door at the end, doing his best to ignore the smell of a badly maintained toilet to his right. A thick green duvet-style curtain with a slit down its middle guarded against the bitter cold. It had been erected early this year, he thought.

'George,' a voice called out. He looked up to see the Director of Foreign Affairs walking breathlessly up the corridor to meet him.

'Oh, hello, Mr Zhong,' he said, praying he hadn't arrived to present him with another invitation to watch Beijing Opera.

'There was a telephone,' he said, his expression solemn.

Unless it was the beginning of a joke he probably meant telephone call.

'Your mother is sick.'

Chapter Six

Papa don't preach

Vatican City

In the study of a small apartment behind St Peter's Basilica Cardinal Giovanni Militello waited for the most important conversation of his life to begin. He had a good idea of what lay ahead, but anything short of precognition could not stop him from fidgeting anxiously.

The study belonged to the Dean of the College of Cardinals, Zelijko Adeyemi. Giovanni had seen early on that he was different. Any fool who wanted to could see it. He'd soared high in Rome, higher than many expected, and such wings of influence would be needed in the coming weeks. All those years ago he had reached out to him and perhaps today it would finally pay dividend.

The Dean was born in Nigeria in 1934, the son of a railway worker. He'd converted at the age of seventeen, despite the strong objections of his father, from traditional Animism to Catholicism and was ordained to the priesthood at twenty-six. The place of his birth was a wild country in upheaval and it had been the perfect forge in which to create a reputation. His defence of the Catholic Church against considerable oppression and a stand against aggression during an uprising in 1967 by the Igbo of Biafra made ripples large enough to be felt in Rome. It had helped make him a bishop at the uncommonly young age of thirty-seven.

The Secretary of the Congregation for Evangelisation was the perfect appointment. His life in the retelling of it became the stuff of legend and his presence proved a more effective counter measure to the scandals bedevilling the Church than the empty rhetoric of aged prelates. By the end of 1988, at the age of fifty-four, Adeyemi was a cardinal.

The Dean had come to symbolise the rising influence of the third world. He had spent more than forty years at the Vatican and his tenure had included fifteen years as head prefect of the powerful Congregation of Bishops, a post he resigned when he reached the mandatory retirement age of seventy-five, and four years as Dean of the College. Despite all he had achieved Giovanni believed he'd fallen short of what he might have been. Everything that pushed him forward had also held him back and for each individual who admired his feverish adherence to Catholic fundamentals there was another who perceived him as too inflexible. He had lacked the guile to conceal his opposition to the progressive shifts taking place within the Church, convinced those who railed against him would sink it under the weight of change. Giovanni knew now what others suspected all along. He would never go any further. Adeyemi had played the game well and enjoyed the confidence of four popes, but he had been too conservative, too honest and too black to make any papal aspiration a reality.

He looked restlessly around the study. On almost every surface mementos vied for position. Some had made their way onto the walls and competed with the photographs for space.

'Sorry to have kept you, Giovanni,' a voice boomed from the doorway.

'Not at all,' he said, standing up to greet him.

They both wore the customary red trimmed black cassock and red sash of the vacancy. Adeyemi's skullcap was conspicuous against his white hair.

'How are you?' he said.

'Very well,' Giovanni said, taking his hand and sandwiching it with his left. They stood for a moment both beaming broadly.

'That's Good.' The Dean navigated his desk and sat down. Almost immediately he got up again and patted down the cassock beneath him as if he were getting comfortable for a long talk. The pectoral cross, which swayed as he moved, came to a gentle stop against his chest.

'Well, here we are again,' he said, his breathing ragged from the exertion. 'It's a shame we have to meet under these circumstances.'

'Yes,' Giovanni said gravely.

The two men allowed a moment of silence to pass between them.

'How have you been?' he asked.

'Better than an old man like me has any right to expect.' Adeyemi grinned, but it melted away quickly.

41

The sudden entrance of a slim African woman in a white habit carrying a tray of tea brought it back. She glanced at Giovanni and bobbed her head in recognition.

'We'll have it here, Sister,' he said, gesturing to the desk.

Placing it down gently she started to assemble the cups and saucers.

'Thank you, Akanke,' he said. 'You can leave the tray.'

After she had gone the Dean picked up the teapot and held it up in front of him.

'Yes, thank you,' he replied.

'*Akanke... to know her is to love her,*' he continued, pouring tea into his cup. 'I've known her since she was a child. Her parents were good people. They gave her a good name.' He moved the pot towards him and watched the brown liquid spill out.

Giovanni remained still. He would allow him as much time as he needed to finish with the formalities. Always listen to the first few bars and find the rhythm before stepping out to dance.

'How long have we been friends?' he asked.

'Too long to remember,' he replied warmly.

Adeyemi chuckled, treating him to an impressive display of teeth. He took a long sip of tea and considered his next words.

'Usuque ad sanguinis effusionem,' he said, putting down his cup.

'Even unto the shedding of blood,' Giovanni translated.

'The red,' he said, rubbing the trim of the cassock in his fingers, signifies, as you know, our duty to God and the Church.'

He nodded politely wishing the Dean would get to the point.

'And that is why I want you to remember that what we discuss here is not motivated by friendship.'

Giovanni pursed his lips together, unsure how to respond.

'You've probably heard by now I'm returning to Nigeria.'

He nodded again. Adeyemi had requested to return next year. His duties as Dean would pass to someone else.

'When I sent my letter to the Pope I suspected he would not be too anxious to let me go, but I waited three months before he asked me to lunch and gave me permission to leave. An act of kindness I'm sure. A decision which takes that long flatters the man receiving it,' he said, chuckling again.

The laugh was a nervous tic of character and Giovanni suspected the reason for it now was apprehension about what lay ahead. It would take time to re-adjust to Nigeria, time he didn't have.

'Soon I will preside over voting to determine a new Dean and the transfer of my title. Perhaps in my remaining years I can contribute in some small way to the growing Catholic Church in my homeland.'

'I am sure there are many good reasons to compel you to stay,' Giovanni said.

'You are a good friend but not such a good liar. I'm an old man. My health is declining and my mind, I'm told, is narrowed by age. I can't say I entirely agree. My feelings are now what they were then, but perception so often triumphs over fact.' He stopped and stared across thoughtfully at the younger cardinal.

'What is it, Zelijko?' Giovanni asked, tracing the raised wood in the arms of the chair. Looking down he saw a lion staring back at him.

'There are many problems facing us. The world is changing fast and it requires constant vigilance to keep up. But some things never change. Structure and scripture are the threads that hold the fragile souls of men together. It's men like the Holy Father who galvanise the will and make demonstrable the goodness of God. People need to be reminded of this.' He looked across at the wall, picking out one particular picture at the end.

'I moved toward the Church as a boy. It's a decision that has given me nothing but comfort in my life.' He took another sip of tea and composed himself.

'My conversion and loyalty were not due to any fault with the underlying ideas governing the spiritual path of my country. In many ways Animism coheres and compliments the teachings of Church. God in all living things...in the lightning and in the wind...in the beauty of nature...in the power that organises and animates it. Is that not God made less concrete? But as a principle to guide the hearts of men?' He shook his head sternly. 'In that it fails for it says nothing of God and the sacrifice of His only begotten Son and it reveals nothing of our place in creation. Man needs to understand both the wonder and the obligation of his birth. Tradition, scripture, belief and belonging are what save us from ourselves. Each year that passes the terrain becomes more treacherous and there are those amongst us who do not see that the march of modernity must be tempered by its bonds to the eternal. These are dangerous times, Giovanni. Who can be relied upon to steer the Church out of harm's way?' He said, offering his palms.

'We've been here before, Zelijko.' He kept his features flat, suppressing a grin welling up inside. He knew exactly where this was heading. 'I'm sure whoever is chosen will act for the good of the Church.'

'That's diplomacy, Giovanni,' he said tersely. 'Speak to me plainly. You know as well as I do the problems confronting us.'

'These problems have always existed.'

'Not like this. Each day the conflict between the traditionalists and the reformists grow. Who would have thought so many among us would seek decentralisation and collegiality? This is the Catholic Church not a democracy. A strong centralised papacy gives it unity and strength. I am right to be troubled.'

'You worry for all of us, but it's been through worse.'

Giovanni breathed shallowly, trying to loosen the knot of excitement in his belly. The dance had started. A few more bars and he would take the Dean's hand.

'And what of the debates this disunity has created?' he asked. 'Married clergy? The legitimacy of divorce and birth control? Doctrinal flexibility? Compromise is the beginning of the end. If we allow ourselves to bend to every change, to every caprice of modernisation, the Church becomes nothing more than a psychiatrist's couch bartering peace of mind for money. We might as well go back to selling indulgences.' Adeyemi sighed resignedly. 'But, if we don't move at all we will be left behind and God will disappear from the minds of generations to come.'

'Then what are we to do?'

'We must choose wisely. It has never been more important.'

45

The dance had begun.

'You're a born politician, Giovanni and you have the heart of a pastoral priest. You have the rare gift of perceiving both the strategy with the righteousness of its aim. These are general reasons, but they are amongst many which recommend you for the task ahead. I pray together we might encourage a favourable outcome.'

'What of the Dominici Gregis? Is a pact not forbidden?'

The cardinal studied him for a moment.

He began again carefully, 'Does it not also state that in electing a successor we should have before us the glory of God and the good of the Church? It is not vanity that motivates me.'

'I'm sorry,' Giovanni said, his countenance flushed with discomfort. 'I never intended-'

Adeyemi waved away his apology. 'There is talk. You do your job well enough to be thought well of and quietly enough to be noticed. A man who screams his attributes is often not heard. This is something you appreciate I think. You are a man who acts for acting and not for those who might be watching.' Giovanni looked down in feigned embarrassment. Modesty was an attribute prized by the Dean. He was right to see him that way. It was how he wanted to be seen.

'Thank you, Zelijko, but I think you over-estimate my virtues. There are many more deserving than me.'

The older cardinal's features darkened. 'Deserve has nothing to do with it, only what's right.'

'Why would the College favour me? The Church is a global concern. There are over one hundred and thirty million Catholics in Brazil alone. Is it not time for their interests to be represented? And what of Africa?'

The Dean let out a heavy nasal breath.

'Then you understand?' Giovanni said.

'I understand numbers mean nothing. There hasn't been an African pope in over fifteen hundred years and I fear we are less enlightened now than we have ever been. We have to deal with the realities of the world. And so long as the Church speaks with one voice, what does it matter?'

'Things have moved on, Zelijko.'

The Dean smiled. 'I'm not sure you believe that. Anyway, the numbers seldom tell the whole story. There are multiple homelands and multiple perspectives. Disagreements do not stop at borders...they are alive and well within them. The outcome of all of this division.'

'Then what use are they?'

'The voting structure by its nature must produce a candidate with broad support. The middle ground is where we will make our stand. You are well disposed to many groups, Giovanni. The moderates and the progressives view you favourably. My endorsement will send the right signals to the more conservative elements.'

'But the moderates will not endorse a candidate favoured by you. They will suspect an ideological alignment.'

'I will not support you publicly. Any influence I have will be brought to bear discreetly.'

Giovanni was speechless. It was really happening.

'I think perhaps you are hesitant about taking on such a role.'

He couldn't be more wrong, Giovanni thought.

'I know this must sound distasteful,' he continued, misinterpreting his silence as unease, 'but this is too important to be left to chance.'

'Yes, of course,' he muttered.

'Despite internal divisions the Italians are united by a desire to see an Italian elected. The Archbishop of Milan is the other major contender for these votes. He's a good man, but he is not equipped for the job ahead. Those voting for him will recast their votes in your favour once it becomes clear you are backed strongly to win.'

'I never knew you were such a shrewd tactician, Zelijko.'

'I will do what is necessary.'

'But there are other candidates suited to this. What of the Archbishop of Salvador Bahia?'

The Dean gave the name some consideration.

'Cardinal Marzano is a strong contender... descended from Brazilian slaves and likely to appeal to both the Latin American and African voting blocs. He's involved in the Congregation for Bishops and considered to have considerable knowledge of the Curia and Vatican bureaucracy. On issues of doctrine, however, he is perceived as notoriously rigid, which goes against the current climate of moderation. He vehemently opposes birth control and stridently endorses celibacy for priests. This will not endear him to those looking for change.'

'We can't assume they will turn to me as a replacement.'

'You underestimate yourself, Giovanni. Besides there's been talk of a caretaker.'

'A caretaker?'

'They're being cautious. They worry about another lengthy pontificate. They need some time to decide how the Church should move forward but not so much to prevent that from happening. Rumours about your health have made you attractive to those still uncommitted.'

'But my health is fine,' he said confused.

'I know that.' The Dean smirked. 'The gossip started after you fainted at the consistory last August.'

'That was the heat.'

'I'm afraid I may have failed to discourage any speculation which might have arisen from the incident.'

He laughed at the amazement spread across Giovanni's face.

'Even a man of the cloth is not immune to sin,' he smiled. His expression became serious once more. 'His Holiness had been ill for some time. You may find it ghoulish that I sought to prepare the ground so early, but I have always been a practical man. If I am guilty of pride then I will repent when the time comes, but God has given me strong principles and I must follow them. The cardinals are polarised and consensus is ever harder to reach. A compromise candidate may well be the only outcome in such fractured times.'

The Dean held Giovanni's stare for a moment.

'I think you share my convictions, but your subtlety of execution has enabled you to avoid the pitfalls I have stumbled into. Your greatest asset is your ability to mask the strength of your passion. I know in my heart that if you are victorious you will tackle the issue of decentralisation head on and staunch the tide of liberalism. Autonomy for the dioceses can never happen. There must be one authority and one message. This future has to prevail and you must realise it.'

'A caretaker pope?' he repeated quietly, momentarily forgetting the Dean was sitting in front of him.

'That is pride, Giovanni. Does it matter under what pretext you lead so long as you lead?'

'I suppose not.'

'You're in good health and you'll defy expectations like others before you. Look to Pope Francesco XXIII for comfort in these doubts.'

'What about the Ukrainian, Volodymr Lytvn? I've heard good things.'

'Ah, yes, the Eastern Patriarch...sympathetic to decentralisation of papal power...educated in Britain and comfortable with the processes of the western world. He has a keen understanding of theology and politics and is at ease in English, the lingua franca of international discourse. He's also pretty media savvy and I hear he is still riding a wave of approval after his efforts at rebuilding his country following the floods of last year.'

'That sounds impressive,' Giovanni said, suddenly aware of the uncertainty of what they were proposing.

'His relative inexperience of the Roman Curia and his youth also go against him. The College is not ready to elect a fifty-eight year old pope. The Europeans won't back him and the Latin American bloc is more likely to vote for a candidate that will represent their interests.'

'I don't know if I am the right man, Zelijko. There are so many who might make a better compromise than I. Cardinal Ricardo Antonio Vasques of Honduras is-'

'Enough,' he said brusquely. 'You know what your strengths are. You're used to the bureaucracy of this place, which is a skill not to be underestimated. It's a cranky old machine and needs to be oiled in the right places. Many are looking for the next pontiff to spend more time supervising the Roman Curia than the last. You're well skilled in secular politics and equally adept at theological discourse. You are known as a talented politician with a knack of delivering on what he promises...Political acumen is a form of divine assistance.'

Giovanni was nodding. He could hear the rustling of ballots and his name being read out over again.

He waved his hand dismissively. 'There is no more to be said. We'll do everything we can. The rest is in God's hands.'

Giovanni smiled. 'Then let us do what we must.'

Chapter Seven

Terms of endearment

Wiltshire, England

Kent tramped into the room hoping it sounded weary enough to discourage any energetic displays of affection his sudden entrance might bring. A young novice from reception trailed behind him.

'Mother, I'm here,' he announced to a high-backed lime green armchair on the other side. He readied himself for the inevitable shriek of excitement but was greeted by silence instead.

'Mother!' he said, annoyed at having to repeat himself.

Getting no response he stepped gingerly to the side so the back of her seat no longer obscured her from view. He could see she was purring contentedly, wrapped in a blanket of bright sun that streamed in from the patio doors next to her.

52

Kent hadn't wanted to come, he'd been summoned. The mention of sickness to Mr Zhong was a ruse he had quickly seen through. She had shown uncommon resolve in her pretence and had lain in bed for three days endlessly calling for him to come to her side. The staff at the home had fetched a doctor to assess her claim she was dying and quickly diagnosed a serious case of bullshit. That should have been the end of it, but her persistence, aided by a stash of gin, had coerced Sister Aggs into making the call anyway. Kent was wise to such artifice. He had expressed his sympathy and sent a counter offer to call again later in the week. A threat to his financial well-being shortly afterwards ended the negotiations in her favour.

Kent had a fractious relationship with his mother. She'd spent most of his childhood preoccupied and distant, overlooking many of the concerns that should have been hers. He didn't understand the reason for her behaviour and only a range of vices she indulged hinted at any cause for it. But she was his mother and as an adult he was doomed to gravitate around her, caught in a fluctuating state of compulsion and repulsion.

He crossed the room and took a seat.

'Well?' he said loudly as he molested his sagging breasts. They were bruised and painful after so much travelling.

The snuffling continued uninterrupted.

He moved closer to her ear and repeated the question. He was shocked to see her eyes were open. They were glassy and unresponsive.

'I thought you said she wasn't sick?' he said, aiming the accusation at the young novice retreating towards the door.

She turned around. 'She isn't.'

Kent thought the response was a little supercilious and would have taken umbrage were he not worried a rebuke might squander the miniscule potential for a ménage a deux later on. Unlikely but not impossible were odds he'd become used to over the years, like an acquaintance you invited for parties but never wanted to see on your own. There was no point in being a realistic optimist. That sounded too much like pessimism.

Kent was a big man, a fact he accepted as easily as his reflection in a mirror. And like a mirror he did not see it as a bad thing. His mother had taken a different view, shipping him off at various points during his adolescence to whatever *phone book* certified psychiatrist she had found. The only person who seemed to feel any better about it was her. She used verbs and nouns like *healing* and *issues* where he preferred adjectives like *moronic*. There was no breakthrough or insight, weeping or catharsis but merely clinical contempt for the time wasted. His weight was due to dense bones and an arthritic metabolism. Any witch doctor who said otherwise was deluded.

'The healthy tend to respond when being addressed. I note a distinct lack of dialogue here,' he said pompously.

'It's difficult to be garrulous when asleep, Mr Kent.' She stifled a laugh, which caused him to blush in embarrassment. It was disorientating to have his disdain thrown back so easily.

'Then why are her bloody eyes open?'

'She's your mother, Mr Kent.'

'You may leave us,' he said, dismissing her rudely with his chin and losing more pride in the process than he managed to salvage.

He waited until the novice had left before grabbing her.

'Come on, wake up you silly cow,' he said, rattling her into consciousness and berating himself for not having done so in the first place. How the hell was he supposed to know she slept like that?

An appreciation of the hours he would have to endure with her was starting to trickle in and it was mixing badly with the jet lag. It had taken over a day's travelling to reach her and the lack of blood or violent coughing incensed him. He had been told not to expect it, but he nursed a vague hope nevertheless. A blur of planes, trains and automobiles had lasted more than thirty hours and the lethargy he now witnessed emphasized his own fatigue. He longed for his bed and the soothing tones of shaded afternoon light that filtered through the pink curtains of the guest suite.

Kent loved to sleep during the day and he also adored eating out, but until his favourite restaurants made the switch from daylight hours he would be forced like Sophie to choose.

'George, you came,' his mother said, her face wrinkling into a smile as she blinked up at him.

'Yes, five thousand bloody miles give or take and there's not a damn thing wrong with you, unless I count the 'orrible way you sleep. How the hell can you doze off with so much heat bearing down on you?' He grinned at an image of her shrivelling up where she sat like an ant under a magnifying lens.

The day was not warm, but the sun, concentrated by the curved panes of glass, made him consider removing the orange cravat, which rested like a crown at his neck. He fingered it half-heartedly and reluctantly stood up, taking off his duffel coat instead. He threw it into the armchair opposite and remained standing.

Mrs Kent adjusted her skirt and sat up.

'Can't you be happy to see me for once?'

'No, and can we skip the old woman routine? You're sixty not one hundred and eight,' he said.

'Seventy,' she corrected.

Kent knew that, but if he gave her an inch she'd take twenty years.

'Whatever.'

The image his mother presented to the world was a fiction. The infirmity was a trick of posture and a slackness of limbs. At seventy she remained stubbornly youthful even if she, in her perversity, could not accept it. She had given up the house in Malmesbury and sold the London flat following the death of his father five years ago. Soon afterwards she'd moved into a nursing home, which was run by a gang of enterprising nuns in the small county town of Lechlade. The decision had lacked necessity as she was financially comfortable and in enviable health. He found it incomprehensible she had opted for a life watching the hours, weeks and years drip away.

'George, is such hostility necessary?'

'Probably about as necessary as the florid blue rinse you've dribbled on your hair.'

'You like it?' She used her fingers to fluff up some curls, which had been flattened by the back of the armchair as she slept.

'If you will insist on your ostentatious displays of pseudo-decrepitude there's little I can do about it.'

'Thanks.'

Kent sighed and looked around purposefully for something to hang the conversation on. The room was cluttered with objects his mother had hoarded from the move. His father had acquired most of them and he felt the reason she hung on to it was to try and forget he was gone. Sometimes it seemed to him as if she feared the space itself, as though an excess might create a vacuum which she could lose her mind to.

A large bookcase dominated the right wall, filled with hundreds of classics he knew she had not read. Along the left side four Georgian Chester-drawers lined up at even intervals. They were adorned with trashy romantic novels, celebrity lifestyle magazines, perfume and empty wine bottles. Her favourite was the rather presciently named Blue Nun. *Blue hair* and *nuns*, a life summed up on the back of a cheap bottle of plonk.

Her alcohol intake complimented her general malaise. She had reduced her consumption over the years, maintaining that incremental reductions would one day result in a dry version of herself. This was fantasy, but at her age she had increasingly less to lose. In the meantime he was able to mine cheap entertainment from the irony of a woman trying to kick a habit being nursed by those trying to get one.

'How about a kiss for your dear old mother?' she said, puckering up like a fish. Kent could smell the alcohol on her breath and wondered when she had started drinking.

'The only thing dear about you, Mother, is the price I've paid to see you.'

'Sit down, George.' She patted the seat in front of her. He didn't move despite his natural inclination to sit.

'Would you like some milk and bread with chocolate spread?' He regarded her suspiciously, unsure if the offer was genuine hospitality or an opening gambit. Despite her physical presence it occurred to him she might be fishing in the past. She spent a lot of afternoons vacationing there these days.

'Mother, what year is it? Perhaps you've detected I am sporting a beard now, which should signify to you I've passed adolescence.' A beard was a grand name for what looked like a patch of dry grass scorched by fire. 'If you were less drugged up you might have noticed the transition.'

'So you don't want the chocolate spread then?'

He considered this for a moment. 'If it will make you happy.'

'And what do you mean by that?' she said crossly, as her brain processed his previous remark.

'By what?'

'Drugged up?'

'Do we have to go through this pretence every time? Mother, I spent half of my childhood looking for the dragon you were chasing.'

Her eyes widened innocently. 'What are you talking about, George? What is this *chasing the dragon?*'

'You know bloody well what I'm talking about. I thought Lady Morphine was an aunt until one of my friends asked me if I was an aristocrat.'

'Okay, George, enough. A small amount for recreational use does not make an addict.'

'Whatever you say, Mrs Morrison. Just tell me why I am here?'

'Why can't we talk before we get down to that?'

'Because I'm not in China and you're not on the phone. You've dragged my delicate constitution through countless indignities, not to mention a number of Beijing toilets, so spit it out.'

Conditions on the plane and in various other Chinese establishments had not been optimal. His evacuations were the highlight of his day and not occasions to be rushed. In a while he would excuse himself and go to the room Aggs had prepared for him. With a little luck he'd snag a paper on the way up and deliver the next batch serenely into the great beyond like Viking kings of yore.

'I know you don't respect me, George.'

'I've never tried to hide it.'

'Listen to me! Can you do that?'

'Okay, that was a touch theatrical.'

'Please.'

'Fine, get on with it,' he said, cautiously retaking his seat.

'I don't know where to begin.'

'As long as you don't start with *I was born,* I don't care.'

Mrs Kent began to cry. The abruptness of it sent tiny shock waves through his stomach.

'What is it?'

She looked up at him, shook her head and looked down. He gazed out at the garden and waited for it to stop. It had been a few years since he'd witnessed anything like that. He thought those days had passed.

Emotionally turbulent scenes had punctuated his youth with nauseous regularity. Each time the trauma of finding her in such a state would give way to disgust as he realised it was nothing more than the highs and lows of a chemical reality. Loaded with drink and who knew what else, shattering self-pity would give way to tearful euphoria as untethered emotions vied and clamoured for position. But this felt different and it unsettled him. The sentiment was not erratic but controlled and focused. The sound was softer, as though it had been dragged over a long distance and tired along the way.

'What I'm about to tell you is something I've carried with me for almost thirty years. Believe me, not a day has gone by without me thinking about it.'

'I'm listening,' Kent said. He didn't like where this was going. Chats that began like this did not end with port and cigars.

'I haven't spoken about this to another living soul.'

'Well, then maybe you should weigh up carefully whether it's time to break your silence. It might be better to carry it to your grave.'

She flashed him a glare that would have sent Medusa scuttling for her cave.

'It has to be now. It's important.'

He shrugged with feigned insouciance. 'Shoot.'

She returned to the sanctuary of her hands, looking for a way to begin.

'Important,' she murmured to herself, as if evaluating the word and its ability to convey her meaning.

'For God's sake, what is it? I've travelled further than a caribou migration to be by your side and so far the only sickness I've seen is an eighty pence rise in the price of rum.' He had ordered the taxi to stop by a Tesco Express on the way. He couldn't bear the idea of spending the weekend sober. He chastised himself now for not buying more. 'Now either cough up a lung or tell me what you're jabbering about.'

'I don't know where to start. How can I begin to make you understand?'

He contemplated the door and the bakery that lay beyond it in the village.

'Out with it or I'm going upstairs,' he said, irritated by the tangible absence of the éclair his mind had conjured up.

'Slivers of things come to me now.'

Kent salivated. The word sliver for him was inextricably linked with cheese and the association provoked a Pavlovian response, which although not unpleasant, was unattractive hanging from his lips.

'It began in the weeks before I met your father. He was a good man, but he couldn't help me. I was already headed to where I was going. It takes a while for the light to penetrate the darkness.'

'You should write fortune cookies. You have that same vague unsatisfying way of making statements.'

'Today I can almost believe it never happened. But of course it did.' She wiped at her cheeks. 'The drugs messed everything up...made everything crazy.' He swallowed uneasily as his mother eased herself up and walked to the glass doors. She was rarely bipedal.

'I thought you didn't take dru-' He let his observation die.

'The memory of what I've done, what I did to him...to you.' She glanced to check he was listening. 'It has never left me you know...how I felt...what I still feel. You'll ask me, how I could believe such things were real? And I can't explain it. You have to accept that, George. You see my mind...the drugs.' She touched the side of her head. 'I took all those things he said and turned them into something monstrous. He called me his Mary Magdalene.'

'Say what?'

Somewhere deep in his mother's brain everything made perfect sense, but she had all the pieces that filled the gaping chasms in her rambling narrative.

'My life was different before your father. If I had met him sooner, who knows? But it was already too late by then. It had been fixed in here.' She touched her head again. 'You see that, don't you?'

'What in God's name are you jeffing on about?'

'It was HIM. He made me do it. He knew how I was...the distortion...and he didn't care...' Mrs Kent's arms were juddering in front of her.

'Who made you, Dad?'

'No! You're not listening.'

'Listening to what, Madame Zelda? Can you hear your own nonsense? Who are you talking about?'

Mrs Kent had gone somewhere, lost in a cavernous recollection in which he was unable to follow.

'The timing was disastrous. Isn't it funny how the mind can be persuaded to accept such crazy things?'

'Yes, bloody hilarious. Anyhoo, I can see I'm not going to get any sense out of you so, if that's everything, I am going to take a nap.' Kent levered himself upright. 'I'll bill you for my travel expenses.'

'You already did,' she said, frustrated.

'Fine, then I'll bill you again.'

'Sit down, George! I haven't finished.'

He thought about it and took a step toward the door.

She fixed him with another glare. 'I mean it.'

He hesitated a moment and then slumped sullenly back into his seat.

'George?'

'What?'

'I barely recognise the woman. She was mad.'

'And she still is by the sound of it.'

'You have to believe I didn't know what I was doing.'

'Sure,' he replied distractedly.

'I've delayed telling you and now time has run out. Soon he will come to find you.'

'Who's coming to find me?' he said, alarmed. 'You haven't sold me to a cult, have you?'

'I'm glad he's coming. He deserves the right to punish me some more and you're entitled to meet him.'

'Punish you? For pity's sake woman, you're making about as much sense as a drugged horse trying to explain quantum mechanics to a gypsy's testicle.'

'I didn't want to do it this way. I should have told you, but I could never find the right time.'

'I swear talking to you must be some perverse attempt at self-flagellation. Who will come? What haven't you told me? TELL ME'

'I'm not doing this very well am I?'

Kent finally lost control. 'MOTHER!'

'You have a brother,' she said quietly.

Chapter Eight

Frankenstein's Monster

Congregation for the Causes of the Saints

Piazza Pio XII

Giovanni tapped his pen nervously against the desk sweating profusely despite the loose robe he wore. He sent for McCarthy over thirty minutes ago and was growing impatient. The source of his discomfort was a white envelope delivered the previous afternoon. Unable to resist any longer he yanked open the draw, snatched it up and spilled the contents on the desk. He dismissed the photograph and picked up the letter. Starting two thirds of the way down the page he began for the hundredth time to read the spidery crawl:

Now justice is finally being done I hope I can learn to feel pity instead of hate.

What did it mean, he wondered? All night he had trawled his mind for an explanation, but the letter had been frustratingly opaque and he was struggling to make the connections. It had come sealed in a small envelope inside another. The sole function of the larger envelope appeared to be the inclusion of a separate note, which contained just one menacing line:

I'll be in touch

The veiled warning seemed to be at odds with the manner of the letter, which was an odd coupling of restrained anger and tentative forgiveness. It had rambled on for more than six pages accusing him of things he didn't understand. Two sets of contact details jotted down at the end added to the incongruity. Blackmail and intimidation did not usually come with a return address. But it had arrived at his office when it had no call being there with a note that needed no interpretation. This was a threat and a demand was coming.

He looked at the photograph he discarded. The petulant expression of a teenager scowled back at him. He had so many questions, but they would have to wait. He had to act now, even if he didn't fully understand it.

A gentle knock halted the tapping of his pen. He put it down and straightened it so it was parallel to the phone before brushing the photograph and letter into the open drawer and slamming it shut.

'Enter,' he announced, picking up the pen again.

It opened to reveal a tall thin man dressed in black.

'You wanted to see me, Your Eminence?' he said, waiting uncertainly by the door.

'Yes come in, Matthew, come in.' He gestured to one of the two seats in front of a large oak desk.

As the priest settled Giovanni grew quiet. He was thinking about the order he was going to give. The problem was delicate, but its solution required blunt force. That's why he needed a man like McCarthy. He just had to find the right words.

The priest was comfortable in the silence. He understood the reason for it. The decisions they made when they came together demanded it and the deeds they shared left no space for awkwardness.

\#

A sixteen year old boy lay spluttering on the cold tile floor of the swimming baths. He'd been dead for almost three minutes before he was dragged from the bottom of the pool and revived. The bright red trunks, flat now and empty of air, had saved him, billowing three metres down like the sails of a yacht. They should have noticed him sooner, but the baths had been busy and the lifeguard that should have been watching him was busy organising a date for the coming weekend. A girl not much more than a toddler but good with her colours had spotted him. She pointed and shouted to her mummy what she had learned in school. Onlookers said the guard brought the boy back, but he knew better. He had died down there and was reborn with the truth of Lazarus.

He waited six long years to enter the service of the Church and was twenty-two before the seminary agreed to put his name forward. They made him wait because they did not believe in the miracle he'd shared with them. Those who had accepted the paradox of the incarnation and the mystery of the crucifixion could not conceive that an unremarkable boy had been touched by a remarkable grace. They'd calculated the cost of training over risk and he'd come out badly. When they interviewed him years

later he down-played those events and it still felt like a betrayal.
#

Giovanni looked up and met his vacant stare. He fancied he saw a terrible abyss in those green eyes.

'Matthew,' he said. The priest flickered into life. 'There is something I need you to do.'

McCarthy shifted his gaze a few inches above the cardinal's head to the predatory smile of his predecessor.

'I know,' he said softly.

He contemplated what lay ahead with a mixture of trepidation and resignation. He knew why he was here. The specifics were only a matter of form not substance. Each time he was called into this office he was asked to do things he would have recoiled from in another life. Many years ago the cardinal had shown him a different way. He had been irrevocably changed, transformed by his hand into a warrior of God. He'd taught him to move beyond interpretation and yield to a divinity outside his grasp. Religious life was composed not of joy but of fear and trembling that was born of incomprehension. It was the story of Abraham and Isaac and the answer to the riddle. God's command indicated the nature of faith. To have not seen and to believe; To accept that without a beginning or an end; To understand his dominion over all things; To submit to a power that suspends and transcends the domain of the ethical; To embrace without question the will of He who strides beyond it. The first step towards redemption was to accept the inexplicable and embrace His paradox. Only in his darkest and weakest moments did he worry why so many had to pay in blood for it.

'Something has come to my attention, which represents a danger to the security of the Church.' He paused as he let the words sink in. McCarthy sat still. The cardinal always began like this. 'An unholy alliance is gathering strength as we speak.'

Chapter Nine

Revelations Verse Two

Kent fished with his tongue for a globule of jam that had slid from a hot scone and escaped to the corner of his mouth.

'So let me get this straight, I want to be sure I understand everything,' he chewed, spreading a large chunk of butter on a second scone ensconced safely within the grasp of his left hand. 'I have a brother who for unarticulated reasons is not here.' Kent slurped his coffee calmly.

'Let me explain-' his mother interrupted.

'Please, allow me the courtesy of finishing. God knows I allowed your dribbling frenzy to go on long enough. I think we should try to get the ball rolling in a more coherent direction.' He pushed the remainder of the scone into his mouth, chomping noisily as he waited for her to settle.

Thirty six hours had passed since his mother's revelation. He'd spent most of it quarantined, alternating between his bed and the table by the window where he demanded his meals be served. To this end he had permitted Aggs limited access, forcing her to bear the brunt of his flatulence and vituperation. He filled the time gazing soulfully on the English countryside, ruminating upon life's transience and his mother's depravity. An embargo on all food entering his room had ended the stalemate. He'd capitulated under terms of fresh scones and strong Colombian filter coffee.

The French Canadian order was a formidable culinary force and Clotilde's was the envy of other care homes surviving on reconstituted dinners and indifferent carers. They acquired the manor in the 1960s, which like so many grand houses cut from their pecuniary umbilical cords had fallen into disrepair. Uncomfortable financial realities in the 1990s had led to its current incarnation as a house of prayer and frailty. Mrs Kent paid her residential fees and gave generously when additional funds were needed. For her support a son with a sour tongue and a pungent aroma was tolerated and allowed to stay once in a while.

'I believe his absence lies somewhere between criminal drug use and someone who is keen on biblical references,' he finished.

'You don't understand. You can't comprehend the state I was in... if you heard *the voice* you would see...I can hear it now...warm and thick like honey heated up in a pan.'

'I must insist you refrain from speaking. Your attempts at elaboration are like watching a used condom trying to juggle bagpipes. But, adding that to my summation, we have an unspecified party, possibly your drug dealer, with a mellifluous tone who is in some way responsible for my brother not being here. Now I'm going to go for best-case scenario and assume you gave him away. So my question is, when did the deed occur? Who with? And why?'

Kent laughed. This was ridiculous.

'Please George,' she said.

'Can we move this on? Can we at least agree on that?' Mrs Kent moved forward and clasped Kent's plump hands in mid-action like a hawk. 'I trusted it,' she hissed.

'Jesus Christ, Mother, this isn't Macbeth. Answer the bloody question?'

'Only if you're ready to listen?'

'Sure, whatever, just give it to me without the garnish of crap,' he said, pulling away from the discomfort of her touch.

'That is not as easy as it sounds.'

'Yes it is,' he said.

She fidgeted with her cardigan as she thought about it. 'I suppose I should start with the key person in all of this.'

'And that's the father of my half-brother?' Kent asked, feeling a twinge of sadness as he said it.

'I think so.'

'What the hell does that mean?'

Mrs Kent held up her thumb and index finger as though she were holding a small ant between them. 'Well, that's where it gets a little complicated.'

'Hmm?'

'The truth is I was kind of seeing his brother too.'

'Oh dear, Jesus, tell me the day isn't going to start like this?'

She clenched her teeth awkwardly. 'And perhaps another guy from town.'

He winced at the bile which had risen to his throat. It made him cough as it burned.

'He was a very sweet guy actually.'

'And I take it he is germane to our discussion?'

'Oh, he's not German.'

He grunted derisively. 'Who is he?'

'Don't worry, he's nobody. The dates are all wrong. There are only two men who matter in this.' Kent detected a slight smugness in the way she informed him as though she were secretly pleased with the accuracy of her ledger.

'You're disgusting.'

'It was a very difficult time for me, George. I had a lot of wild oats to sow.'

'I really don't want to know about your oats.'

'It's hard to know where to begin.'

'I'll give you a hint. The last piece of information had no relevance whatsoever. The only thing we gleaned from it is you have the sexual appetite of a Bonobo chimp.' He pointed at her mouth. 'Think before you open it.'

Mrs Kent nodded meekly, choosing her next words carefully.

'He called me his Mary Magdalene.'

'Yes you mentioned that. I'm assuming it wasn't Jesus.'

'He said he was special...that genius lay in his genes-'

'Do you mean *genes* or *Jeans*?'

'Huh?'

'Never mind.'

'He told me that man's evolution had reached a spiritual plateau and had begun to stagnate. He was born to complete the journey. He was the first of the end stage and his role was to disseminate the truth and the promise of the divinity he carried inside.' She scrunched up her face at the effort of recalling his words. 'Um... millennia of progress had culminated in him...he was its zenith and the seed that would strip back the universe and remove the obstacles of illusion.'

Kent was flabbergasted. What had this woman done with his mother?

'How is it you remember that drivel but have difficult remembering what you had for lunch?'

'It's tattooed on my back.' She lifted her shirt and shifted around to reveal several lines of small gothic lettering. 'See.'

'What the fuck?'

She gave a sheepish smirk and covered it up. 'Like I said....wild oats.'

Kent couldn't take his gaze from her midriff. 'And you found this attractive?'

'It was the dru-'

'If you mention drugs again something bad is going to happen.'

'I took his words to heart. I was messed up. I believed him and I wanted to be a part of it. I thought if I was the one who mothered his offspring it would make me....' She stopped talking, afraid suddenly how it would make her sound. 'We had joked around about the possibility. I thought maybe...'

'What is it like to go nuts? Does it feel real?'

'My biological clock was ticking, George,'

'Maybe you should have ignored it.'

'Anyway, one night I hinted it might be a good idea to have a baby for real.'

'That's sweet and so well thought out. Conceiving on drugs with a self-proclaimed prophet. Great idea.'

'I don't expect you to understand, George,' she said defensively.

'Good, because I don't.'

Mrs Kent studied him for a moment. 'But when I suggested it, he went crazy.'

'Doesn't that sort of assume he was sane before?'

'George, are you going to let me tell this or not?'

'It occurs to me in order for someone to go crazy one has to be sane in the first place. I tend to think of the word *went* as indicating a transition.'

Mrs Kent took her cup from the table and turned it slowly in her hands.

After a minute of silence Kent gave in. 'Okay fine, finish your story.'

She put it down and smiled in satisfaction.

'He said he could never allow that to happen and if it did he would have no choice but to do something.'

'That's nice and ambiguous.'

'He was very angry,' she said.

'What are you doing climbing in out and of bed with a man like that? '

'It was a strange time, George. You can't imagine what I felt.'

'Oh, for fuck's sake, I've read existentialists that make more sense. I want you to explain why you allowed yourself to be intimate with that obvious loon.'

Mrs Kent fell silent.

'I don't think you're in any position to start sulking,' he said.

'It was the dru-'

He stopped her with his hand.

She looked at it forlornly and said, 'Then the best and the worst thing happened. I found out I was pregnant.'

Kent smacked his face in exasperation. 'Can we speed this up a bit? Why is this shit dripping on like Chinese water torture?'

'I need to tell this my way.'

'Let me help. We've established I have an older brother. So start with why he isn't here?'

She looked at him surprised. 'Why do you say older?'

'Well, obviously it happened before you were with dad. He would never make you give up your baby.'

'You're right, he wouldn't.' She smiled sadly. 'The night we met I was two weeks pregnant.'

'The brothers had gone and I was left trying to make sense of it. I wasn't looking for anything with your dad but then something happened that changed everything. I knew in that instant he was the only way I could save my unborn sons. I was so afraid for them. I thought they were in danger...marked out.'

'Hang on a second.' He squinted as a thought started to take shape. His heart thumped uncomfortably as she rambled on obliviously.

'I don't believe it any longer of course. I can see now I was mixed up. I was lucky finding your father. He was such a gentleman-'

'Stop!'

'What?'

'You said unborn *sons*.'

'Oh yes, I did, didn't I?' She combed her hair uneasily with her fingers. 'I was hoping to do this better, but there's no point in putting it off.'

'What do you mean?' His voice was hoarse. 'You've told me everything, right? I have a half-brother and you gave him away. What is there to put off?'

Kent's eyes were darting around wildly as if they might be able to escape what Mrs Kent was about to tell him.

'In a way you could say he's half, she said.

'What do you mean, *in way half?*'

'Her shoulders drooped as though no longer willing to put up a fight.

'I think you already know what I am about to say, George.'

'Mother?' The question came out as a frightened mew.

'*I mean in a way,* no'

'What?'

'I was carrying twins.'

'What?'

'Your father is not your father.'

'What?' His lips moved, but he had already departed. He was deep inside himself looking up at a pinprick of light.

'Don't worry, it's definitely one of the two brothers. I'm ninety-nine percent sure. I think it was the dangerous one.'

'She doesn't know. She's almost sure. She thinks it's the dangerous one.'

Kent laughed hysterically, farted twice and passed out.

Chapter Ten

The importance of being earnest

London

Jim Elliot pinched the bridge of his nose and let out a heavy nasal sigh.

'I'm worried about this, David. You must see how strange this is?'

He watched his flat mate pick contemplatively at his jumper. He knew he shared his concerns, but he had more to gain in ignoring them. In the growing quietness he felt compelled to justify his reservations.

'Who phones in the middle of the night, taunts somebody with the promise of personal information and then suggests a clandestine meeting without even introducing himself?'

'I know, Jim, I answered the call, remember?'

'You asked me what I thought. Don't get upset because you don't like my answers.'

David exhaled irritably. 'I'm sorry, but you're making too much of this. Just because someone is reluctant to give a name doesn't mean he's some psycho. This is sensitive for everyone involved. He probably didn't want to go into detail over the phone.'

'The first time he rang you became hysterical and yesterday you didn't talk for the rest of the day. Be honest, this isn't normal.'

David looked astonished. He didn't think Jim knew about the second call. He sometimes forgot his friend was around. His unintrusive nature was one of the reasons he invited him to stay. The arrangement suited them both. Jim got to live rent free, which gave him a chance to pay off his mounting debts, and he got to have someone familiar around him who didn't ask too many questions.

'It was unexpected and I overreacted,' he said.

'Why all the cloak and dagger? Why doesn't he tell you who he is or what he wants?' David was surprised by his friend's persistence. The last time he had been this vocal was when he climbed inside a bottle for three months.

If you think about it, the way he's behaving sort of makes sense.'

'Why is that?'

'Well that's just it.'

Jim finally understood. 'Oh my God, you think he's him, don't you?'

Trimble's expression remained impassive.

'Aren't you're jumping the gun a little?'

'How else would he know about my visit with her? They must still be in touch. Think about it, his reluctance to tell me who he is? It's obvious. He wants to wait until we meet.'

'I think you should be careful.'

'What for? Why he would be a danger to me?'

'The whole thing smells funny.'

'You're being paranoid. Anyway, it's my decision.'

'You're right, it is, except of course you want me to be here,' Jim said, annoyed by his flatmate's blinkered stubbornness.

'Is it really too much to ask?'

'In normal circumstances I'd say no, but this isn't normal, is it?'

'Are you saying you won't be here?'

'No, but I do have a right to be concerned.'

'I know, I'm sorry,' he muttered, 'but even if I'm wrong about him, he might have information that can help me draw a line under this.'

'I want you to be cautious, that's all. I don't want anything to happen to you.' His flatmate tapped the cushion on his lap uneasily, embarrassed by his own emotion.

'I will, but you are worrying too much. He's coming here, doesn't that say something? What's the worst that can happen?'

'Why are you doing this anyway? You were furious when you returned from visiting your mother. What do you expect to happen?'

'She's not my mother.'

'Precisely, and this guy is not your father.'

'Dad left me the letter for a reason.'

'And what's that?'

He shrugged. 'I don't know, guilt maybe.'

He looked puzzled. 'Guilt?'

'When I went to see her I found out some things.'

Jim watched David light a cigarette. He could see his hands were shaking.

'What?'

'Well, for one thing, the adoption wasn't strictly speaking official. It seems she needed to offload me in a hurry.' He cringed at the rancour in his voice. 'And my father stepped in to save the day.'

Jim's jaw dropped. 'What? Why?'

'I don't know.'

'What did she say? Why did she-?'

'Give me up?'

He nodded.

'She told me lots of things. She was afraid of someone hurting us...she was ill...all bullshit. If she believes half of what she told me then she's mad.'

'I'm sure something must have happened. I imagine it's not an easy thing to give up a child.'

He laughed humourlessly 'Child? She had twins for Christ's sake.'

Jim looked at him in stunned disbelief.

'What kind of person does that?' Trimble glared at him as anger rushed in like a tide. 'How could she give one away?'

'Why didn't you tell me when you came back?'

'And say what? That my whole existence is down to some crazy woman?'

The way he felt confused him. He didn't want the past to be different, so why couldn't he let this go?

'The point is I think my father came to believe he'd taken advantage of her and deprived me of something.'

'Do you think he knew about your brother?'

'If he did I don't blame him. She was giving me away whether he took me or not. She chose to do it that way, not him. If he held himself responsible then I'm sorry for it. As far as I am concerned there is nothing to forgive.'

'I don't understand why your parents didn't go through the normal adoption channels?'

'Apparently they tried for years, but it didn't happen. They got tired of waiting I suppose.'

Trimble took a long drag on his cigarette. Putting it like that made him feel sick, as though he were a commodity to be obtained in one place or another. But it wasn't like that. His parents were his parents because they were meant to be.

'Do you ever think about it? What it would have been like?'

'No.'

'So why are you doing this?'

'I need to understand why he left the letter. I owe him that much. But whatever I find won't change anything.'

Jim stared at the rippling furrows on his friend's forehead.

'When is our friend arriving?' he said.

'Sometime this evening.'

\#

Father McCarthy sat by the window, his hand nervously playing at his throat. He felt awkward without a collar and he yearned for its restriction. He considered re-buttoning the top of the blue Oxford he wore but decided against it. He'd caught sight of himself in a mirror in the men's toilet at Heathrow and thought it appeared odd. He didn't want to stand out.

For the last hour he had been sitting in a restaurant off the Fulham road. The place was sandwiched between tall white town houses and was a bubble of quiet in the bustling city. The effect was accentuated by swirls of leaves falling from nearby trees and a soft autumnal light that bounced off its warm interior. The serenity was an ill-fitting glove at odds with the tempest inside him.

The name and address the cardinal had given him wasn't much to go on, but a reconnoitre of the property had revealed more. The houses in the area were packed like a fortress and crammed with tenants. There were few opportunities to break in unobserved. The only viable option he decided was through the front door.

The basement flat was accessed from a flight of steps below street level, which told him the twenty something guy in a business suit who flew down them earlier had an obstructed view of anyone approaching the main entrance. An elderly gentleman occupied the top dwelling. He had gone out in the morning and returned later in the afternoon. On the basis of his tortuous pace and the length of time it had taken for the light to appear in the upper window McCarthy guessed such trips were infrequent. He wouldn't be a problem. The two men he observed chatting in the living room on the first floor were his only concern. One of them had to be the target, but the other man's identity was a mystery. The cardinal had not warned him about anybody else.

The plan he'd created in his mind wasn't solid, but it was best he could devise in the circumstances. He ran through it in his head. He'd wait until the cover of night and allow time for the mystery man to leave. If he remained after that he'd have no choice but to kill them both. He'd ring the bell and take out the first man in the hall. The risk of exposure was unavoidable, but a decisive push, strike and drag would minimise the danger. He'd need to enter fast and hit the second man hard to maximise the advantage of surprise. In such high density housing a noisy struggle would not go unnoticed. That was as far as he had gotten. The rest he would take as it came.

As the restaurant started to fill up he watched a group chatting underneath a painted brick archway, which divided the place in two. They were loud and happy and he envied them with a strength of feeling that made him ill. He tried to ignore them, but they forced their way in like water through sand.

McCarthy thought about what lay ahead. *Thou shalt not kill.* He used to believe in the inflexibility of moral law, but such absolutes disregarded the permutations of an unknowable universe. The cardinal had taught him this. Morality was a malleable thing that wrapped itself around a time and place. It was shaped and reshaped by function and the forces of a world that ignored it and embraced it in equal measure. Only trivial truths could be observed. The important ones were defined by circumstance and coloured by a palette of impulse, emotion, reason and motive; Cause and effect. He trusted the cardinal in these things because he had no choice. The suspicions he sometimes had could not be expressed for they would taint the virtue of the things he'd done. If it was all a lie then he would cling to his ignorance as though it were innocence. There was no going back.

#

As a young priest McCarthy had worked in a small rural parish outside Turin. He'd mastered the Italian language as a seminary in London. From the very beginning he longed for a post in Italy. When he learned about the position he immediately made an application to the bishop of the diocese. His reasons for going were thin, but a suggestion that he was reconsidering a life in the Church secured the position. Training and cost over loss. He'd remembered the lesson they taught him.

The transition from England had not been easy. The last incumbent had been popular, long standing and more importantly local. He had passed away loved and still in his post. It had taken patience and perseverance to win them over, but gradually their resistance became acceptance. His tenure lasted longer than was customary and for a number of fortuitous reasons he had missed the Quinquennial repostings. The end finally came with his involvement in what the papers would refer to as the *Disrobing of Turin*. It was this that brought him to the attention of the cardinal.

The Shroud of Turin was a piece of linen in which the body of Christ was said to have been wrapped following His crucifixion. Imprinted on the delicate cloth was an image of a body purportedly with the five wounds of Jesus. A gash to the forehead and lesions to the torso were clearly evident, suggesting a crown of thorns and a public whipping. Puncture marks to the feet and hands hinted at a nail, which might have fixed them to a cross. A slash at the side echoed the narrative of a centurion spear.

The shroud had been the subject of a number of high-profile investigations during the twentieth century, but the results had been inconclusive, providing just enough tangible evidence to fuel the controversy. When a new radiocarbon test emerged it ignited the row once again. The scientific community believed it would be able to conclusively settle the dispute. In October 1988 the Archbishop of Turin broke the news. The Carbon-14 tests confirmed the shroud was a fake. Scientists in Oxford, Zurich and Arizona had verified the age of authenticated samples and concurred they were a blend of linen and cloth woven between 1260 AD and 1390 AD. It could never have covered the body of Christ.

McCarthy understood the attraction. The mere possibility of standing in the material presence of the divine was enough to remove all reason. Two million pilgrims had visited during the first month of public display. But desire was not enough. The robe was a medieval tourist gimmick, a sideshow distracting followers from the real nature of faith. The resurrection was not a sorcerer's trick to be uncovered, but a mystery beyond understanding.

His vociferous support of those wishing to subject it to scientific scrutiny had won him enemies. A Catholic daily newspaper had described him as an *atheist prostrate at the altar of empiricism* and likened his role in events to the serpent in the garden of Adam. In a particularly melodramatic flourish a source identified as a leading Church official had commented:

McCarthy represents the drive of modern man. In this he has undermined what he does not understand. He is, for everyone to see, a contemporary Judas trading silver for notoriety.

In the end it didn't seem to matter much. The sightseers continued to come and coins continued to fill the coffers. He suspected the effects on his ministerial career would be more profound and was astounded when only a few months later he received the call to serve in

Rome. The architect of the move had been the cardinal. It was the beginning of the end.
#

The priest got up abruptly and the chair let out a squeal as the two back legs caught the floor. He dropped a twenty-pound note on the table and walked out.

In a few minutes it would all be over.

Chapter Eleven

A Death in the Family

Wiltshire

If it were not for a peculiar quirk of habit Kent would have fainted where he sat and slumped under his own momentum into the armchair. Instead, he lay sprawled on a rug beside his mother's feet. His natural propensity to pitch himself forward when expelling noxious gases had been his undoing. The unforeseeable onset of unconsciousness had left him vulnerable to gravity causing his head and breasts to act as a counterweight to his arse. His mother looked on helplessly as he nose-dived like a Spitfire to a thin Persian landing strip.

She looked down on the crumpled figure of her son as he rubbed the lump on his forehead. It was his first collapse and he contemplated it with a degree of scepticism.

'Why are you doing this to me?' he said groggily, picking up with remarkable speed from where they'd left off.

'I'm not doing anything to you, George. Please get up. I need to tell you everything.'

He rolled over on his front and propped himself up with his elbows, looking remarkably like a walrus trying to impersonate Marilyn Monroe.

'That's really not necessary?' he said, pushing against the ground with a grunt and dragging himself onto the sofa.

'Let me start at the beginning. Things are so much easier to remember in order,' she said.

He pulled at his shirt, which had bunched unattractively over his breasts. 'You know how they say every story should have a beginning, middle and end. Well, you should forget that entirely.'

'Perhaps, I should tell you how I met your father.'

'Which one?'

She scowled at him. 'The one who raised you and called you son.'

'I don't think you're in any position to take that attitude.'

'Do you want me to continue?' she asked, treating him to a waggle of the trademark Kent eyebrow.

She interpreted his look of contempt as a cue to begin:

'The night started out in The King's Head in Malmesbury. I was in high spirits because I'd had a good win on the bingo. With everything that was happening in my life I needed nights like that.'

He nodded impatiently. 'Go on.'

'Bingo was a proper night out back then...before Mecca jazzed it up. It's all flashing lights and no soul these days.'

'I don't want to hear about the bingo, you fool.'

'Well, it was a bad time for me back then...' Mrs Kent stopped, suddenly aware she was navigating an area she had locked away for nearly three decades.

'Bad time,' he prompted with a circular motion of his hands, like a basketball referee signalling a travelling violation.

'The situation with the brothers was complicated. Thank God I stopped seeing Robbie the month before. That would have made things really thorny.'

'Robbie?'

His mother's tendency to swing from the hazy recollection to idiosyncratic knowledge was one reason he loathed chatting with her. He was no clearer at either end of a conversation.

'He was sweet but far too young. Boys don't know what they want at twenty-one.'

Mathematics had left him alone until now, but it decided at that moment to punch him in the face. 'Oh dear, God,' he retched.

'What's wrong?'

'You were in your forties for Christ's sake.'

'So?'

'What do you mean, so? You were in your forties. What the hell were you doing pedalling around like the town bike at that age?'

'There's no need for that,' she said.

'Of course there's no need for it. There's no bloody need for any of it.'

'Women reach their sexual peak later in life, George and there were reasons I had not settled down by then.'

'Please.' He held out his palms like a shield. 'I can't take any more detours.'

'I don't think-'

He cut her off. 'What did we say about relevance? Remember, if it's not important then no talky.' He pantomimed a talking mouth and slapped it with his other hand to illustrate.

'So, I knew Robbie wasn't in the frame,' she said, finishing off her earlier point.

'The frame?'

'As the father.'

'That's a lovely turn of phrase you have'.

'Thank you, dear,' she smiled. 'I knew it was one of the brothers but, as I said, I wasn't sure which one.'

'No, I'm pretty certain you said it was the mental one.'

'Oh yes, that's right,' she said, scratching her neck.

'What do you mean, oh yes, that's right. Do you not remember?'

'Of course, it was just a slip of the tongue.'

Kent stared at her mistrustfully. 'How the hell does that happen anyway? Two brothers at the same time?'

'Well, I was only seeing one of them at first.'

'Congratulations.'

She ignored the jibe. 'And then by complete chance I met the other one. There was a spark and we were on fire.' She giggled, amused by her metaphor.

'What's wrong with you?'

'I didn't know they were brothers at first. We were both drinking and one thing led to another. You know how it is.'

'No, I don't.'

'Well, I'm sorry, but that's the way it happened.'

His lip curled in revulsion. 'How did you not know?'

'Why would I?'

'Well, their last names would be similar for a start.'

'Yes, there was that,' she conceded, 'but it didn't click immediately. The names were foreign sounding and difficult to remember.'

'All the more reason to associate them. Jesus, you must have a waffle iron for a brain.'

'I wasn't myself.'

'Oh yes, the drugs. I apologise.' He shook his head in frustration. She seemed so completely unapologetic, he thought.

'Over the course of the next few days we fell for each other hard. I didn't put the family thing together until later. When I did I knew it couldn't continue.'

'You make yourself sound so virtuous. Where was your conscience when you thought you were cheating on two strangers?'

'Hey, we never said we were exclusive.'

'That's really classy.'

'I was a modern woman,' she said, offended.

'If modern means a bit of a slag then you were positively futuristic.'

'Now look-'

He waved away her look of indignation. 'Fine, I'm sorry.'

Without a word Mrs Kent got up and walked to the patio doors. She leant on the handle and pushed it open. The sound of the wind and rustling leaves filled the room.

'Are you going somewhere?' he asked, surprised they were unlocked.

She secured each door with a latch to the wall.

'I came clean and confided everything to him. I promised I would end it with his brother...' she said, as the rest of her words disappeared outside.

'Which one?'

'Are you not listening?' she answered, turning back and retaking her seat.

'Yes, that's right. My confusion is down to a lack of attentiveness. Who couldn't follow a story in which none of the protagonists have a name?'

'Are you making fun of me, George?'

'Yes, Admiral Slow, I am. Stephen Hawking would have a brain haemorrhage trying to make sense of this sordid mess.'

'He forgave me straight away,' she continued, filtering out the insult. 'I was relieved...I really liked him.'

'But?'

'But, our continued relationship would come at a price.'

Kent groaned. Here it comes, he thought.

'I had to carry on with the affair.'

'Of course you did,' he said, slapping his thigh for effect. 'What could be more natural?'

'He told me breaking it off would make things worse.'

'And why is that exactly?'

'Because his brother would want to know why.'

'So?'

'Well, he was convinced that would be very bad for everyone involved.'

'You make him sound like a Bond villain. Are you telling me you couldn't make up a reason to split? You've managed to deceive me well enough.'

'I didn't deceive you, I just didn't tell you certain things.'

'And I suppose the dog didn't shit on the rug, he just forgot to do it outside. There's still a big pile of poo either way.'

'That's not the same thing, George.'

'No, you took the crap and hid it under a cushion instead. And I just sat in it.'

Mrs Kent watched some leaves dance on the carpet by the door. She would have to clear them up, she thought.

'He was adamant his brother would find out. Honestly, I think he was scared of him.'

'Then why not end it with your one true love?'

'I was smitten. I thought there was a real prospect for us.'

'What, sneaking about?'

'I thought that maybe in time the other relationship would naturally finish and we could pretend we had met afterwards...by accident...like we sort of did.'

'Please tell me you told him no.'

'I'd rather have two of them than nothing.'

'And that was the only option?'

'There was no other way.'

'In your world perhaps.'

'We lived in the moment, George.'

'Where are they now, tell me that?'

'Sometimes you have to take what you can where you can.'

'That's lovely. You know Grace isn't just one of the simpletons at your coffee meetings.'

She raised her eyebrows. 'What's done is done, George,'

He sighed. 'So what happened?'

'Of course, after I found out I was pregnant it changed things. I had to tell him.'

'Tell who?'

'My sweetheart.'

'Which one was that again?'

'Don't be facetious, George.'

'I will when you stop being fatuous.'

'I was upset because I wanted it to be Frank's, but I was certain it was Vinnie's.'

'Oh, so they have names now?'

'Of course, I'm not an animal.'

He regarded her sceptically. 'They don't sound very foreign.'

His mother grinned at him as though he were a girlfriend she was about to share some sexy tale with. 'Well, they were sort of pet-names, ones I thought went well with their faces.'

'*Special* names for a *special* lady.'

'That's right,' she said, misunderstanding his meaning.

'Why were you so sure Vinnie was the father?'

'I knew inside.'

'How scientific.'

'Women's intuition' she said. 'It's not like I wanted it to be his, but I just knew.'

'I thought Vinnie didn't want children.'

'I thought he might change his mind once he found out. I was wrong.'

'What did he do?'

'I'll get to that.' She paused and stood up. Kent had never seen his mother so mobile. He knew she was capable of it, but she rarely flaunted her ability. She picked up the leaves that were bothering her off the floor and sat back down.

'I went to see Frank first. It was too much for him. We argued and I left. When I returned he'd gone.'

'Where?'

'I don't know, but he never came back.'

'The course of true love never runs smooth, eh?'

'Don't be cruel, George,' she said, inspecting the dry brown leaves in her hand.

'What about Mad Dog Vinnie?'

'I didn't have a chance to tell him. When I went to talk to him he was already gone.'

'So he did a runner then? Franky boy must have spilt the beans.'

'No, he didn't,' she snapped. 'His leaving was coincidence.'

'And how do you know that?'

'Don't worry about that.'

'Are you telling me he ran for no reason?'

'No, I'm saying he left. Whatever reason he had to be in Malmesbury was over.' She crushed a leaf and felt it disintegrate in her palm.

'And he didn't tell you he was going?'

'Nope.'

'You obviously made quite an impression. Didn't you try to find them?'

'I didn't know where to begin. They were foreign. They must have gone back there.'

'Nice place *foreign*. Drinks are a little expensive but I hear the weather is gorgeous.'

'Don't start, George.'

'And you never saw him again?'

'Not physically...not in the flesh...'

'On the telephone then?'

'Not exactly.'

'Am I going to guess until the monkeys on typewriters get past Hamlet or are you going to tell me?'

'I saw him the night I met your father...or at least I think so.' Her tone took on the dreamy quality he had learned to fear.

'Or at least I think so,' he mimicked. 'This isn't the matrix. Things are or they are not. Now, which is it?

'You need to understand how I was...know the things that led up to that point in my life. Nothing was normal. Anybody might have cracked.'

'Cracked?'

'I'm running ahead of myself. Can I start again?'

'I'd rather you didn't.'

'I've got lost somewhere,' she said, looking for a place to connect her narratives. 'Let's go back a bit. Remember, I was in the in The King's...pregnant and alone.'

'We've been here before. I really don't need to hear it again. Although technically it's actually forward chronologically speaking.'

'While I was there I met this man. For the life of me I can't remember his name?' Her features contorted as she tried to recall it. 'Doesn't matter,' she said, 'but he had an arse that could crack walnuts.'

He considered putting his hands on his hips but decided it wasn't natural sitting down. 'How much have you had to drink today?' he asked.

'I'm telling you how it was.'

'Well don't, it's repellent.'

'He said I had the bestest body he'd ever seen.'

'Obviously not a Booker Prize winner then.'

The idea that his provenance had any relation to a stranger that approached unfamiliar women with shards of English grammar and invented adjectives was upsetting.

'Don't be nasty, George. He was just being nice.'

'I suppose he could have meant you were the most bestial thing he had ever seen.' He sneered his bestest sneer.

'We got talking and after a line of coke in the toilet and a crack pipe he invited me to the Red Lion where he was meeting friends.'

'You know for a second there I thought you said a line of coke and a crack pipe.'

'It was the 80's, George. They were wild times and I was raising hell. I deserved it.'

'You were pregnant!'

'So he invited me to the Red Lion, ' she continued shrugging him off, 'that's the pub in Avebury opposite the mystical stones-'

'You were pregnant!'

'Opposite the mystical stones...' she repeated loudly, trying to rejoin her sentence.

'Pregnant!'

'Opposite the mystical stones....' she shouted over him, refusing to get pulled into an exchange of insults.

'I know where it is,' he fumed. 'And just because some Stone Age idiot suffered a hernia dragging a large rock from one field to another does not make it mystical.'

'So I thought, why not?' she said, ignoring his interruption. 'He had some lovely friends and I would have happily let any one of them butter my toast.'

'And pregnant!' he cried, crumpling under the effort of trying to banish the image of his mother getting her toast buttered.

'After a few more lines of coke and what not, I was starting to feel woozy. I should have been enjoying myself, but instead I felt inexplicably sick.'

'Maybe you should have nipped back to the loo with your friend. There's nothing like a crack pipe to settle the stomach.' He may not have been fussy about what he put into his body, but that was a pretty good place to draw the line.

'Am I telling this story or are you?'

'You are and sadly it's not a story.'

'I decided to go back to my mother's because she lived nearby. So I asked this lad if he would give me a lift.'

Kent looked at the ceiling. 'What lad?' he said, tracing a brown mark that looked like a tea stain.

'The guy with the tight buns. You're not following this very well are you?'

He gazed at her in disbelief. 'It's difficult to keep up with the sheer number of suitors. What were you doing in cars on crack and pregnant at the age of forty-two? You make Moll Flanders look like Mother Theresa.'

'I had come to the end of my parole. I was letting off steam,' she said.

'What?' Kent saw purple spots in front of him. His heart was whispering mutinous threats to him as his mother's face faded in and out of focus.

'Oh Jesus, Oh Jesus, I'm not hearing this. I've gone insane. Please God let it be that. I can recover from that.'

'Don't judge me, George. You don't know what I went through.'

'Are you trying to kill me, is that it? Do you want me dead?' he said, clutching his right breast.

'Anyhow, this lad got it into his head that I wanted more than a ride home, but I wasn't up for it...not that night.'

'I need a drink,' he groaned, pondering what improbable turn of events had caused him to wake up in this dystopia he found himself in. It could be bad shellfish, he thought. If only he'd eaten some.

'George, stop being a baby. Real life is not all dinner parties and canapés. Sometimes you get dirty and it's fun. If you gave into your feelings once in a while you might not be so miserable.'

Kent thought of the Lithuanian, his first stolen love, writhing away on his continent of flesh and her eyes clenched tightly shut as her flushed countenance groaned upwards in an obstreperous benediction. But that sort of thing was for him. His mother's sex was functional. That was the way it was supposed to be.

'You know what I think it was?' Mrs Kent said, her voice and then her likeness forcing itself rudely into his reverie.

'What what was?'

'Why I was feeling sick?

'Crack and Tia Maria I would imagine.'

'I think it was grief.'

'Grief?'

'Yes, it was the Fourth of July,' she said, as though its meaning was obvious.

'Am I supposed to be guessing the answers here? What were you grieving about? Lives lost in the American War of Independence?'

'It was our anniversary and I missed Charlie. I was the wrong side of forty, pregnant, broke and alone.'

'Who's Charlie?' he said irritably. 'You do realise that I can't see inside that water balloon you call a brain.'

'My first husband.' Kent's gut exploded. He couldn't be sure, but it felt like there might be a bit of last night's dinner in his pants.

'I was forty-two,' she said. 'A lot of living was done before I met your father.'

His countenance took on a greasy sheen of panic.

'What? Did you think I lived like some spinster in one of those Jane Austen novels?'

He arched his eyebrows uselessly. Speech had left him.

'I remember the first time I saw him in town. I thought he was so handsome, I nearly wet my knickers. He was like a fifth Beatle. In my mind it's like yesterday. I was twenty-one years old. I'd just got off work from the Woolworth's in town. It was a Saturday. Payday.'

'Who are you? What have you done with my mother?'

'I know you don't understand this, George, but this is who I am. So many years with your father watching my Ps and Qs. Don't get me wrong, I loved him, but I changed for him.'

Kent had often wondered how his father and mother got together, but now was not the time for answers.

'Why are you telling me this?'

'You need to know where I came from so you can understand and make sense of what happened the night I met your dad.'

'You're talking about events twenty years apart.'

'But they made me what I am.'

He rummaged in his pockets for his iPhone. 'I'm ordering pizza.' He hit a number on speed dial and ordered two large meat feasts. After he had hung up he called back and added a bucket of chicken wings.

'What can I tell you about Charlie?'

'How about nothing?'

'It could have been so good,' she panted, breaking off momentarily. Kent swallowed painfully at the images in her head. 'But then I wouldn't have had you. I'm grateful for that.'

'But not enough to stop using crack apparently.'

'I was young and beautiful then.' She paused, waiting for her son to reassure her that she still was. An awkward silence told her the compliment would not be forthcoming.

'It didn't take long for him to notice me. He came right up and said he'd seen our future. We were married six months later. Poor old Dad never got to see it, but Mum cried enough for everyone,' she sniffed.

'Where is Charlie now?'

Her features darkened. 'I'm coming to that.'

He watched the rain that had started and wondered just how deep the rabbit hole went.

'In the beginning it was wonderful. He was romantic...considerate...funny. He took me out every weekend. Sometimes we would pretend we weren't together and he would pick me up like he did the first time. Occasionally we'd let it play out with the other fellas...tease them a bit...but Charlie would always get to take me home. It made us both feel good...it was exciting.'

'You sicken me, do you know that?'

'Then you're probably not going to like what I'm about to tell you.'

The hole went deeper. A Guatemalan sink hole in the middle of his life.

'Me and Charlie were coming up to six months married. I was working permanently by then at the Mcilroys, the department store in Swindon that used to be on Regent Street. I'd finished work and arranged to meet Charlie at The Kings. We were going to get something to eat and hit the dance halls. I was waiting at the bar for him to arrive when this man came over.' The cheap aftershave he wore lingered on malevolently in her memory. Even now her tummy would flop and flounder like a dying fish at the smell of it.

'He was probably no more than forty, but he looked ancient to me then. I still remember how his breath stank and his horrible brown teeth. He was an awful man...arrogant. He reckoned if he bought me a Babycham and threw some smut I'd fall over him.'

'On the basis of what you've told me over the last few days, I'm amazed it didn't work,' he said.

'That's not funny, George.'

'It wasn't meant to be.'

'I'll be honest, it made me angry. I wanted him to know how stupid and how up-himself he was. I wanted to embarrass him.'

Kent snorted scornfully.

'So I led him on. When I got bored I told him to piss off, but he wouldn't accept it. He grabbed my arm and said I was a tease. That was when Charlie arrived and the situation got ugly. He couldn't accept being flipped off like that. In the end the landlord had to intervene.'

'And he left?'

'Yes.'

'That's okay,' Kent said with relief. He didn't know what to expect, but that didn't sound too bad.

'I wish now they'd come to blows. It might have stopped it from happening?'

Tension swooped on him like a rabid owl. 'Stop what?'

'When we left the pub a bit later we saw him waiting outside by his car. I told Charlie to shut up and keep walking, but that was like a red rag to a bull. Things got out control.'

Kent was trying to stay in charge, but rage was kicking down the barn door. 'What did you do? His voice was strained.

'He wanted to kill us, George. Charlie was only defending himself.'

'Tell me.'

'There was a struggle and Charlie accidentally stabbed him.'

He fought the urge to pass out. 'Accidentally? What did you think he was carrying the knife for?'

'How do you mean?' she asked, baffled.

Although screaming seemed the most appropriate response Kent forced himself to calm down.

'Was he an amateur surgeon? Or a compulsive whittler perhaps? Maybe he intended as a postmodern commentary on the emasculation of men in an increasingly matriarchal society.'

'There's no need to be sarcastic, George.'

'There's no need for about three-quarters of your life, but you did it anyway.'

She could see beads of sweat trickling down her son's face.

'We left him bleeding on the ground, not knowing whether he would live or die.'

'I need some water,' he croaked, exposing an undulating mass of pink flesh as he dabbed his brow with the tail of his shirt.

'I always regretted that, even when I read in the paper he'd been found and taken to a hospital. We lost a lot of sleep worrying about what happened. It took a long time to put it behind us.'

'How brave of you.'

'And then we saw him again or at least I did.' She gazed out at the statue of St Francis of Assisi in the garden and composed herself. 'He was standing there by the bar in The Kings like nothing had happened. Charlie didn't see him until it was too late...the glass made a mess of his face.'

'Will you stop saying *The Kings?* You sound like an old lag. Use its full name.'

'He begged him to stop but he wouldn't...everyone just stood around too scared to do anything.'

'Yes, I'm sure it was dreadful,' he said. So Charlie was killed in a pub brawl, he thought. He could live with that.

'But that wasn't the worst of it. Maybe some people reckoned Charlie needed a good thrashing, but no man deserves to be urinated on in a room full people. What kind of creature does that? Can you understand someone using you as a toilet?'

Several blood vessels on Kent's cheeks and forehead popped. She was trying to kill him, he thought. She aimed to shock him into a heart attack. She was trying to get away with the perfect murder.

'It hurt a lot worse than the bruises. The Charlie I knew died that night. He started drinking heavily and it wasn't long before he lost his job at Reaps Construction. That's when things turned really sour. You see, he blamed me in a way for what happened...and I sort of understood that. I had been a part of it yet I had not been punished like he had. I was a constant reminder of what he wanted to forget. With him out of work I had to support the two of us, which made him resent me more. While he drank my wages he'd tell me I was useless and gloat about other women he'd been with. I ignored it hoping things would get better.'

'So you left?'

'I put up with it for seven years. I hid the bruises and paid for his drinks. I suppose I felt it was my problem...my responsibility.' The skin around her jaw tightened. 'Until one night I snapped.'

'And then you left?'

Kent felt the bitter taste of bile in his throat again. Reason dictated that she was the victim, but he couldn't bring himself to feel sympathy. She should have known better and he hated her for bringing this to him. The bond between mother and son would tie his past to hers and he could feel the injustice of it mushrooming inside him.

'I killed him,' she said.

Kent opened his mouth to let in the flies as his insides reared like a stable of prize stallions. He could feel the air in his bowels increasing in pressure and he gripped the arms of the sofa in preparation.

'You see, that night he came home and passed out without saying a word.'

'That's good, that's good. That's good, isn't it?'

'No, it wasn't. Don't you see?'

'No, no, no. I don't see.'

'He didn't beat me and that made me mad.' She studied him a moment, checking to see if he understood. He hadn't.

'It brought everything into focus. It was as if reality had suddenly been unveiled and I could see everything as it really was. I was furious because I'd expected it. As he lay there snoring I was filled with rage at my stupidity. I hated him more than anything in my entire life and I despised him for making me the way I was. He was the most pathetic thing I'd ever seen and yet I allowed my life to be ruled by him.'

Kent felt like crying.

'I have no doubt had he beaten me that night I would still be married to him and that's the hardest thing of all to live with. Looking back I should have walked away, but I didn't. I took the leg of the table and I hit him with it until I was sure he wouldn't wake up again.' Mrs Kent started to weep. 'They locked me away for ten years.'

Kent always assumed bad things happened in other places. It was incomprehensible that it could touch the mundane safety of his life. In this place, in the village, he should have been protected.

'Inside they're supposed to *cure* you,' Mrs Kent sobbed. She used her fingers to punctuate the word, 'but it was in there that I developed real problems.'

Kent blacked out.

Chapter Twelve

Worried

The Vatican

Giovanni wiped his glistening forehead. The fire had been a bad idea. The housekeeper had thought so too and after dinner she left him alone with a quizzical look and a glass of whiskey in a flickering room. The night was mild, but he felt cold when he returned and it had seemed urgent then.

Two days had passed since he'd spoken to the Dean and fewer than twenty-fours since making contact with McCarthy. Giovanni tried to picture the priest at that moment but found it abstract and unsatisfying. He'd been to London many times and his appearance was familiar enough, but placing him there moving and thinking seemed impossible. He imagined himself a giant instead, strolling across Italy and stepping over the puddle of Austria into France. He took a couple of steps and leapfrogged over the English Channel before the vision finally disintegrated and became the bright orange of a fire again. He poured himself another whiskey. It had to be done by now.

Chapter Thirteen

The Virgin Whore

Wiltshire

Kent batted away the napkin in fright, taking a moment to register his mother's presence as she stood over him waving it uselessly. That was twice now in as many days, he thought worriedly. At least he'd passed out in his chair this time.

'Get that thing away from me,' he said, as a feeble current of air tickled his nose.

'How are you feeling?' she asked.

'Hungry,' he groaned woozily, aware his stomach appeared to be convinced it was breakfast. The blackout must have screwed with his internal settings. He never hankered after bacon and eggs this late in the day.

'In a minute, George. We have things to finish first.'

'What things?' he said, reaching for a glass of water which had materialised by his side.

'Concentrate, George.'

As Kent braced himself for it to start again he spied an open pizza box by his mother's feet. He noticed several pieces were missing.

'Is that my pizza?' he asked incredulously.

'You were snoring, George. I didn't know how long you would be.'

'You're unbelievable.' He leant across and tore off a slice. 'Is nothing sacrosanct?' he grumbled to the drooping triangle in front of him.

'Maybe you have *the narcolepsy.*'

'Why are you saying it like that? You sound like the Amish.'

'It's not my fault you respond to stress so ineffectively.'

'You're right, I should avoid these situations. Shall we get this done and agree not to see each other for a while?'

'You never come to see me anyway.'

'And now you know why.'

'I don't have time to argue, George.'

'Then I suggest you proceed.'

She reached for a slice of pizza and was stung by a lightning fast smack on the back of her hand.

'Not on my watch.'

'Fine,' she said, rubbing her wrist. 'Well...I'd finished parole and I was celebrating. I made up my mind to have fun. After the brothers I had sworn off any relationships. I wanted to get to know me again.'

Kent leant back in tired disbelief. His mother, the ex-con.

'So you thought you'd have a no strings sex session with some fellah you'd befriended over a crack pipe in a pub toilet?'

Mrs Kent let the comment go. 'That night changed everything. My needs no longer had any relevance. There was something far more important at stake.'

'What?'

'I'm getting ahead of myself again. You're pushing too hard, George.'

'Yes, I imagine questions which demand you explain what you're drooling on about can be quite gruelling. However, I will agree to endure another session of you meandering through the entire English language without actually saying anything if you answer one question.' He paused for her to object.

'Go on,' she said.

'Why would Dad take on the kind of baggage you were carrying?'

His mother considered it for a moment. 'He was a good man.'

'But not a saint. What was in it for him?' he asked, picking a piece of pepperoni off his trousers.

'Are you saying I wasn't much of a catch?'

'You are correct, Madame.'

'Why do you have to be so blunt, George?'

'A reactionary trait borne from your inability to summarise I should think.'

She frowned, unsure what he meant. 'Let's say he didn't know everything about me,' she replied cryptically.

'Oh, it was one of those relationships.'

'What do you mean, one of *those* relationships?'

'Built on duplicity and dishonesty.'

'Don't judge me, George. I might have left out one or two things, but I loved your father'

'I guess murder with a table leg isn't a great conversation starter.'

'Charlie got what he deserved,' she said, hurt.

'Mother, not wishing to be invidious, but I recall you saying you felt... what was it?' Kent squinted and pressed his fingers theatrically against his temples, as if summoning the word from the deepest recess of his memory. 'Grief?'

'I still get emotional on our anniversary. We had some good times you know?'

'Bar a few months of salacious fornication he beat you for almost the entire length of your marriage.'

'Yes, but we still made love from time to time. He was a fine looking man-' She caught sight of her son's disbelieving glare and crossed her arms in protest. 'I was a very sensual woman.'

Kent winced.

'To answer your question, your father knew nothing about my other life. I behaved myself around him.'

'What about the pregnancy?' he said, the question fighting its way through chunks of half masticated pizza.

'I'm getting to that.'

They were interrupted by a sudden knock at the door. Before they could object it opened with a creak and an old woman of indeterminate age peeked around the thick wood. It was his mother's neighbour, Mrs Knight.

'Hello, dear,' she said to Mrs Kent. 'Are you busy?'

'Not now Beryl.'

'Are you coming to the market?'

'No, Beryl, I'm in the middle of something with my son.'

She smiled at Kent. 'You telling him about his dad, then?'

'Wonderful' he said. 'So, you've filled in your cronies?'

'Go, Beryl,' she said sternly.

She disappeared without further argument.

'Very nice' Kent said, after she'd gone. 'It's nice that you've shared more with her than the man you were married to for twenty-five years.'

'Never mind about Beryl. She doesn't know what she's on about half the time. Now, where was I?'

'You were about to tell me what improbable circumstances enabled you to snag my dad.' Putting it like that made him feel miserable. He was his father, wasn't he? As a teen he'd always seen himself in his dad, not his mother. What did he do now?

'Fate threw us together.'

'Can't you just tell me what happened and spare me the cosmic sound bites?'

'Well, I was in the car feeling sick.'

'Whose?'

'The guy with the tight buns...the one that could crack walnuts? Try to keep up, George. That's the second time I've had to explain.'

'Sorry, I was thinking about you doing porridge.'

'What?'

'Forget it,' he said, fanning her away.

'He'd agreed to give me a lift home from the Red Lion, but it turned out he wanted the fare in advance, if you know what I mean?'

'What's with the *if you know what I mean* schtick? It's like talking to a cockney spy.'

'There's no need to be grumpy, George.'

He stayed quiet. There was every reason.

'I couldn't help myself, I swear but...I vomited on him.'

'Uh huh,' he said breezily, resisting the growing compulsion to start punching the walls.

'Well, he became very angry.'

'Ooh I can imagine,' he said.

'Suddenly he's tearing at my clothes. I cried out for help, but the music in the pub was too loud.'

'Why would he do that?'

'He was going to rape me, George. And he would have done if your father hadn't come along.'

'Puke must be quite a potent aphrodisiac around those parts.'

'He pulled my attacker out of the car like a bag of shopping and the next thing I know he's looking at me and asking if I'm alright.' She shivered as though someone had run a feather across her back. 'My Prince Charming.'

'Go on honey, you tell it.'

Mrs Kent eyed him distrustfully.

'He wanted to call the police...'

'Naturally.'

'But I was embarrassed.'

'You didn't want him to discover you had form, did you, sweetheart?'

'Form?' she said.

'A record of your criminal endeavours.'

'You probably think that's silly, don't you?'

'No, not at all babe.'

'What's wrong with you? You're being very understanding. You sound funny.'

'I hoped you would ask,' he said, leaning forward. 'Quite disconcerting, isn't it? Now, take that sensation and multiply it by the number of atoms in the universe and you'll have some idea of how I'm feeling.'

'George, what are you talking about?'

'Absolutely nothing,' he sighed.

She looked melancholily at the slice of pepperoni which had fallen on her son's crotch. 'My sadness was lifted like a curtain and I'm not ashamed to say I desired him.'

'To do what?'

'I mean sexually speaking,' she said.

'Ugh,' Kent groaned.

'I persuaded him to walk with me amongst the stones and I forced him to take me then and there.' The old woman's countenance glazed over. 'I remember the moon and the feeling of cold stone against my bare buttocks.'

'Mother!'

'Sorry,' she said sheepishly, her cheeks red from the recollection.

'Dad did that?' he asked sceptically.

'He never did anything like it again,' she said, reading his mind. 'People behave out of character when they're sad and lonely. Both of us had suffered in our lives. Perhaps that's why we were drawn to each other. Your father didn't like to talk about it, but he'd lost a son before we met. He was married then. They turned their backs for just a second and he drowned. The endless recriminations finished them off. That's what grief does, George. It gets between people.'

Another undisclosed sibling, Kent thought, and a dead one at that.

'Fate's a funny thing, George. She seems so random and so personal all at once. Our mutual misfortune had given us something to latch on to. I was a widow and he'd lost a son.'

'A Black Widow more like. You were a convicted killer who'd done ten large in the big house for bashing your husband's brains out with a piece of furniture.'

'George, don't be nasty.'

'Whatever you say, Slick.'

Shrivelling under his mother's scrutiny Kent occupied himself jangling some loose change in his pocket until she was ready to move on.

'We talked for a bit afterwards, but it was awkward. I could sense he wanted to leave. He was polite...offered me a lift home and so on...but I turned it down. I needed space to think. He gave me his business card and we said goodbye. I never had any intention of calling him again. I wasn't ready for anything and neither was he.'

'But you did see him again?'

'Yes, I called and he agreed to meet me. We had dinner and I told him about Charlie.'

'Wow, you told him everything...all the lurid details? Why? I thought you weren't ready for anything?' Kent was secretly impressed. So the old girl did have some decency after all.

'Well, not the entire truth. I sort of said he died in a car accident.'

He moaned in disgust. Decency had well and truly left the building. 'You mean you played on his tragedy to establish a connection?'

'Do you want me to go on, George?'

He said nothing. For better or worse he couldn't allow her to stop now.

'I had to lie. I needed to him see a future for us. His belief in my pain was a foundation on which to build. That would be important after I broke the news to him.'

'Oh, God,' he said, horrified. 'Tell me you didn't.'

'I didn't do it for me, George.'

'You tricked him. You said the babies were his, didn't you?'

The revelation made Kent feel like an imposter. His father's real son had died and he'd taken his place, positioned in his affection like a cuckoo's egg in another bird's nest.

'You're detestable.'

'Let me explain.'

'Go on then.'

'The night with your father, after we made love-'

'Yes, yes,' he flapped, squeezing his eyes tightly shut as he tried to lock out the image.

'Something happened, something which would make being with him long-term vital...or at least it seemed so then...'

Kent drew a question mark in the air with his finger.

'It's difficult to explain,' she said. 'It was like a break.'

'Break?' What had she broken, he wondered?

'With reality,' she said.

'You must try to organise your thoughts. I can't sit through another episode of you drivelling on like a cockatoo with learning difficulties. What break? When?'

'There's no way to explain it logically, George. I mean I didn't go crazy and start running up and down the street. After it happened everything appeared to be normal. Trains were still trains, buses were still buses, shops were still shops, but this thought that was bonkers and crazy existed alongside all of that. And it changed everything.'

'And there she is,' he sang. 'Completely fucking nuts.'

'It was fantastical and unbelievable, but I believed it with all my heart. That's why I had to deceive him.'

Kent's head fell into his hands. 'What are you talking about?'

'If you listen you'll understand.'

'Why don't you tell the truth? You lied to Dad and told him the babies were his because you were scared of being on your own.'

'Baby,' she corrected. 'And you're wrong about that.'

'What do you mean, baby?'

'For him there was only you.'

His brow creased in frustration. 'Meaning what?'

He tried to anticipate what was coming but as with all of his mother's disclosures he was like a blind man trying to follow breadcrumbs.

'That night I walked home along the field parallel to the road. It was late. The moon was large and bright and the sky was cloudless and full of stars.'

'You're not Hemingway. I don't need you to set the scene.'

'The point is I felt happy. In that moment I believed things would get better.... and then...bang.'

'You were shot? '

'No, I mean, bang, it happened.'

'What?'

'I've never been able to recall everything, but I remember falling and the cold wet ground slipping away beneath me... the sensation of my arms and legs melting together as my mind dripped into the starry dark. And I remember I was not alone. There were so many voices...desperate sad voices...whispering and crying out....like a colony of nesting birds on a rock in the sea,' she said distantly, ignoring the puffing noises emanating from her son. 'Their cries were lost in each other...I couldn't make out what they were saying. At first I thought that I'd died...had a brain attack or something.'

'Ah, the brain attack, that well-known medical diagnosis.'

'I wondered if I'd gone to hell or maybe some place in between.'

'Why?' he asked, pushing to one side the urge to slap some real sense into her.

'For the life I'd taken from Charlie. I thought maybe they were eternal echoes damning me for what I had done...the voices of the people he might have touched or helped had he lived.'

'Touched or helped?' he asked, confused. 'Charlie didn't sound like the type of guy involved in charity runs or inspirational speaking.'

'But then one voice grew louder,' she continued, 'pushing its way deep inside my head.'

'And you don't believe this anymore?'

'The human mind is capable of so much, George, of building worlds within worlds and inhabiting them as though they were as real as we are now.'

'What are you talking about?'

'It was like a cascade of warm honey washing over me...a wave of pure rapture enveloping me in absolute joy. I never wanted it to end.'

Kent discarded the empty pizza box and picked up the next one. What a sideshow, he thought.

'But then I heard something else...something lurking inside. It said terrible things about you...about me....'

'Sounds a little Freudian. Possible fears of motherhood perhaps?'

'You're not hearing me, George.'

'Unfortunately I am.'

'It was *him*.'

'Who?'

'Your father.'

'Didn't he just leave?'

'I mean your other father.'

'I think at this point it might be prudent to add something to distinguish between the two.'

'Your biological father,' she said. 'At least that's what I remember. I'm not so certain anymore. He may not have been there at all.'

'Thank God you cleared that up.'

'Who knew what chemicals were in my system?'

Who knew? Jesus, what a wreck, Kent thought.

'The words were lost, but I understood the message. It was a warning. Someone was coming for you and your brother.'

'And who's that, sweetheart?'

She scrutinised him carefully, unsure if he were making fun of her. 'Do you understand what I am telling you?'

'Yes, absolutely. You're saying you had a bucket load of drugs and took a magic carpet ride.'

'You're mocking me, George, but when I felt the wet morning grass beneath me it remained with me.' She pressed her finger into the bridge of her nose. 'Everything I knew had been fractured into a hundred pieces and put back together again differently.'

'Are you actually listening to yourself? I can't believe I've been sitting here like a potted plant absorbing this shit for two days. I mean, Jesus Henry Christ,' he choked, working himself up. 'You are a mad, gin soaked, over-sexed, under-brained and drug dependent mental person. Seriously, enough. What in Satan's ball sack are we doing here?'

'Visions, George, visions. My mind was close to bursting. I had no choice but to listen.'

He expelled a masticated bit of beef from his throat and coughed. 'And what did they tell you?'

'That you were special.'

'Okay, I'll give you that one.'

'No, I mean SPECIAL,' she said.

'I'm not following.'

She pointed skyward and whispered, 'Sent by him.'

He exhaled vehemently. 'Absolutely mad.'

'The two of you were born for a purpose and my duty was to protect you from those forces seeking to destroy you.'

'And those *forces* would be my sperm donor father?'

'I'm not sure. In my head he was connected, but the whole thing was greater than him. I didn't know everything, but I knew I had to keep you safe until you were able to fulfil your destiny.'

'Mad, utterly mad.'

'Years later I began to suspect I'd made a mistake.'

'And it took you that long to figure that out?'

'But I was convinced back then that giving one of you away was the only way to keep you both safe.'

'And not even a tiny part of you thought, hang on a second, I'm fucking nuts?'

She shook her head.

'How would splitting us up help anyway? Wouldn't I still be in danger?'

She muttered something he couldn't hear.

'What was that?'

'The prophecy said two, not one. They'd be looking for twins.'

'It's a prophecy now, is it?'

'Tell me, how can somebody be so mental and come back? How have you escaped committal?'

'Giving up your brother ripped me in two, George.'

'Do you know what I think? This is all some dementia led delusion. Charlie, twins, the drugs, prison.... it's all bollocks. I think you've bordered the senility bus while I've been away. I mean, at seventy you're hardly a spring chicken. You almost had me,' he said, jabbing a playful finger at her.

'He's come looking for you, George.'

'Who has?'

'Your brother came to see me. He found a letter from his father. I tried to explain to him what I've told you, but he wouldn't listen. When he left I thought I'd never see him again but then he called about a week ago looking for you.'

'So you've come clean because you had to?'

'I know this is difficult to take in, George.'

'Sent by the maker indeed. You didn't actually think your children were going to grow up and become...'

Mrs Kent turned away.

'Actually, what did you think?'

'I don't know,' she said quietly.

'You're hardly the Virgin Mary. There are rabbits with more discretion. How could Dad not see the problems you had?'

'It's complicated.'

'Well, try to explain. God knows you're lucid enough when explaining nonsense.'

She began to cry.

'Your father and I more or less lived apart and when we came together we were strangers. Did you ever wonder why he was so busy?'

George didn't answer.

'It didn't work out like I thought it would. I knew I could never replace the family he lost, but I hoped I might become something he could live with.' She wiped her cheeks. 'But we didn't fit and no amount of trying could change that. He stayed in London during the week and most weekends too. He made-believe he had a beautiful wife...a perfect family....but I was better in the imagination than in the flesh. Why do you think he took you to London so many times instead of staying here with me?'

'Then why get married at all?' Kent asked.

'He was an honourable man. He accepted you were his and he wanted to legitimise you. He didn't see you as a burden, George. You gave him a reason to carry on. He loved you. Our marriage was built around his need for you.'

'Well, I'm sorry as a foetus I lacked the moral fortitude to stop you.'

'He was happy, you know' she said defensively.

She waited for him to speak.

'Don't you have anything to say?' she said.

After a long pause Kent said, 'No, but I do have a question. How did you convince Dad to let you give up the other baby?'

'He didn't know I was pregnant with twins.'

Kent clicked his teeth a few times and ran the tip of his tongue irritably over his top lip.

'Okay,' he said slowly, as if he were speaking to a small child. 'Let's pretend for the moment that not everyone speaks the language of the insane. Tell me, how does that happen?'

'I had a doctor issue me with a death certificate in India,' she said, mimicking his tone. 'There's a big black market out there for fake documents.'

'Are there many people up to that kind of thing?' he asked curiously.

'The main interest is in insurance claims for bogus hospital stays and expensive medical treatment. Death is the extreme con. Not many people will try that.'

'How does it work?'

'They buy them over there, combine it with a holiday in some nice resort and make a claim when they get home. The doctor gets a percentage up front of the fabricated bill. Everyone's happy.'

'How do you know this?'

'You learn lots of things in prison.'

'So you went to India?'

'Seven months before you were born. I stayed a week in Delhi and told your father I was visiting relatives in Cumbria.'

'What about the birth. Wouldn't he found out then?'

'I left a note and took off. I said I needed some space and he needn't worry.'

'And he accepted that?'

'As far as he was concerned I had over a fortnight to go. I told him I'd be back before the due date. What could he do?'

'But the baby would be early?'

She shrugged. 'Lots of babies are premature. I waited a few more days after it was over. I wasn't that far out in the end.'

'Where did you go?'

'Yorkshire. I figured it would be remote enough to avoid any chance occurrences.' Mrs Kent wiped away a tear. 'I said goodbye to your brother two days later.'

'Did the hospital not ask about the father?'

'There was no hospital.'

'What do you mean?'

'I mean there was no hospital?'

She waited for him to put the pieces together. His expression told her he hadn't.

'I hired a cottage. I read everything I could and then I let things take their course.'

Kent's jaw hit the floor and carried on walking. 'Isn't that dangerous?'

'Nature been doing it millions of years.'

Why did she suddenly sound Creole, he thought?

'A hospital would mean records,' she explained.

The image of his mother screaming on the floor of a dilapidated shack assaulted his brain like a triad gang. The knowledge she had taken not one but multiple trips into the heart of darkness was tougher to take than a sandpaper enema. He wondered what else was left to confess.

'So you returned home with a baby?'

'In life things happen unexpectedly. Your father learnt that lesson the hard way. He didn't ask too many questions. I'm afraid our relationship was not a normal one. And I had come back with a healthy boy, which was all he really cared about.'

'Why go to India at all?'

'To get the certificates. I couldn't risk them fobbing me off with a worthless piece of paper. I made certain it came from the right people and was filed in the right places.'

'So what do these certificates say?'

'Officially you were born in Delhi. You lived and your brother died. There's no record of his birth in this country and nothing to contradict the official story should anyone come looking. As far as anyone is concerned your brother is buried in a grave in Lechlade.'

He gasped in horror. 'What's in it?'

'An urn and some ash.'

'How is it nobody has asked any questions?'

'Like what?'

'Like why a woman about to give birth would fly to India?'

'Who would ask?'

Kent thought about this for a moment. 'The hospital where you went for check-ups?'

'What check-ups?'

'God in heaven. How have you hidden such colossal insanity?'

The rabbit hole was a bottomless chasm. He hoped he had enough fuel in the tank for the journey back.

'Things are not joined up, George. Besides if I needed a reason I'd make one up.'

'Like what?'

'It doesn't matter.'

'Indulge me.'

'I don't know...perhaps I wanted to bless my unborn son in the water of the Ganges. There are no laws against doing stupid things.'

She'd thought of everything. It was amazing when he considered most of the time she liked to dance on the lower end of the IQ scale.

'There is one thing which doesn't make sense. How did you know it was twins?'

'What do you mean?'

'In the field...when it happened....you were no more than a couple of weeks pregnant.'

She shrugged. 'You tell me?'

'I have to admit I'm struggling here.'

'Take your time, sweetheart. Don't rush it.'

'Where is he?' George asked.

'I found a family through a prison pal.'

'Lovely.'

'It wasn't like that,' she said. 'I was in an open facility toward the end of my sentence. They put you in there so you can reintegrate. My friend was in for fraud or embezzlement or something....quite posh. She had some rich friends looking to adopt. I thought they'd give him a future.'

'And everyone went along with it?'

'She found good people. They were desperate for a child and willing to move away and start again.'

He felt sick. 'How could you manipulate a broken man to be a part of this?'

'Things would have been a lot worse without your father.'

They acknowledged the truth of this in silence. His life was a sacrifice for the two of them.

'And in all the months before we were born you never considered what you believed was utter pig drivel?'

'No.'

Kent had had enough. He forced himself to an unsteady standing position. "I believe it was the great Desmond Tutu who said, '*When your dreams turn to dust, vacuum*'. Now if you'll excuse me, I need to purchase some Shake n' Vac."

Mrs Kent listened to her son's laboured breathing as he made his way out.

'You don't have to like it, George,' she said after him, 'but your brother's coming and he's bringing someone who can help you find your biological father.'

The sobbing came in shuddering intervals like a bicycle pump venting air. She had cried a sea of tears over the years, but there was no salve of grief for her. Her son was out there judging her for the death that became their separation.

Chapter Fourteen

What's the time Mr Wolf?

London

The orange glow of the tunnel lights played against the rivulets of water running down the window of the train carriage as it bumped and jolted on the track. His breathing had started to slow, but his throat was still sore from the run. He'd walked at first, but after a couple of streets he'd broken into a flat-out sprint. Fortunately the route had been quiet. The only person he encountered was an elderly woman in a clear plastic rain-hood, but she'd been too preoccupied with the stubbornness of a terrier to notice him.

The adrenaline in his system made him jumpy as he sat. He threw a furtive glance around him. The only other occupant of the carriage was a pinstripe suit engrossed in a copy of the Evening Standard. He felt safe enough to risk a peek at his own clothes. He didn't see any blood; No sign of what he had done. The priest felt inside his coat and slid his finger reassuringly against the

cold steel of the blade. He hadn't liked using the knife. Killing a man was a personal thing. He dipped into his left pocket and touched the cord, which lay coiled like a sleeping snake. In the struggle of a rope there was no place to hide, but he realised the moment Trimble opened the door it would be too perilous.
#

It was dark when he rang the bell. The lights in the flat were on, but the curtains were drawn. As he stood waiting on the step his heart felt engorged in his chest, pulsating like a separate beast, hungry to accomplish what he'd been sent to do. The sound of commotion from within upped the tempo in his ears and drowned out the noise of the city. As the chain rattled on its hook he readied himself.

The door opened to reveal one of the men he had seen earlier. He hadn't looked as big from across the street. He gripped the knife. This wasn't going to be easy.

'Hello, I'm-'

'So you're him?' he said, cutting him off.

The priest was stunned. He'd not been expecting that.

'What?' was all he managed to say.

A flicker of unease crossed the man's brow.

Realising his mistake McCarthy rallied his scattered thoughts. 'Yes, I'm him.'

The other man considered him a moment. 'Then you'd better come in,' he said, leaving him standing at the entrance.

'Please shut the door behind you,' he called behind.

The priest closed it with a gentle thunk and followed him in. The hallway was almost black and the only illumination came from the door of the flat, which had been left ajar. With the broad back of the man obscuring the way ahead he failed to notice the cushioned bench with mail strewn across it. He caught it with his left leg and fell heavily against the wall.

'What are you doing?' asked a jittery voice in the darkness.

'Sorry,' he said, 'it's hard to see. I'm a little disorientated.' The young man sounded edgy, the priest thought.

'Needs a bulb,' came an unapologetic reply.

What was going on, he wondered? *So you're him,* he had said. Clearly he was expecting someone, but the way he was acting suggested it wasn't anybody he knew or trusted. So who the hell did he think he was?

McCarthy ran through the options available to him. He wasn't foolish enough to think the easy entrance was luck. Whoever he was supposed to be was still due and that was a problem. He didn't have much time. His intuition told him to leave, but he was here now and he wanted it done. He should have taken out the big man straight away, but the unexpectedness of his remark had thrown him. He hoped it wasn't a mistake he'd regret.

In contrast to the cold hostility of the hall the flat was warm and softly lit. The sitting room was tastefully decorated with expensive brush linen sofas and shelves full of artefacts from foreign places.

'I need a stiff drink. Would you like one?' the man asked him once they were inside.

'Thank you.'

'I've some chilled vodka in the freezer or would you prefer something else?'

'Vodka sounds fine.' The condemned deserved one last drink. He was an emissary of God not a stone cold killer.

He watched the young man fumble self-consciously with the glasses on the draining board and tried to connect his gentle manner with the cardinal's grave warning. He'd killed enough bad men to know a bigger plan was in play, but something about this didn't sit right. He dismissed the thought from his mind. He couldn't afford to get lost in that now.

'Are you alone?' he asked.

The man hesitated. 'Yes...why, is that necessary?'

'No, but preferable.' The priest was grateful. Only one person would have to die tonight. 'The matter is delicate,' he explained, edging quietly towards him.

'What is this about?' He unscrewed the lid and poured out the liquid. 'On the phone you said you knew some things? What I can't work out is why it concerns you?' The bottle hung over the second glass waiting for a response.

The priest tingled all over. Was he talking to him? Did he know? He wanted to ask the question, but the thought of where the answer would lead terrified him.

'That's why I arranged this meeting,' he said, staring at the boyish curls on the back of his head. The murmurs of doubt had started. They always came, but they never made any difference to the outcome. The first time he killed a man it knocked the wind from him, but the Rubicon had been passed long ago. Repetition just added to the number of ghosts that turned up in between.

'You must have a lot of questions.' The words faded away as he eased the knife out of his pocket.

'You can start by explaining why he didn't come in person?'

The cardinal never came, he thought, squeezing the handle tightly as a gelid calm of inevitability wrapped itself around him.

'I'm sorry,' he said quietly.

'And why is that?'

'Because he couldn't do the things I do.'

McCarthy had become the angel of death.

In one fluid movement he drove the knife deep into his neck and took a large step backwards, clenching his hand in discomfort at the reverberation in his fingers. The blade was embedded to the hilt. He must have glanced bone, he thought, as he watched the blood pump out of the gaps around it.

Distance was a trick he'd learned after the first one. Dying was never gentle when he came calling and he knew better than to get too near. The flailing arms and grasping hands always sought him out as if seeking a connection to anyone who might appreciate the magnitude of what was happening. He had seen this performance more than once during his time with the cardinal. It was always the same. The first act was instinct, the second terror and the finale a cry for comfort.

The young man was different. He remained quietly standing as gluey threads of saliva swayed from his bottom lip like branches in a breeze. The only sound hinting at his distress was a soft wheeze of air as it dragged its way through clogged passages. It seemed to the priest that, in some confused final logic, he believed the stillness might somehow slow or prevent what was happening.

Galvanised by a sudden realisation the man took a laboured step forward and collapsed in a heap, his legs folding with an audible crack beneath him. Slumped against the fridge he clawed at his throat, nails scratching skin, until without any preamble they stopped and died against his neck with the grace of a landing butterfly. The head jerked a little longer, unable to quite accept the body's resignation, as a pool of black red spread on the shiny linoleum like an oil slick on water.

The priest crouched down on his heels and checked the pulse at his wrist. His song had almost finished. He studied the dying green eyes as they stared quizzically at the swirling carpet beyond them. What was in that gaze, he wondered?

Getting up quickly he looked down and for the first time in a long time he became afraid. The murmurs came again: *How could a man redeem himself by losing his soul?* He hurdled the body and vomited into the sink. He regarded it with shock. He hadn't done that in a while. Wiping at his mouth with his sleeve he ran the water and grabbed a cloth from the side. He hurriedly cleaned the knife and slid it back into his pocket. He scanned the room one last time before hurrying into the cool night air.

\#

At St James's Park station the doors slid open with a whoosh and four young men in jeans and puffers climbed aboard. They stood, despite abundant empty seats, in a group beside the exit holding on to the rail above them. Their loud banter unnerved him. Had they noticed him? Of course not, he thought. Why would they? No one was coming for him. Not yet. He needed to keep it together. There was more to be done. Tomorrow it would be over.

#

Behind a slit in the curtain separating the sitting room from the rest of the flat an unblinking eye fluttered back into life. Pushing through on his knees Trimble crawled towards the blood. As he reached his friend's crumpled body he slung his arms over his shoulders and hauled himself on to his chest. He lay there with the tenderness of a lover and listened for a sign that someone had heard his pleas.

The blood on his cheeks and chin were dry before he found the strength to push himself up again. He sat for a while with his back against the fridge and Jim's head cradled in his lap. He rubbed at his face, staring in disbelief at the rusty-red flakes falling on his lap. That was Jim's blood. He had laughed at his friend's warning and now he was dead. How could he tell his family that? How could he tell them Jim stepped up to do what he should have done? How could he tell them Jim had died because he was too cowardly to confront his own demons? How could he tell them he was dead because everyone around him died.

Without any idea of where he was going Trimble grabbed his things and hurried out the door.

Chapter Fifteen

Tears before bedtime

'What is it, Mother?' Kent said into the mouthpiece as he lumbered about restlessly, his movement a response to the gadfly on the other end. He cradled the phone under the fatty folds of his left cheek, encasing it like an octopus devouring a crab. The arrangement left one hand free to give physical expression to his demurrals while the other dragged the wire behind him like a saline drip.

'George, I need to talk to you,' she said nasally, which made him wonder if she were coming down with a cold.

'You should have considered that before you opened the proverbial can of worms,' he said.

'You have to come out some time,' she squawked.

'Do I? ' he said absently, distracted by a fox that had traipsed into the still landscape outside. Kent didn't approve of its sudden appearance. Its brisk trot through the preternatural stillness was an insolent daub on a masterpiece of tranquillity.

'Fooking vermin,' he said, as his brain inexplicably urged him to imitate the voice of Ted the gardener. He was famous within the residential community for his disinclination towards the creature.

'Don't be rude, George,' came a tinny rebuttal.

'I wasn't talking to you. It was Ted.'

'I may be old, but I know my own son.'

'I think coming downstairs would be a mistake.'

'Why, what's happened?'

'What indeed,' he said, turning the right side of his face to the warmth of the sun.

'We'll talk about it when you come down.'

'That's a somewhat circular suggestion,' he muttered.

Kent spotted a lone piece of toast covered with marmalade on a plate beside his bed and moved over to introduce himself. He was unable to say how it had survived the earlier assault, but the effort of juggling the cumbersome rotary phone combined with the low height of the table made acquiring the malted temptress quite difficult. He clawed at it with his free pinkie, stubbornly refusing to compromise on his possessions.

'George, are you there?' his mother asked, her voice swimming against the backdrop of the drama.

He finally yielded to the demand for greater movement and dropped the base unit on the bed. He pinned the slice down with one of his talons before scooping it up with the aid of the other four. In three noisy crunches and a short swallow it had disappeared. He immediately looked down at the golden crumbs and lamented his impetuousness. It would take time before they could be replenished.

'George, I can hear you breathing,' Mrs Kent continued. 'Don't make me come upstairs and get you.'

'Hmm,' he said, picking the unit back up.

'Do I have to do everything, is that it?'

'Mother for every one thing you do I get an ulcer the size of a camel's hump.'

Kent had spent the last twenty-four hours in grave isolation. With the aid of a mobility cart, leased from another resident in exchange for a box of fudge and a packet of fruit pastilles, he'd managed the quarter-mile journey to the village shop. Once there, he gathered enough alcohol and finger cakes to sustain him for his withdrawal. The early hours of the binge had resulted in severe inebriation and a self-examination of such brutal honesty that it had left him weak. He took to bed for the rest of the day and night, weeping and expatiating on scented lilac note paper. He decided just before dawn he would regain his strength and escape his albatross before he shot it.

'What are you doing anyway?'

'I'm finishing breakfast.'

'Breakfast! It's the middle of the afternoon.'

'It was a miracle I managed sleep at all. The skeletons in your closet make quite a racket in the dead of the night.'

'It's two thirty, George. You need some exercise and I need you down stairs.'

'I'm well aware of the time, Mother,' he snorted. 'However, we are in agreement that a postprandial stroll would probably do my constitution some good. Therefore, I propose, that you arrange for some lunch to be brought up. I would consider it a conciliatory gesture.'

'We don't have time for this. A gentleman is here to see you,' she said, lowering her voice until it was barely audible. She glanced over her shoulder at the tall man sitting beside her and smiled awkwardly.

'What gentlemen? Walnut boy?'

'You'll find out when you come down, George.'

'That's a rather large assumption, Mother.'

'If you're not here in five minutes no more food will brought to your room...ever.'

He stroked his beard thoughtfully while he considered this.

'Fine, but I do so under protest.'

'Why can't you do what I say without complaining all the time? I am your mother.'

'And that's something I have to live with every day.'

He hung up. He didn't answer to threats and would never succumb to anything as base as blackmail. It was fortunate she'd fallen into the grey area of venality.

Kent strolled leisurely to the loo. The laxative effect defecation had on the mind was a fact rarely extolled. Auguste Rodin, his favourite artist, was one of the few to recognise this. *The Thinker* was a perfect depiction of mental concentration facilitated by excretory exertion.

\#

Trimble pressed his foot down on the accelerator of the Volvo and the speedometer climbed to eighty-five miles per hour. He looked nervously in his rear view mirror unsure what he expected to find there. He'd spent last night sitting on the edge of a bed in a hotel in West London drinking himself into a stupor. He'd awoken fully dressed on the bathroom floor just before noon. Getting drunk had not been the most sensible thing to do, but it had helped get him through the night. The shaky sickness of his hangover had unexpectedly restored a measure of calm.

As he slumped under a cold shower, two things wandered groggily around his head. Jim was dead and he should have been. For all his guilt he knew he didn't want to die, not like that. But what did he do? The prospect of the police terrified him. What could he say to them? The situation was crazy. Real life wasn't like this. How was he going to convince them this story was true? Before he could persuade himself to go, as he should have done the day before, the thought he had been avoiding all night finally hit him. *Had Mrs Kent been telling the truth?* He stumbled out of the shower in panic. They were in danger. If he didn't get to them they were dead.

Trimble blinked his headlights impatiently at the car in front of him and it chassed to the middle lane. As he punched the pedal again a shrill ring from the cell phone on the passenger seat startled him causing the vehicle to veer to the right. He looked at it in disbelief. The caller ID said it was Jim. He picked it up.

'Hello?'

'David, are you there?' He recognised the voice straight away. How did he know his first name?

'What are you doing with his phone?' he trembled.

'I saw what happened to your friend.'

'You're a murderer.'

'I know you're frightened, but you must listen to me.' The cool indifference of his previous calls had been replaced by concern. 'Are you alright?'

A surge of outrage coursed through Trimble like a flash flood. He wasn't going to let this bastard dictate events any longer. He wanted to kill the son of a bitch.

'You're a fucking murderer,' he said.

'This wasn't me, David.'

'I'm going to find you and I'm going to fucking kill you.'

'I saw the body on the floor and-'

'You killed him.'

'I can see what it looks like, but ask yourself, why would I do that?'

'You thought it was me.'

'You're right I did and I'm glad it wasn't. I checked his wallet and saw his driving license. I just pray whoever did this will not uncover their error. I saw your friend's phone and found this number. I am sorry.'

'You're a liar. Don't you dare touch him.'

The image of the black handle protruding from Jim's neck rested like a dead weight in his mind. Why had he hidden behind that curtain? The two of them might have had a chance. Perhaps he would have seen the knife and reacted. They'd be at the station now recounting their absurd story together. But that was the fiction. He hadn't been there for him. He had left him like a beast of slaughter in a pool of blood.

'I understand how you're feeling-'.

Trimble punched the steering wheel. 'You have no fucking idea how I'm feeling.'

'I didn't know it would go this far. That's the truth.'

He gripped the cell angrily. 'Tell me why?'

'I promise you, I will work this out.'

'And how are you going to do that?' he said, shaking with rage.

'Your friend was a mistake. He was in the wrong place at the wrong time.'

'That's bullshit. Nobody else knew we were meeting. There are no *they*. You killed him.'

'I know how this looks, but things are not what they seem.'

There was a hostile silence.

'Fuck you.'

'There are others involved in this...those who do not want you to know the truth about your father.'

'Who are you? What do you want?'

'I didn't want this to happen.'

What the fuck did that matter, Trimble thought? Jim was dead and he was never coming back.

'Just stay the fuck away from me.'

'Let me help, David. I can make sure no one else gets hurt.'

'So do it. You don't need my permission for that.'

'I'll do everything I can, but you need to get your mother and brother and find somewhere safe.'

'She's not my mother you prick. My family is dead, just like my friend.'

'Okay, but you don't want to see her hurt, do you?'

Trimble didn't answer. He was already on his way. He didn't need to be told the right thing to do, not this time.

'Don't tell anybody where you're going. I'll contact you on this number.'

'I'm going to the police,' he said, taking pleasure in the consternation he imagined it would bring to the other end.

'And that's the right thing to do, but please wait a couple of days. That's all I need.'

'Fuck you.'

'Don't be stupid, David. If you go to the police you won't be safe.'

'Is that a threat?'

'It's a fact.'

He listened to the ragged breathing on the other end.

'Just give me some time,' he said. 'I swear this will be over soon.'

Trimble stabbed the disconnect button with his thumb and threw it on the seat beside him. It would never be over.

\#

'I said five minutes, George.'

'My, aren't we the pedant,' he sniffed. 'It's a pity you weren't so concerned with details when you omitted to tell me that for the man I thought was my father was actually some chap you ensnared into the role and that my real paternity lies in some atavistic copulation of befuddled insobriety. On top of which, I might add, you also failed to mention that I have a brother, a twin nonetheless, that owes his conspicuous absence to the ramblings of some immaterial being slash bloke, also undetermined, with a God complex.'

'George, don't start,' she sang, winking mischievously at her guest as if to indicate that this was a purely playful admonishment. 'I told you before, I wasn't that drunk.'

'Cut the act, Mother,' he said, pushing aside her attempts at levity. 'Once you get a thirst on Russian sailors go into hiding.'

'You break my heart, George, you break my heart,' she replied, patting her breast lachrymosely.

'Not so difficult to do when it can be purchased for half a pint of stout and a gin and orange.'

'I'm not going to argue with you. You've kept this nice man waiting long enough.'

Kent's expression narrowed as he debated the effort of walking across the room against the likelihood that it would either be a waste of time, or worse still, yield more disturbing facts to besiege his troubled mind. The intelligent look of the stranger, a stark contrast to the ambling insanity of his mother's, gave him some cause for optimism and with a cursory nod of greeting he began the migration. Twenty surprisingly small steps later he took a seat.

'Who are you?' he asked, adjusting his weight so it settled comfortably. 'You're not my brother and I take it you're not the man responsible for persuading this wretched creature.' He indicated with an accusatory finger that his mother was indeed the creature in question. 'To give away one of a priceless pair. So who are you and why is he not here?'

'I don't know,' the priest said truthfully, taking this as his cue to sit down. Unbuttoning his suit jacket he took a seat in the armchair opposite.

'Please do not make the mistake of treating me with the same regard as this fool.' He directed five chubby splayed digits towards his mother. McCarthy glanced at her anxiously, hoping for some intimation of what the fat man was tub-thumping about. She gazed blankly ahead.

'I will try to remember that,' he said, bewildered by the behemoth in the ill-fitting bathrobe.

The priest had arrived almost half an hour earlier and was astonished when once again he was ushered in with barely any need for fabrication. After a maze of corridors and steps he found himself being presented to a lady with blue hair. She looked him up and down just as the other man had done and invited him to sit without another word. In the intervening hour she'd neither inquired who he was or what he wanted, explaining only that she would rather they talk to her son together. She had filled the wait with odd monologues, questions he didn't understand and inane small talk.

'Who are you anyway?' Kent asked.

'I've told you, George,' Mrs Kent interrupted. 'He's going to take you to see your brother.' Her knees were moving up and down, excited at a prospect she had waited nearly thirty years for.

'Why didn't he come himself?'

McCarthy opened his mouth to say something but shut it again. Something about all of this was beginning to sound unnervingly familiar.

'David said he might be bringing someone along. I suppose he sent you in his place,' she speculated, providing him with a neat answer to the big man's interrogation. 'I'm sure he's very busy.'

'When did he phone?' McCarthy asked.

'Yesterday morning.'

She didn't know he was dead, the priest thought.

'And you didn't think to mention that?' Kent said.

'I forgot?'

'Oh yes, that's right, you have a memory like a sieve, unless of course it involves manslaughter, forced sex or amphetamines.'

'That's unfair, George.'

'By your own admission you caved your ex-husband's skull in with a table leg. You also alluded to a sex attack, which I seem to remember was precipitated by you emptying the contents of your stomach over some ape's upholstery. And it's no secret you've had more drugs than a Glasgow heroin convention. So how exactly am I being unfair?'

'That's unfair.'

'Anyway, moving on...what did he say?'

'He said he was meeting someone and if it went well he would bring them along. What does it matter now? This man is here to take you to him. Get ready will you, George.'

'First, tell him to answer my question,' he said, gesturing rudely to the priest.

Why don't you ask the nice gentlemen yourself?'

He turned and looked at him expectantly. 'So?'

'Excuse me?' McCarthy answered, mystified as to what he was supposed to be commenting on.

'My mother says you know where he is. Now out with it or bugger off.'

'Where who is?'

'Hare Krishna on a Ferris wheel. Who do you think? My BR-O-THER,' he said, breaking the word into three angry syllables.

'And you want me to take you to him?'

The fat man's bizarre ferocity was giving him a headache. The incident in London hadn't settled well and combined with the torrential abuse it made him feel as if he were standing on the precipice of reality.

'Jesus wept,' he said, slapping his hands against the sides of his chair and muttering something inaudible to the floor. 'It's like talking to a monkey on smack. Yes, my brother, my sibling, un frère...a fraternal counterpart in my misery...a consanguineous cohort to share the burden of my parentage. Isn't that what you are here for?' He wobbled to his feet treating the priest to a glimpse of thick blotchy red goose pimpled thighs through his loosely tied robe. 'Or perhaps this chat is over?'

'Yes, I know where he is,' he answered speedily, realising their appearance signified the obese man was about to leave. 'I'm sorry, I'm a little tired,' he explained. 'Your brother is dealing with other pressing matters. I've been instructed to take you to him.'

'Hallelujah, it speaks. Welcome back to the human race,' Kent said, light-headed from the exertion of divorcing his bulk from the armchair so rapidly.

'Yes, he's in a meeting. He's very busy, but he wants to meet. Don't worry, he's perfectly fine I assure you.'

'I didn't ask you about his well-being. I'm sure any man devoid of this pitiful woman's company can only prosper from it. I asked where he is.'

'At his office.'

'And who are you?'

'I'm his assistant.'

'Ooh very nice,' Kent said, impressed.

Mrs Kent moved her skinny frame to the edge of her chair. 'So, what now?'

He wanted it over, but he knew he'd have to wait. It was foolish to think he could have done it here. He was too exposed. He ought to be grateful to them for giving him a pretext to lure them away.

'I'll take you to his home. He'll meet us there.' The priest jangled his car keys to emphasise the point.

'I can come?' she asked, rocking up and down like a young girl in the presence of a lolly.

'Yes, of course.' the priest said. She was on the list too.

'No, you bloody well can't,' Kent bawled. 'The last thing your abandoned progeny wants to see is your beaming face.'

'Actually, he's asked to see you both.'

'Then that's something for me to take up with him when we arrive. Go and get ready, Mother.'

The priest gave her a smile of encouragement, which Kent noted with disapproval.

'Where are we going anyway?'

'Oxford.' He had no idea why that place sprang to mind, but the fat man accepted it with a grunt.

'I've always thought Oxford was a beautiful city, steeped in history,' Mrs Kent burbled excitedly to herself. David hadn't said where he was from. She was looking forward to finding out more about him.

'Oh shut up, Mother. You're about as interested in history as a Klansman is in rap music.'

Satisfied with his rebuke he addressed McCarthy. 'So we're good to go?'

He nodded.

'Then lead on my good man,' he commanded with his index finger.

'Don't you want to get dressed first?' he asked, trying to disguise his revulsion at the thought of what lay under the bathrobe.

'Yes, George, put some clothes on and make yourself decent.'

'If you knew anything about decency we wouldn't be in this mess.'

'That's no reason to go around half dressed.'

'Wait here,' he instructed. 'I won't be long.

The priest nodded wearily as Kent swept imperiously out of the room.

Chapter Sixteen

A Time to Kill

Clotilde Manor

Trimble had arrived to see his friend's killer ascending the steps that led into the manor and the sight stiffened him like a board. The man was a devil and his long black trench coat became a cloak billowing in the gusty wind. The dark clouds gathering for rain seemed to understand the terrible nature of the monster it threw into gloom. He imagined it might snatch his scent from the heavy air and discover him, bounding over in great lupine leaps to correct with snarling savagery the mistake it had made.

As he disappeared inside Trimble felt an uncomfortable mixture of fear and shame. The strength of his self-loathing was powerful enough to propel him from the vehicle to the entrance before he realised he had no idea what he was doing. Rushing in would get everyone killed. On a bench under the shade of a willow tree two nuns regarded him curiously and accepted a thin smile as he returned to the safety of the Volvo. Whatever he did next had to be decisive.

He had parked some way back from the front in a hastily erected area of asphalt, which served as an additional car park. The approach to the main entrance gave little cover. If he tried to tackle them as they exited he'd not have enough time to cross the open ground on foot before he was spotted. He contemplated going in and walking them out. But could he gamble on the killer's unwillingness to act in a public place? Everything was a risk from where he sat and he had to use whatever leverage he had. Right now, that was being dead.

In his wing mirror he observed three nuns walking down the oak drive and in his rear view an elderly man in a wheelchair left unattended on the front lawn. People were everywhere. There was little chance of getting away unseen. His gut told him the killer would lure Mrs Kent and her son into an environment he could control. So what was taking him so long?

Trimble glanced at the photograph taped to the dashboard. He had no idea why he'd stuck it there. He wondered whether he had always intended on coming back, perhaps to sit and watch for different reasons than he did now. He looked for commonality in the face staring back at him but found nothing of himself. It wasn't just the weight or the height which set them apart but also the angular bald head which soared like a mountain peak above a fertile brown tree line. From a distance it had the appearance of a goose egg resting precariously on half an egg-cup. Below it bushy eyebrows were cast furiously down, seeking out the bright orange cravat which rested at his neck like a tumour.

He had obtained the snap from Mrs Knight, a resident at Clotilde Manor. She'd burst in on him and Mrs Kent during his first and only visit there, clutching the dog-eared photograph as though it were a ticket to their exclusive club. Her incessant chattering filled the remaining ten minutes as she tried to offset the awkwardness her entrance created. Mrs Kent, unable to find the words to drive her friend away, wandered off to arrange more tea in the hope his reluctance to talk would do the job for her. It was in this moment Trimble found himself presented with it. She had been reluctant to part with the picture as her grandchildren enjoyed showing it to friends, but she'd insisted.

The shot had been taken several years ago at a barbecue in the village. A scowling Kent held a can of Heineken in one hand and three burgers in the other, resembling a row of tyres in a bicycle stand. He was, Mrs Knight confided, an odd duck, prone to unexpected outbursts. She suspected for a time he suffered from Tourettes until she realised the sole focus of his invective was his mother. His behaviour had on occasion given the community grounds for concern. She recalled in particular a staged sit-in at a local cake shop dressed in nothing but a cravat and a pair of moccasins. She'd not really understood how the incident was connected to Mrs Kent or why removing his clothing strengthened his cause, but ten hours later he was hospitalised for gluttony.

The sudden appearance of Kent and the man in the black trench coat brought intense relief. He had been right to wait. He watched the two of them descend the steps to the entrance and make their way to a green Renault Clio parked off to the left. The stranger moved swiftly around to the driver's side and motioned impatiently for him to get in.

'What did I do to deserve this?' came a disembodied shriek.

Trimble located the source of it teetering above them, heavily sprayed hair blowing about like blue candyfloss on a stick. The tilt of the fat man's head below and the pronounced jut of his chin made his feelings clear. The assassin, however, unsure where to place himself in the mother-son dispute, had switched his attention and was motioning for her to come down and join them.

A thunderous roar broke the stalemate, followed a split second later by a frenzy of lightning arms and spittle, reminding Trimble of some old black and white footage he had seen of Adolf Hitler at a Nazi Party rally. Mrs Kent shifted from foot to foot like an over ripe prize-fighter as she evaluated his display. The black trench coat gave up his appeal and nervously divided his focus between the two of them.

'Are you coming or not because I'm not coming up there after you?' Kent finished yelling. 'You have five seconds.'

The threat seemed to do the trick and she scuttled down towards him and disappeared through the open car door. The fat man swore a couple of times and slammed it shut behind her. He walked around to the front passenger seat mumbling to himself. After a game of twister, a cry for help and several expletives he was wedged firmly inside. It confirmed his decision to wait and follow. Kent would be no help in facilitating his escape. He might well need a fire crew for that.

Trimble wished he'd treated Mrs Kent better when they met. She'd waited nearly three decades to set things right and he robbed her of the opportunity to properly explain. After his previous hostility she'd no doubt guessed he had no intention of visiting her again. If it wasn't for the events of the past days he probably wouldn't have. When he telephoned to tell her he would come she had welcomed it with disproportionate gratitude. He saw now it had blinded her to the dangers she'd spoken to him about. Why else would a woman who knew so much be so careless? She should have seen it coming.

The engine started and the Renault pulled off quickly. Trimble followed at a crawl until he saw the indicator light blink left as it came to the end of the drive.
#

'More space at the bloody inn,' Kent said, shifting irritably.

The priest glanced sideways at the prodigious girth of his neck. The photograph he'd been given did not do justice to the grumbling oddity beside him. As he listened to his heavy breathing he resigned himself to the knife. Size like that was a weapon and such immense limbs, however untrained, would become hazardous in a struggle. In the rear-view mirror he considered the slender form of its mother. Even *in utero* his appetite must have taken a toll, he thought. He would need to be careful when the time came.

'So, what do you know?' McCarthy asked, breaking the silence. So far the man-child and his mother had not made much sense and he only had a short drive to get some answers.

'About what?' Kent said.

'Don't tease him, George,' his mother said from the back seat. 'He means your brother. Isn't that right?' The priest nodded. That was a good place as any to start.

'Well,' he began, dislodging a piece of well-masticated toffee from the back of his mouth whilst fishing out a chocolate bar from one of his pockets.

Food had been appearing for the last twenty minutes at increasingly smaller intervals from the folds of his coat like contractions before a birth. McCarthy pictured a gruesome baby made up of mashed up food held together by gooey marshmallow and chocolate slime.

'My mother is not exactly J.S. Mill, but from her demented drivel I've managed to retrieve two salient facts. I have a brother who was pronounced dead by an unscrupulous doctor and my biological father is undetermined.'

The priest ignored the obvious possibility which presented itself. It couldn't be that, he thought. The cardinal wouldn't be involved in such things.

'Go on,' he said.

'That's about it, except for some drug induced nonsense about how important we are,' he said, patting himself down for any promising lumps. A quick check of his inside pocket completed the interrogation. 'Whatever that means,' he said with a burp.

'What do you think it means?'

'I think-' Mrs Kent began.

'That she needs to get into a methadone program,' Kent cut in. 'As for my brother, I know very little about him. Why the hell do you think I got into this tin coffin for?'

The priest's hope the fat man and his mother would provide some answers was rapidly diminishing. He considered a quick stab to the jugular vein. It would be unexpected and fast. The mother would be easier. He rejected the idea. Driving around with a mammoth dead body, a screaming woman and blood soaked seats was not a good plan. He was allowing anxiety to get the better of him. A few more miles and he'd reach the deserted farm track he had scoped out. It would be almost dark by then and nobody would be around for miles.

Kent reached down to the calf of his right leg. There was a tearing sound.

'What was that?' The priest said with concern.

'Auxiliary rations,' he replied matter-of-factly. A packet of Opal Fruits was clenched in his right hand.

'What?'

'The chewy sweets with the fruit flavour? I would offer you some, but I'm down to my last pack.'

'He's a guest, George,' Mrs Kent said.

'No, Mother, I believe this is his car and therefore we are the guests. He should be sharing his sweets with me, a fact I've overlooked on the basis he doesn't have any.'

'Not the sweets,' McCarthy said, ignoring the woman. 'The sound.'

'Sound?'

'The ripping noise.'

'Oh, you mean the Velcro.'

'Velcro? Aren't those corduroy trousers?'

'Made in Britain and customised in China,' he said proudly. 'I find corduroy to be an entirely superior fabric but alas not blessed with the storage capacity of the Khaki pant. The pocket comes in very handy. Ten Yuan very well spent.'

'George is very creative,' Mrs Kent said proudly.

'Shut up, Mother. It was practical necessity not creativity.'

'Why?' the priest asked, feeling guilty that this ridiculous conversation would be the fat man's last.

'Emergencies.'

Kent did not elaborate any further and he did not ask for more. He spent the next three miles watching him work his way through his hoard, carefully unwrapping each one before dispatching it with a snap of his wrist.

The light was fading as he turned into the track. He continued on for another few minutes, snaking through undulating fields of corn before coming to a stop and turning off the engine. He took a deep breath, surprised no-one had questioned the route.

'Why are we stopping?' Kent said.

'I need to ask you some questions.'

'I thought we already did this,' he said crabbily. He'd had enough of detours.

'Well, I'd like to ask a few more.'

Kent wasn't the most perceptive of people, but he sensed a subtle change in his driving companion which made agreeing with him a better option than abuse.

'If you must,' he said.

'What are we doing here?' McCarthy said.

Kent squinted in confusion.

'What is this all about?' he asked, reformulating the question in the hope that it would produce some shoot of understanding.

'What are you talking about?'

'You know.'

'You're going to start the same crap as her, aren't you?' The instinct for caution was lost in a haze of indignation. 'Now look, I'm tired and hungry and if I don't get something to eat soon-'

The fat man's preoccupation with food was becoming tiresome. 'Tell me,' he demanded, his composure slipping. 'A man isn't killed for no reason.'

'Don't shout at my son,' Mrs Kent hollered behind him.

'Yeah, don't shout at me, you mongrel,' he chimed, just before the man's last sentence snuck up and kicked him in the balls.

'Who's been killed?' he said timidly.

McCarthy's fingers closed around the handle of the knife in his pocket.

'It doesn't matter, but the same people want you dead too.' He let this sink in, allowing fear to lubricate the wheels of thought.

'Me,' he whispered incredulously. 'Why would anyone want to hurt me?'

'George, George,' his mother bleated. 'George, what's happening?'

'For the last time, Mr Kent, what are we doing here?'

'Last time? What do you mean last time? Are you going somewhere?'

He pulled the blade from his pocket and held it up in front of the fat man. He didn't care about the risks anymore. For once it felt personal.

'Get away from my boy,' Mrs Kent squawked, her arms flapping around McCarthy like a trapped bird. He brought his elbow back quickly and silenced her. She slouched back into her seat, blood streaming from her nose.

'Tell me what I want to know.'

'Mum,' he cried out.

'Then I'm sorry. I truly am.'

Kent swung out his leg in self-defence with an agility that surprised both of them and then squandered the effort by waving it around and letting it fall on the gearstick with a painful thunk. He followed it up with an impressive display of flopping and then passed out.

McCarthy brushed away the dusty tread of a gym shoe from his knee where the fat man had made contact and rubbed the inside of his ears, which were still ringing from the high-pitched falsetto of his scream. He picked up the knife from where it had fallen on the floor.

Suddenly the door gave way and he fell backwards. He looked up in confusion.

'Who are you?' he croaked.

Chapter Seventeen

Lazarus

Kent opened one eye and looked around. From where he was slumped his field of vision was limited to the roof and the top four inches of the window opposite. He was on his back. During the flopping and the subsequent period of unconsciousness he'd managed to defy most of the laws of physics and ended in a supine position across the two front seats. After some wheezing and a glacial grinding of chin he saw the driver's side door was open and the seat empty.

'What the fuh?' he muttered, before the muscles in his neck gave way and he hit the hard plastic of the armrest behind him. Where was his mother?

Lunging at the dashboard with one arm and the back of the seat with the other he jacked himself up to a sitting position. He grimaced at a sharp stab of pain from the hand brake, which poked against his spine. He surveyed the scene and caught sight of his would be assassin lying on the ground fifty feet ahead. Beside him was a man patiently driving a knife into his chest as his hands fluttered feebly around the handle. It reminded Kent of an old couple cutting an anniversary cake.

McCarthy coughed as the steel moved slowly through his lungs. The sweaty warmth of his blood flowed down his sides and pooled in the cracks of the broken earth beneath him. He struggled to get up but fell back again. The blade had stuck deep in the soil and movement was painful. His head was throbbing. His attacker had brought the rock down hard. He wished he could unpin himself so he could die sitting up.

The man Kent had been observing had completed his gruesome task and was advancing toward him. He tried to move but discovered to his horror a feeling of fizzing paralysis caused by the steering wheel's restriction on his legs. Cursing all small car manufacturers he thumped his useless trunks with his fists and went for his heart like a gun. He listened to his arse make a journey through most of the musical scale as he clutched his breast tightly, perhaps worried it might use the opportunity to escape, and rather improbably passed out again.

When he came around, he first wondered if he might have diabetes and then quickly noted two other things; the man was staring at him and he was still alive. As he assessed what this meant, he utilised a trick of the animal kingdom and remained motionless.

'What are you doing?' asked a richly layered tone, the sort of sound an espresso might make if it could talk. He stayed still.

'I know you can hear me.'

Kent abandoned the ploy. 'Oh, hello,' he said. From a lying position his confidence sounded hollow.

'You need to come with me,' Trimble said, signalling for him to follow.

'I do?'

'I'm the person you're looking for.'

'You're the one I'm looking for?' he repeated. Why did nobody tell him these things?

'Where's my mother?' he asked, getting up.

'She's fine,' he said, pointing to a burgundy box shaped Volvo someway behind them. He could make out her silhouette in the back seat through a fogged up window dabbing at her nose with a tissue.

\#

Kent grappled with the car's seat belt, which was a delayed reaction as the Volvo had been moving at speed for the last ten minutes. He'd spent most of that time uncharacteristically active, negating its pregnant emptiness by a flurry of pointless activity. He'd been undecided whether to devote his energies to divining the mechanics of the electric window or fiddling with the buttons on his duffel coat. The former came to an abrupt end when he caught sight of the annoyance on the driver's face.

The seatbelt found its cradle with a satisfying click. Kent hadn't spoken to the man since he'd got in and he was trying to decide whether this was a good or bad thing. His mother had clearly made her choice, staring contentedly at her captor as though she were exactly where she intended to be. He wanted to be a braver man, to punch, kick and hurl obscenities that curled the hair and got the blood dancing. In more fecund imaginings he saw himself despatching the stranger with a carefully placed karate chop before ejecting him from the moving car, and shimmying over to the driver's side. Afterwards, it would be a quick stop at Clotilde's to pick up some things, and then on to the airport. But, as with all plans there were flaws. He lacked the stamina for sustained activity and the limb dexterity required for the shimmy. He didn't even have a driving license. In any case, the image of the man they'd left staked to the ground ranting deliriously like a Seventh Day Adventist babbling in tongues cautioned him against any foolish heroism.

'Who are you?' he said, mastering the courage to speak.

Trimble threw a confused look at Mrs Kent.

'I'm here to help,' was all he could muster. He couldn't utter the word brother and in its absence there wasn't a lot to say.

Kent took a look at his mother's serene expression. She was nuts but not that nuts.

'In which case would you mind if we make a slight detour?' he asked.

'Why?'

'I need to pick up some things.'

'What?'

'And if you really want to help you could drive me to the airport.'

'What?'

Kent hadn't expected that to work. 'Fine,' he said. 'I'll play your game. How can you possibly help me?'

Trimble looked at him in disbelief. 'You do understand that man was going to kill you?'

'Allegedly.'

'What?'

The volume of the reply made Kent's sphincter twitch. The man was trembling and he doubted it was because he was cold.

'I want to know where we're going,' he said, retreating to safer ground. 'And if it's not too much trouble I'd like you to tell me who you are and why that man was trying to kill me.' He added some aerial punctuation to the word kill, which caused an angry dimple to appear in Trimble's cheek.

'Why don't you ask your mother?'

'I'm asking you?'

'I'm taking you somewhere safe,' he said frostily. He wanted to take his fist and smash it into the fat man's nose.

'Somewhere *safe*,' Kent muttered, turning the word over in his mind. *Safe* was one of the sweetest words in the English language. It implied responsible sex, an object with money inside and an adequate distance from danger. But it also meant something or someone was looking to change that.

'Yes, we'll work out the rest later.'

'We'll work out the rest later? You don't think that little bit of butchery back there merits a confab? I don't know about you, but it's not every day I witness a man hammered into the ground like a washing line. And what do you mean by safe? Are we in danger?'

'Look mate,' Trimble said. 'I'm as much in the dark as you are. If you want answers then ask the old lady on the back seat.'

'Don't talk about my mother like that. I'm the only one who has earned that right.'

Kent turned around. 'Come on, out with it you old tart. What's he talking about?'

She smiled.

'What's wrong with you?'

She smiled again.

'What's wrong with her?' he said, redirecting the question to Trimble.

'My name is David Trimble,' he said.

'Um, is that supposed to mean something?'

'I haven't told him, David,' Mrs Kent said softly. 'George, this is-'

'What haven't you told me now? Please tell me you didn't have sex with this one as well?'

'George, that's disgusting.'

Kent was warming up. Anger had replaced terror and he basked in it like a Mediterranean sunshine.

'Ooh, pardon me, I'd no idea indignation could accompany your level of promiscuity.'

'You don't understand, George,' Mrs Kent said.

'I'm not listening,' he replied, rummaging in the glove box.

The unauthorised exploration yielded some wine gums and a packet of extra strong mints. He opted for the former, calculating the sugar rush would best offset his depleted energy levels. He ignored the driver's withering appraisal and opened the bag. He hit the contents like a hyena on a wounded zebra. Happiness spread like a yawn. His blood sugar level had been topped back up to dangerous. The Kent equilibrium had been re-established. Not long after that the bottom dropped out of his world.

'Your brother's name is David Trimble,' his mother said tearily. 'He's your brother, George.'

This was the reunion she'd waited a lifetime for.

For the first time since they had met Kent truly looked at him and what he saw hit him like a claw hammer.

'It's true,' Trimble said.

He began to nod uneasily like a puppet on a string.

'Well, George, say something,' she said.

His bottom lip quivered. He could feel drops of moisture tickle his ribs as they fell from his armpits.

'George,' she said impatiently.

'...tinker, tailor, soldier, sailor... twenty-two, she'll have you...fifty-three, she's yours for free.'

Trimble thought he heard the fat man calling out bingo numbers.

'George!' she shrieked, causing both brothers to wince.

It brought Kent back to his senses. 'What's the matter with you?' he said, attempting to conceal his micro breakdown with bluster, but the truth had been unveiled and it jeered at him like a turkey in a polka dot bikini.

David Trimble stood six-foot five, whereas Kent strained to remain upright at five-foot five and a quarter. He was muscular, a fact noticeable even beneath his jumper, whereas he was morbidly obese, a fact blatantly obvious despite his attempts to hide it beneath a thick coat. The deep green of his eyes were piercingly intelligent, whilst his were a dull shit brown with a hint of soullessness. His brother had a visage to shame the gods. He had a mug only a mother could love. All of this he might have taken stoically were it not for the mop of luscious black hair deriding his pallid glabrous mount.

'Okay then, okay. That's great,' he said, nodding erratically in an attempt at nonchalance, unaware his jittery glassy-eyed rocking was having the opposite effect. He wrestled for control of his eyebrows, which he relied upon to express the subtler of his emotions, and tried to sandbag the deluge of jealousy. The wretched hunchback creature he'd envisioned in those first terrible hours after his mother had told him the truth was nothing but a fairy tale, a pernicious and cruel hope destroyed with brutal indifference. There was no one to rescue or become a mentor to. This man had spent a lifetime prospering from his mother's absence and it seemed he got the lion's share of the good genes too.

'Fine, so what do we um...?' For the first time in his life words left him. Trimble had to be mad, he thought. Mental superiority was the last refuge open to him and only a mind like a rancid cabbage would offset the damage his appearance had caused.

'Say hello to your brother, George,' Mrs Kent said, leaning forward. She had pictured this moment many times and was desperate to see it reproduced as she imagined.

'Right, yeah, of course,' he coughed. He collected himself and clapped his hands. 'So, let's get down to brass tacks, shall we?' He didn't like the expression, but in his new no nonsense mood it felt appropriate. 'So what now, David? What do we know?'

Trimble was doing his best to dampen the resentment he felt. The two of them had no right to expect anything from him. They were not his kin. They were gone and he wasn't looking to replace them. Mutual love, shared values and a singular belief in the absolute necessity of the other were the everyday crayons that defined a family. To allow them in was a betrayal to those who had spent a lifetime giving him substance. His gaping emptiness was beyond their reach.

'Well, I know someone wants to kill us and my friend is dead because of it.'

'Oh, baby, I'm so sorry,' Mrs Kent said, weeping quietly behind him.

'What's with the water works?' Kent said. 'You didn't know him.'

'I'm so happy,' she wailed.

'Why?' he asked. 'Because his friend is dead?'

'Shut up, George,' she sniffed.

'I think this has something to do with our–' Trimble let the sentence hang half-finished.

'Our what?' Kent asked.

'Your biological father,' Mrs Kent finished from the back.

'And where might we find him?'

'I don't know.' Trimble said, looking behind at Mrs Kent.

'Ooh, I think you might be disappointed if you're looking there for answers,' Kent said, following his gaze. 'I'm afraid my mother is somewhat of a spotty record keeper.'

'George, not in front of David,' she hissed.

'Why the hell not? He's had the luxury of not having it in front of him for almost thirty years. It's about time he took some of the load.'

'I'm not listening, George.' She covered her ears to illustrate the point.

'Do you know anything about our biological father, Dave?' he asked, cocking his head expectantly to one side and then cocking it back again. The movement felt quite feminine and although not entirely objectionable he decided not to do it again.

'Don't call me that,' he said flatly, focusing on the road.

'Tell me he's an emeritus professor or something and not some carnival freak.'

Trimble frowned. 'Why are you asking me? Why doesn't-' He turned around again to direct the question at Mrs Kent before turning back. 'Your mother knows who it is?'

'*Our* mother,' he corrected. 'You can't get out of it that easily.'

'Mrs Kent, how can you not know?' He asked the small figure in the rear view mirror.

'I tried to explain last time, David.'

'I'll field that question, Mother, if you don't mind,' Kent said. 'Well, it's like this, bro. On the auspicious occasion of our conception our mother was, how can I put this delicately...putting it around.' He paused to enjoy the look of perturbation on his face. 'The principal characters involved have three things in common. They're brothers, they did not leave a forwarding address and they are comfortable with monikers assigned to them by the vegetable on the back seat.'

Kent's features contorted as he rubbed his chest in pain. This was his mother he was talking about.

'You see, Mater loves a man with an alias, I'm afraid. Or rather I should say she loves unnecessarily furnishing a man with an alias because she has difficulty remembering anything with more than one syllable. These two mystery men are the likely, but I fear not certain, candidates for our paternity. From what I can garner from our mother's feverish narrative, they left her like rats deserting a sinking ship, but not without first indulging her predilection for chemical substances and persuading her in a language that bordered on Elvish to give one of her children away.'

Trimble reached inside his coat and brought out a bottle of pills. He handed them brusquely to Kent.

'What do you want me to do with these?'

'Open them,' he said curtly.

'You didn't tell it properly,' Mrs Kent said.

Kent laughed as he wrestled with the childproof safety cap.

'Tell it properly,' she cautioned.

'And blah blah blah blah blah, at which point I lose the thread and start to self-harm,' he said, handing it back. 'Oh, and later she ensnared my father into the role of Dad by claiming the baby was his. You might have noticed I said *baby* not *babies*. My mother told me she filled you in on that particularly demented chapter. I think that about brings you up to date.'

Trimble lifted the bottle to his mouth and swallowed a number of pills dry.

'What are they for?' Kent asked.

He stroked his temple but didn't answer.

'Okay, but that doesn't tell us why he wants us dead,' Trimble said.

Kent felt a twinge in his gut. He wished he would stop reminding him of that.

'Well, the obvious question is, why now?' he said, clicking his jaw nervously. 'Logically something must have changed to affect whatever status quo existed before. And since I've been in China for a nearly a decade, it means it has to be one of you two clowns. Who was the man you were aerating back there?'

'I don't know.'

'You knew enough to kill him.'

Trimble shivered. He'd killed a man.

'Don't listen to George, sweetheart, you had no choice,' Mrs Kent said reassuringly.

'Yes, Dave, and my mother would know all about that sort of thing. She's quite the raconteur. Has she regaled you with her table leg anecdote?' Mrs Kent glared at him.

'He killed my friend,' Trimble said softly. 'He would have killed you too.'

'Why did he kill your friend?'

'Because he thought it was me.'

'What does that mean?'

'It means that being us is bad.'

'Please tell me you're not going to continue the tradition of vague anagogic statements enjoyed by Mystic Meg back there.'

'It means, I don't know...some guy phoned me. He had an accent. He said he knew about our...biological father. We arranged to meet. I got cold feet and asked Jim to stand in for me.'

'Somebody else turned up instead. He was younger...he sounded different and didn't have an accent. I thought maybe he sent someone else in his place...like I had...so I waited to hear what he had to say.' His voice cracked. 'I made the wrong choice.'

Kent was trying to apply some cold logic, but his mind didn't seem to want to comply. It taunted him with the idea that he was on an elaborate secret camera show. That wasn't impossible, he thought. The budget would probably be higher than the usual fare but was eminently more possible than any of this.

'It all happened so quickly. I didn't see the knife until it was too late. When I did I was too scared to move.'

'So the guy who killed your friend and the guy on the phone are working together?' he asked, looking around for some sign of a lens.

'Maybe,' he shrugged. 'I don't know.'

'So how come you're here?'

'The things your mother said...a hunch.'

'So you believe her nonsense?'

'Well, something isn't right. You'd be dead if I hadn't arrived.'

What kind of people had his mother messed with, Kent thought? What had she done? Whatever it was, it had come back to take a chunk out of her derrière.

'On the way here I got another phone call. It was *him*. He denied any involvement in what happened to Jim. He told me to get somewhere safe and wait for his call.'

'You didn't tell him where you were going?' Kent asked, alarmed.

'No, of course not.'

'But you believe him?'

'I don't know.'

'Why don't we go to the police and get this crap sorted out?'

'Because I'll be chief suspect in two murders. With no motive and nothing to explain this I'll be detained, you'll be released, and whoever wants you dead will send somebody else. We should wait.'

'Should *we*?'

'Yes *we* should.'

'For what?'

'For a phone call.'

'That doesn't sound like much of a plan, Dave.'

'It's not up for discussion.'

'Really? And that's up to you, is it?'

'I've just killed a man. I'd say that makes the decision mine.'

Kent sagged against the seat and watched the rolling English countryside blur into one.

'Where are we going?' he asked, hoping it involved a restaurant or cafe.

'North.'

'Okay, Davy Crockett, more specifically?'

'Later,' he said.

The danger of their situation snuck up on Kent unexpectedly. They might really die, he thought. A dizzy panic descended, causing a sympathetic dilation in his ass. Normally he was not averse to such personal effusions, but the pungency was immense. Distress seemed to give it a spicy kick. He gagged as he tried to dispel the fumes but its viscid consistency made it like trying to blow away treacle.

Trimble rolled the window down in disgust. 'Mrs Kent?'

The old woman sat up and smiled. 'Yes, dear?'

'Can you think of anything in the last few days which might be related to this?'

She examined the roof as she thought about the question.

'Well, one of the brothers came to see me. Does that count as something?'

Kent sat bolt upright. 'You mean one of the two brothers who might be our father. You mean one of those two brothers?' he said in astonishment.

'Yes.'

'And you didn't think that might be relevant?'

'I'm telling you about it now, aren't I?' she responded, unruffled by her son's obvious agitation.

'You, You, You' he spluttered, his words escaping like bullets from a blister red face.

'Let her speak,' Trimble said irritably.

She glowered at her son's flustered reflection and resumed talking. 'Frank came to see me.'

'And what did he want?'

'He said his brother was dying. He needed me to do something for him.'

'Okay, so let's start with what we know. What can you tell me about him?'

'I'm not sure. He's foreign...um...'

'Well, let's start with his full name?'

'To me he was always Frank.'

'Frank who?'

'Just Frank.'

'Which is ironic,' Kent interjected, 'because that's exactly what it isn't.'

'Did he leave a number?' Trimble asked, ignoring the fat man's comment.

'No.'

'Can you tell me anything?'

'I'm sorry,' she said.

'Don't worry,' he sighed in frustration. 'We'll find him.'

'That's very noble of you, Dave,' Kent said. 'But as she sits there marinating in her own stupidity we are running for our lives.'

Chapter Eighteen

A falling out

Somewhere in County Durham

Trimble pulled sharply into the bus stop and cut the engine.

'I have to make a call.'

'I'm getting sick of this,' Kent said.

'As I am of you,' he said wearily.

'Look, I've been as accommodating as I can under the circumstances, but we've been driving for....well, ages.'

He didn't know how long they'd been on the road as he'd slept for most of it. The susurration of fast moving air muffled by glass had a soporific effect and the internal landscape behind his lids had proven far superior to the one outside them. Where else might a man climb vanilla mountains and watch the graceful movement of glamour models astride a cantering horde of chocolate wildebeest whilst being pleasured by a Finnish catalogue model?

'I'm not holding you against your will. I've saved your life once already, something you seem incomprehensibly ungrateful for. Is it really difficult for you to sit there a little longer?' Trimble looked away as he spoke, the act aspiring for a disengagement he was unable to achieve.

'It is when you won't tell me where we're going.'

Kent was becoming tiresome. He reminded him of a boy he'd schooled with. He had the same sense of entitlement and a permanently moist pink glow, which made him appear overindulged and oddly venal.

'Well, if you stop whingeing and let me make a call, you might find out.'

'Shouldn't we all decide that?'

Trimble rummaged in his pockets in search of some change. Getting no answer Kent cast about for something else to take the brunt of his displeasure when it suddenly dawned on him he knew where they were.

'Hey, I know this place. Why are we here?'

'It's dead,' Trimble said, waving his mobile under his nose. He motioned to a phone box fifty yards away and tossed it into the coin tray. 'I'll be five minutes. Don't move.'

'Why don't you use mine?' The offer was greeted by the metal clunk of the door closing. 'I don't have it anyway,' he muttered, checking his coat. He'd left it back at the home.

He watched Trimble jog up the road, trying not to let the sound of his mother's slumbering vex him any further. What was he up to? He looked out the window. What was he going along with, he thought? He might not have a plan, but he was happy to leave his mother and

David to it. Whatever trouble they'd found was unlikely to make its way to China.

He picked up Trimble's mobile out of the tray in boredom and stabbed at the keys. Their illumination was met with a camp gasp. The sign of a healthy battery gauge elicited another. He exited the car gracelessly and stomped towards the phone box.

'What's going on?' he demanded, hammering against the glass.

Trimble's startled expression turned to anger. He shook his head fiercely, spoke quickly into the receiver and slammed it down.

'You're a fucking idiot,' he said, ramming the door open with his shoulder.

'If by idiot you mean blindly going along with your unique brand of outlaw justice then yes I am indeed the rain man of retards, the Champion of Cretins, the Master of Morons, the Lord Protector of Pea-Brains, the Patron of Pinheads, the Sovereign of Saps, the Fuhrer of Fat Heads, the Dauphin of Dullards, the Imperator of Imbeciles, the Deity of Dunces, the Father of Fools-' He gesticulated wildly to ensure the irony did not go unnoticed.

'I told you to stay put you gargantuan circus freak and if you don't shut your cake hole I swear I'll break your skull in two.' Kent weighed up the threat. The length of the drive and the revelation they were brothers made him optimistic about his chances.

'You lied,' he said, holding up his evidence.

A young woman in a blue tracksuit pushing a pram stopped to watch their exchange.

'Because I wanted some bloody privacy. The last thing I need is you in the background giving my mate cause for concern.'

'Huh?' He placed a hand on his hip.

'I was trying to persuade him to help us out. We need some supplies. I have no idea how long we will be down there and we don't have any cash.'

Kent reached for his wallet.

'Don't bother, I've checked,' Trimble said.

'Okay, so where is *down there*, exactly?'

'God knows what Richard thinks after your outburst. He's already suspicious. I hope, for your sake, he's a good enough mate to trust what I told him.'

'And what's that?'

'A lie. He'd phone the police if he knew the truth.'

'What is it with all this shit? You've heard of a credit card. Let's book into a spa and mull this over. A mud pack and sauna can do wonders.'

'And that's why you're not involved in the decision-making process. I don't know what we're up against and without that information we stay paranoid. People are being killed and credit cards leave a trail. You do understand that? We use cash and we go to ground.'

'Well, that certainly is paranoid and your avoiding my question. Where is this *ground*?'

'You'll see when we get there. I'm not having you moaning all the way.' Trimble had Kent figured out and what he'd planned would not make him happy.

'That implies there's something to moan about.'

'It's only for a few days and you'd do well to remember I'm the only thing keeping you alive. I suggest you shut up and say thank you.'

The woman on the path giggled.

'Take a picture luv, it'll last longer,' Kent shouted, his hand back on his hip. The women scowled and pushed on.

'Classy,' Trimble said.

'Look, just because my mother believes you're the new Messiah it doesn't mean I have to.'

'I've only been acquainted with you a few hours and I already dislike you.'

'I'm sorry, I guess we have different interests. I like reading and good food and you like killing and driving.'

Trimble could feel his self-control wriggling beneath his skin. 'You really don't want to test me,' he warned.

'Why? Are you thinking about branching into fratricide?'

'I'm going to hurt you.'

'Well, I don't think that's a very good idea,' Kent said nervously.

'You're right.'

'Good,' he exhaled. 'I think we've all said some things we might wish to rephrase.'

'I'm not going to hurt you, I'm going to kill you. As you keep pointing out, I've already done it once.'

'Whoa, Whoa, Whoa. Where is this coming from? Come on, let's talk.'

'We're done talking.'

'Don't be like that. That's just the stress devil screwing with your mind. Come on bro, look where we are. Being here has to mean something.'

'And why is that?'

'This is where I went to university. That's Hilde and Bede.' He pointed to the buildings beside him. 'It's one of the colleges of Durham Uni. And that,' he gestured to a side road which climbed steeply ahead, 'leads to the street where I used to live. Now, doesn't that mean something? Let's get something to eat and chew the cud. A bit of back and forth, what do you say?'

The thought of food left Kent's mouth wet. Only one other sensation could come close to that feeling.

Trimble was staggered. 'You went here?'

'Yes.'

'So did I.'

'That must mean something, right?' he urged.

For the moment the revelation relieved some of the tension that had built up between them. Was it a coincidence, Trimble wondered, or evidence of something shared? He reached for the pills in his jacket and swallowed a couple more.

'What are they?' Kent asked.

'I've had a tough time recently. They help. And I need to pick up some more.' He shook the bottle to emphasise the point. The remaining pills rattled loudly. 'There's a place nearby.'

#

The clinic was a row of terraced houses dating back to the turn of the twentieth century, which had been knocked through and amalgamated seventy years earlier. A new sign and some paint were all that conveyed the passage of time. It's reputation was local and largely invisible to the world zipping by. Trimble would have missed it himself had he not known where to look.

'Wait here,' he ordered pushing open a door about half way along the row.

Kent was beginning to have serious doubts about his brother's mental state and that seriously pleased him.

He'd worked hard during his childhood to maintain his sanity and he'd rather be damned to eternity in a wire jaw than see it naturally acquired by a sibling that should have suffered alongside him.

'At least I didn't end up here?' he gloated to himself, nudging the toe of his gym shoe against the ground to demonstrate his point.

'I mean you would have to be mad to stay in a place like this.' He looked around to see if anyone had heard and smirked, wishing the sleeping form of his mother in the Volvo were present to appreciate the witticism.

Fifteen minutes later the gentle pacing had degenerated into an aimless dragging of feet. Growing impatient Kent found temporary distraction in a branch which he whacked purposefully against a tree in the middle of the grass quadrangle out front. Eventually the threat of exhaustion overtook the mindless pleasure and he abandoned it. He was grunting with the effort of stretching his arms when his brother finally reappeared.

'Shall we go?' Trimble called.

'Finally,' Kent smirked.

'Thanks for waiting,' came a restrained response.

'I was right,' he crowed, unable to hold back any longer.

'About what?'

'The insane old tart's leg-overs left more legacy than I thought.'

'What?'

'Her defective genes have replicated themselves in you, like some insidious cancer of the genome.'

'What are you talking about?'

'My mother is as mad as a horse on an exercise bike.' He gestured toward the pills in his right hand. 'It looks like you got your inheritance.'

'I lost my family,' he said.

'My mother mentioned it.'

'Back off, Kent.'

He clasped his hands behind his back. 'And I am sincerely sorry for it, but I put it to you that you're being a tad economical with the facts.'

'I'm not in the mood for this Kent.'

'This has to be over two hundred and fifty miles from London,' he continued. 'I'm guessing this is not your usual dispensary.'

'So what?' he asked, despite himself.

'How do you know about this place? I put it to you that you frequented this establishment as a student. And if my calculations are correct that was some time before your current misfortune. In summary you were born mental, Mr Trimble.'

He had nothing to say. Kent was an insensitive clown, but he was right. He had been born this way. Depression had always been part of his life and it crept up on him like a changing season. Reasons chemical, biological or psychological were never able to satisfactorily explain it.

'Were you ever hospitalised?' Kent asked with mock solemnity.

Trimble let him wallow for a few seconds more and then lunged for his throat.

Chapter Nineteen

Out of Time

Giovanni had seen McCarthy for the first time on television. He was one of a number of talking heads enlisted for a feature length documentary on the Shroud of Turin. It had been released to coincide with the new carbon14 dating tests. His interview had been a scathing assessment of what he referred to as a snake oil industry, dismissing his opponents as fringe scientists, self-styled experts and poorly educated church prelates. His testimony had been passionate, candid, and totally fearless. The cardinal saw instantly a man like that could be a valuable asset indeed.

Arranging his placement in the Vatican had not been easy, but he'd spent too much time planning their future to let a simple thing like politics get in the way. Within eighteen months he'd become his mentor and confidant; Time enough he decided to put events into motion.

#

An official visit to Bogotá, Columbia, years earlier, had awoken Giovanni to new possibilities. St Bernardo's

Christian retreat for habitual offenders had been the second of four scheduled visits of a week-long stay. In a dilapidated office the coordinator of the centre drip-fed him statistics and anecdotes over the rattle of an old air-conditioning unit. He was bored and tired and the thought of the sinuous lines of traffic, honking horns and exhaust fumes which stood between him and his hotel grated on his mind. It was fortunate that what the small moustached man said next made it all go away.

The drug Burundanga, as it was known locally, cropped up in much of the crime in Bogota. Derived from a plant of the nightshade family called Barrachea it had been used for hundreds of years in religious ceremonies. The refined powder yielded the chemical variant Scopolamine, familiar in the West for its sedative properties. During the Second World War Mengele, the infamous Nazi physician, experimented with it as a truth serum and later throughout the cold war it featured prominently in CIA tradecraft.

Incapacitation, submissive behaviour and short-term amnesia were just a few of the effects to be exploited. Odourless and tasteless it could be easily administered in food or drink. There were many incidents in Bogota in which people had been persuaded to part with money and ATM codes only to awake with no memory of what had transpired. In one case a Colombian diplomat disappeared shortly after leaving a function and reappeared forty-eight hours later under arrest in Chile for cocaine smuggling. Medical tests had revealed a large amount of the substance in his blood. Relatively inexpensive and easy to obtain it was the drug of choice amongst the city's criminal underclass and there were more than five hundred victims each month.

#

Giovanni disliked involving anyone else, but he reasoned a prostitute with a baby and a blossoming drug habit wouldn't ask too many questions. For triple her nightly fee she'd agreed to perform his rather unusual request. Despite his worries she'd played the part of his niece well. Like a lot of the *lucciole* in Rome she'd not been born to the life and could still remember an existence outside it.

McCarthy had woken in the early hours of the morning with no idea where he was. The last thing he remembered was the restaurant. He propped himself up unsteadily and looked about woozily, allowing a moment for the room to creep into focus. When he saw the puddles of thick red liquid pooled in the creases of the blanket the effect was instantaneous. Scrabbling from the bed he landed with a heavy thump on the floor. His mind raced, but there was a blank spot where an explanation should have been. He staggered to the bathroom and fell to his knees beside the toilet. A short time later Giovanni got the phone-call he'd been waiting for.

When he arrived the priest was on the ground, his arms splayed outwards in a gesture of defeat. The cardinal followed the blood trail to where he already knew it would lead. He did his best to look dazed as he sat on the edge of the bath. His protégé crawled forward and slumped against his legs, sobbing in heaving inconsolable gasps. He resisted the impulse to comfort him. That would come later.

McCarthy could not recall how she'd managed to entice him back to her room. Taking her to dinner had been a favour to the cardinal. She'd turned up in Rome unannounced and he'd been too busy to attend to her.

Giovanni's anguished observations helped fill in the blanks. He was an inexperienced priest and she was an attractive young girl. He had a low tolerance of alcohol. Had she plied him with drinks? The scratches on his cheek and his torn shirt told its own story. The evidence was unassailable. The priest broke down, whimpering in confusion. He'd found God at the bottom of a swimming pool. Was it possible he'd found the Devil in a hotel room in Rome?

McCarthy accepted the instruction to go and wait in the cardinal's apartment without protest. His life was over now. Giovanni lingered a while before he fetched her from the balcony. She was not pleased to see him. The night was cold and she'd been out there longer than she'd bargained for. He placated her with more Lira and a warning before sending her back on to the streets. She didn't need it. Listening to that young priest crying would haunt her for the rest of her days. Any man that could organise something like that was not someone you crossed easily. And her daughter was more important than any sin she had to bear.

Dried cow's blood was difficult to clean and it took several hours for the cardinal to get the place back in order. Afterwards, he took his time washing and changing. He'd allow the priest a little longer to simmer. McCarthy would no doubt go to the police, given time, but saying goodbye to the future took longer than a few hours. Besides, it was not prison he feared but something far worse.

When the cardinal returned he found him sitting like a statue at the kitchen table. With his arrival the crying began again. He listened to his confession once more before he offered him a way out. His words were rehearsed, but he delivered them as if they came from the heart. He believed the priest was a good man and his soul did not willingly participate in the terrible thing he'd done. The devil inside had risen up in a moment of moral frailty and tarnished that which most offended him. He loved his niece and that would not be diminished by what he was about to do. But there was deliverance from this turpitude.

Prison, he told him, was a place for man's punishment not God's mercy. Forgiveness was what the Church preached and it would be his burden to carry. For McCarthy however there would be, if he chose to accept it, a different millstone. The battleground had moved and the fight for his soul would bring him nose to nose with the Devil again. The priest stopped crying. It was a hard road, the cardinal cautioned, but reparation did not come easy. He would have to minister to his own conscience and they would never mention the events of this night again. McCarthy's tear streaked expression wrinkled in bafflement as he tried to understand what he was being offered.

Just as a clear sky was accompanied by the possibility of rain, the cardinal assured him, so a pure soul was plagued by the possibility of evil. The two forces were intertwined, defining and realising themselves through the other. Who, he asked, could object to the altruism born of disaster? That act of evil, natural or otherwise, which replaces indifference with compassion and apathy with love. Sometimes the two opposing states spill into the other and become so entangled that distinguishing them is all but impossible. Who after all could judge the wickedness of ending a single innocent life to save a million? And who could say whether this night had not been a necessary catalyst for the good that might follow? Wasn't salvation itself accompanied by the depravity of a crucifixion? McCarthy listened intently. His redemption would come, the cardinal said, when he accepted into his heart the nature and truth of these contradictions and followed it with a leap of faith. He'd have to work for his deliverance and it would be hard won, for he would be called upon to make these choices. Tonight he would make his first. The girl would disappear and he would begin his atonement.

The cardinal had never been as persuasive as he had that night and the priest had yielded completely. He would go to the very depths of hell to get a chance at heaven and that was precisely what he had in mind. A boundary had been crossed and in time he would cross it again. He would die trying to exorcise a ghost that never lived.

Who could replace a man like that?

#

A deserted farm track, Wiltshire Countryside
A few hours earlier

Father McCarthy listened to the rasping of his lungs, which made him feel claustrophobic as though he were trapped under water with the cacophonously mechanical sound of his own breathing thundering in his ears. He greeted the inevitability of what this meant with an equanimity that surprised him. He thought about who he was and who he'd become. His larval idealism had been infected. He had fed on the promise of forgiveness and re-emerged altered.

He'd done many bad things, the honesty of death made the truth of this transparent, and whether these acts served a greater good he'd never know. A night many years ago and a terrible deed brought him to where he lay. How could such a starting place have led anywhere else? He had wanted to go to the police that morning, but the cardinal convinced him otherwise; persuaded a coward of his own cowardice. The green-eyed man ended it for him and he was glad because he could not have done it for himself.

The wheezing had found a rhythm and McCarthy began his contrition. He saw clearly now and would take whatever came next. The priest exhaled one last breath and looking up at the crisp blue sky died.

Chapter Twenty

My Brother's Keeper

The cardinal opened the draw in the bottom of his desk and took out a bottle of whisky. He poured a large measure into the cup of tea in front of him. He was worried. McCarthy hadn't made contact in over forty-eight hours.

The phone rang and he scooped it up eagerly.
'Hello?'
'Hello, Giovanni,' a voice said.
'Who is this?'
'You know who it is.' He was right of course. He knew the sound of it as well as he knew his own.
'Francesco,' he said frigidly.
'Did you get my letter?'
The cardinal's insides wrung themselves out like a wet dish rag.
'You?' he said, feeling light-headed.
'You sound surprised.'
'What do you want?' Giovanni asked, pushing the earpiece tightly against his face.

'What do you think I want?' Francesco said, allowing his anger to creep in.

'What are you going to do?'

'That depends on you.'

'Why are you doing this?'

'Why?' he said, remembering the dead man in the apartment. 'You know why.'

'Francesco, this is not right. We should be trying to repair what's damaged.'

'You're going to drop out of the election,' he said flatly.

'Drop out?'

'Don't play games, Giovanni.'

'I'm a member of the College of Cardinals, I'm obligated to vote.'

'Yes, but not to run.'

'It's not a vote for club captain. I have no choice in the matter.'

'We both know there are things which can be done to put you out of favour. It would be better if it came from you? You'll regret it if I have to do it.'

'Please, Francesco, let's talk about this.'

'We are talking and it's a courtesy you don't deserve, Giovanni. I would have exposed you already if I were not convinced it would do more harm than good.'

'I won't do it. They're dead. You have nothing.'

'As long as I'm here to connect the dots I have more than I need. And they're perfectly alive, I can assure you of that.'

'You bastard.'

'Don't be silly, Giovanni. We both know it had to be this way. People don't see you the way I do. I've always seen through you. You're a bad seed. The murder of that innocent man in London was despicable.'

There was a puzzled silence. 'Yes, I'm afraid your assassin screwed up. The wrong innocent person is dead.'

'Don't pretend to be a concerned bystander, Francesco,' he hit back. 'You knew what might happen when you sent that letter. Your hands aren't clean in all of this.'

'You're not a good man, Giovanni, I was never in any doubt of that, but I didn't think you were capable of this.'

'If I am a monster, then it was you who let me off the leash.'

'Maybe you're right, but it doesn't change anything. I'm giving you one chance to exit with dignity. I suggest you take it.'

'And if I agree, I have your silence?'

There was a long pause.

'Yes. I'll cease contact with them. Without me they'll be nothing to link you to what's happened.'

'Why would you do that? What's in it for you?'

'People look to you for comfort and moral certitude in a difficult world. I'll not disabuse them of that. But I promise you if anything else comes to light I will hang the both of us.'

'Really?' he said, unconvinced.

'Yes. Rein your thug back in. He's not going to find them.'

Giovanni wanted to reach into the phone and tear out his spleen. It would be worse than dying to withdraw now. He was so close and Francesco knew it.

'How can I drop out?'

'Announce an illness. Cancer, heart problems, it doesn't matter. Do it whatever way you want but get it done.'

'When?'

'Tomorrow.'

'That's too soon.'

'For what?' he said, amused by his transparency. 'A phone call and a public declaration?'

'You'll pay for this.'

'No, I won't, but you will. Justice for that boy might come late, but it will come. Shall we say five p.m. tomorrow afternoon, your office? You can make the announcement then.'

There was a click as the line went dead.

Chapter Twenty-One

Et tu Mother?

Kent brooded like a bull on the soft upholstery, scratching sullenly at the bruised imprints around his neck. Trimble's thumbs were clearly distinguishable as two crimson islands on either side. It was only his mother's intervention which saw off more serious injury. She had leapt on them like a possessed fruit bat and prised her son's enraged fingers from her other son's throat. She'd hurried them away, afraid one of the twitching curtains which encircled the performance would ring the police.

'Why does she get to go in the front seat?' Kent moaned pubescently, unable to maintain his silent protest any longer.

'Because you've been annoying your brother, that's why.'

'Please don't call him that, Mrs Kent.'

'I'm sorry, David.'

'You're sorry? Look at this.' He tugged the duffel coat aside to reveal the signs of the assault.

'George you can be a real trial sometimes,' she said.

'Oh really and what's that like exactly?' he said. 'After all you are the only one that's actually been on trial.'

'Where are we going, David?' she asked, brushing aside Kent's attempt to goad her into a confrontation.

'Somewhere safe, Mrs Kent.'

She tapped him lightly on the arm and said, 'Well, dear, I'm sure you know what's best.'

'I'm sure you know best?' Kent imitated from the back seat. 'Are you seriously entrusting our safety to this lunatic?' He wagged a sausage roll finger at the back of his head. 'Am I missing something? I know you share common interests, like killing and such, but why would you exclude the only rational participant in all of this from making strategic decisions? Who else is going to tell you guys a dog barking is not code for kill the next person you see?'

'What did you say?' he said, spinning around. The car swerved to the left as he struggled to keep one hand on the steering wheel.

'You heard me,' he replied, leaning away from him.

'Boys, boys, please,' Mrs Kent said, like a woman secretly pleased with her new role.

Trimble turned back to the headlights cutting through the dark. 'What a dick,' he muttered.

'And George, stop causing trouble,' she said.

'But, Mother—'

'No, George. That's enough! Nobody is preventing you from leaving.'

'My, aren't we the little traitor. Nearly a third of a century putting up with your horse manure doesn't count for much, does it? I'm only here because Jack the Ripper there was wielding a steak knife like a scalpel when we met. An implement, incidentally, he used to do a whole lot of ripping.'

'Then, get out,' he said.

'It would give me no greater pleasure, Dave, but my mother, the confused perfidious fool she is, would no doubt stay. Although her company produces an unrelenting sensation of acid indigestion she has the distinction of carrying me in that drug riddled pouch of hers for nine months. This it seems, despite my best efforts, has produced an unwanted attachment which forces me to give some consideration to her basic safety.'

'That man was about to kill you and If I had not come along your whale carcass would be beached on the side of the road.'

'That's conjecture.'

Trimble punched the roof three times.

'One more comment, that's all I need,' he shouted. 'Go on you fat fuck, say something else. I dare you.' Kent remained quiet. Only a couple of fingers were left steering the car. He looked beyond Trimble to the road and wondered if they were driving too fast to survive a head-on collision.

It felt like an eternity before he accepted his lack of speech as victory and turned away. Kent blinked a few times as if waking from a coma and then farted in relief, congratulating himself on not aggravating the situation any further.

He waited for some time to pass and asked, 'Why are you being so secretive, David?'

'It was a reasonable question, Trimble thought, but he wasn't going to answer it. 'We're nearly there,' he said dismissively.

Well that told him less than nothing, he thought.

'For God's sake man, can't you just spit it out? You're not Lionel Blair and this is not give us a clue. W-H-E-R-E I-S I-T?' he said, slowly enunciating each letter.

'Oh, George, stop going on,' his mother chided. 'Why are you always trying to whip everyone up?'

'Oh, shut up, Driving Miss Daisy. Take a look around will you? We are so far in the dark we might as well be tied up in the boot with a blindfold on. And since we're on the same side then surely there is no harm in all of us knowing the state of play.'

'Look, you fucking baboon,' Trimble said to the mirror. 'It's not a fucking conspiracy. We're going to a hole in the ground. There is no address or road name. It's a hole. And if you don't stay quiet I'll kill you myself.'

'A hole?' He fell back on the upholstery behind him. 'A hole,' he repeated, as though the word were from some ancient Vedic script. What did it mean?

After many miles had passed in silence, his voice came floating unexpectedly out of the darkness.

'Mrs Kent?'

'Yes, David?'

'I need to know.'

'What, dear?'

'Everything...from the beginning.'

'Yes, I'd like that,' she said. 'There are a few things I didn't tell you.'

'Using the word *few* here is like telling a quadriplegic victim he has a sprained ankle,' Kent interjected.

'Shut up, George,' she barked. 'Well, David, I suppose I should begin with-'

'One thing I would like to know before you do,' he said, cutting her off.

'What, George?' She said tiredly, faintly irritated by the heavy breathing in her ear.

'How did you choose which one to give up? Toss a coin? Paper, scissors, rock... what?'

'For God's sake, you both looked the same at birth. I loved you equally then.' Looking at Trimble, Kent wondered. He must have come out of the womb like Spartacus.

'What's that supposed to mean?' he asked.

'What?'

'You said *equally then*. Are you saying your choice would be different now?'

Trimble couldn't resist the opportunity. 'Well, pound for pound she would be losing out,' he giggled.

'That's really funny.'

'I don't know, I'm lost with all of this,' Mrs Kent sighed.

'Then, get a map,' he snapped, slumping back into the seat.

'My parents knew about some of this, didn't they? That's why Dad left me the letter?' Trimble said.

'Your father was a nice man. I only met him once, but he seemed like the type who would do the right thing.'

'Thank you for saying that Mrs Kent.'

'I don't think he believed the things I told him. I can't say why he left the letter. Maybe he wanted you to reach out...find George.'

'Then why not tell me before?'

'He might have been frightened. It's a tough thing losing the person you love,' she said.

That could never have happened, Trimble thought.

'He left the letter in his will, didn't he?' she asked.

'Yes.'

'Then he knew he wouldn't be around. Perhaps he meant it to help you with your loss.'

'How?'

'A distraction from the pain, perhaps.'

'It can't be as simple as that. With everything that's going on, there must be a connection. I mean, why is all this happening now?'

'I think I messed up. I trusted someone I shouldn't have,' she said. 'I've been thinking about it since that man tried to hurt George.'

'Who?' Trimble said.

'I told you Frank came to see me...that he wanted something from me.'

He nodded.

'I think he sold me a story. He told me his brother...your biological father...was dying. He wanted me to write a letter about George. I was angry at first. I couldn't believe he was asking for a favour after everything that had gone on between us. But he begged...I tried to be the bigger person. I told him about you too...I don't know why. I guess I was excited. After hiding you away for so long...being able to talk about you kind of felt like I had you back. And he seemed excited hearing about you. I thought it was because he wanted to give the good news to his brother but...'

'So what did you do?'

'I did what he wanted and I gave him some details so he could contact you. I thought you had the right to choose whether to see him before he passed away.'

'Brain like a malnourished haemorrhoid,' Kent muttered.

His observation died in the back seat.

'But now, after everything that's happened I can't stop thinking about the meeting...it can't be a coincidence.'

'How did he find me?' David asked. 'I never told you where I was from.'

'I don't know. I said you were a clever boy like George, that you went to Durham University...your name....nothing really...just the few things you told me the day you came to visit.'

'I see.' Alumni records, Trimble thought. He cared about keeping in touch before his world went to crap.

'It's funny, you finding that letter from your father when you did. If you hadn't come to see me I would have had nothing to tell him.'

And Jim would still be alive, he thought.

'And you have no idea where to find this Frank?'

'I'm sorry.'

He grit his teeth and stifled the urge to say something he would regret. How could she not ask?

'You said you wrote a letter?'

'Yes.'

'Was there an address for it?'

'Frank said he would deliver it himself.'

'And you didn't want to know more?' There was an accusatory note in the question.

She shrugged. 'I wanted him gone.'

Kent shook his head in the dark. 'I hope you're starting to understand, David, what I'm up against. By her own admission this dying man, our beloved father, was an absolute whack job. He is the primary reason our life sounds like a bad soap opera....which leaves an open sore of a question, doesn't it? To wit, why has she given out our personal details with less thought than a dog humping a trouser leg?'

'I thought he was dying, George, and a lot of water had passed under the bridge. I didn't think he was a threat anymore.'

'How the hell do you know he was dying? Because the other mad bastard brother told you? Who are you consulting when you make your decisions, a jug of humus wrapped in bubble wrap?'

'I think the man on the phone might be Frank,' Trimble said.

'Then why are you waiting for his call?' Kent replied.

'I think he's trying to help us.'

'Like he has so far? Last time he was given information someone tried to kill us.

'What else can we do?'

'Go to the police?'

'Not yet.'

'Why?'

'Because.'

'That's a great answer, David.'

'He said there was someone else involved. It is possible he's the good guy.'

'And what if there is no good guy?'

'Frank wouldn't do anything bad,' Mrs Kent said confidently.

'You said the opposite thirty seconds ago.'

'Your mixing up my words, George.'

'Didn't you just say *he sold you a story*? That hardly sounds like a great guy, does it? And he buggered off and left you, remember?'

'I don't know anything for sure, George. And he must have had his reasons for leaving.'

'And there we have it, the rewriting of history has begun. She does this a fair bit, David. For my mother, 1984, is like an instruction manual.'

'I think whoever this man is,' Trimble said. 'He has the answers. And my gut is telling me he didn't have anything to do with killing Jim.'

The sheer volume of unanswered questions made Kent's head hurt. He sat up in discomfort.

'What if they find us?'

'They won't.'

'How can you be so sure?'

'You'll see when we get there.'

'I can't take this anymore,' Kent said. ' Assassins, conspiracies...I feel like I'm on acid. And you-' He pointed to Trimble as though he were indicating the accused man in a courtroom. 'Are a fruitcake. Is it not possible,' he whispered to his mother ear, 'that he's the mental one? That he killed his friend for kicks and then, searching for someone else to blame his twisted impulses on, came looking for the one person who'd hurt him the most. How do you know the phone call he's talking about even took place?'

'That's enough, George,' Mrs Kent said, but her son couldn't be stopped. He was mid rant.

'Is it not possible that-?'

She twirled around and slapped him hard, leaving the imprint of a palm and four fingers across his cheek.

'You've gone too far, George,' she said.

'You need to let me out,' he wailed.

'I can't do that,' Trimble said. The cheesiness of the line and the gravity of its delivery made Kent laugh until it turned into a coughing fit, which brought water to his eyes.

'George, you're not helping,' Mrs Kent shouted, switching on the overhead light so she could turn and glare at him properly.

'It's okay, David,' she said, patting him supportively as she kept her gaze on Kent.

The pressure inside Trimble's brain was building. The fat man was the stuff of nightmares. He started to think he'd always been with him, a leviathan prowling the muddy depths of his mind, hiding in the deep until he came to get him.

Chapter Twenty-Two

The Drive

They had been driving for a long time, despite Trimble's earlier assurances they were almost there. Kent had succumbed to a fitful slumber, waking intermittently with a start as his bowels vocalised his distress. The banality of the dialogue between David and his mother guided him like a Zen monk to the black canvas behind his eyelids where he painted a world without them.

His brother's past was a tale of pre-occupation and foreign travel. Trekking for Kent was a nugatory endeavour made more contemptible by the belief it was life affirming. Bumming around like an under achieving tramp on a pig-infested beach in Goa and disavowing a lifetime of eating beef was apparently spiritual. To his mind the same experience could be achieved by sleeping rough in a cow shed and chewing on a used nappy.

He'd awoken a final time to him talking about China. It was here he had fallen in love and married. Soon after they moved back to England and he began a PhD in Archaeology whilst she taught Mandarin at a local college. Some years later, on a wet Wednesday night in May, he'd lost her and his parents to a collision on the M25. He had taken it badly.

Kent had utilised the intervening periods of consciousness for reconnaissance. From his lying position he had garnered information from the audio clues around him, fashioning the scraps of data like a shit bat into a three-dimensional model of his environment. He knew from the speed and manoeuvring of the car they had travelled on B roads rather than A roads. The slow listing of the vehicle and the lack of illumination from passing vehicles indicated that they were now progressing on an infrequently used dirt track. This suggested some degree of isolation and once he ruled out a barbecue or a spot of dogging he greeted this particular development with some trepidation. He pictured Trimble laughing demonically as he held aloft a shiny spade against a background of fork lightning and rain- sodden mud.

They came to an abrupt halt and his insides squirmed like a dog trying to get free of its lead.

'Okay Kent, you need to get up,' Trimble said, switching off the engine.

He sat up and blinked myopically at the black landscape.

'Why is it so dark?' he bleated, gripping the handle above him until his knuckles turned an almost luminescent white.

'It's nine o'clock and we're in the middle of the country. Are you ready, Mrs Kent?' he asked, opening the door.

'Yes, thank you, David,' she beamed, still unable to quite believe he was with her after all this time.

Kent stepped gingerly into the night. He noticed in the interior light that had activated with his exit that he'd snagged a fibre of cloth on a crack in one of his finger nails. It seemed like a bad omen to him, like it might be the only evidence to his abduction and disappearance.

'What are we doing here?' he said, fiddling with the thread.

'This way.' Trimble signalled ahead of him with a torch. The beam cut a cone through the darkness, illuminating the mottled browns and greys of the tree trunks that surrounded them. Mrs Kent scampered alongside him.

'Why won't you answer my questions?' he called, stomping after the two silhouettes.

It was three-quarters of an hour before he stopped again and reached into his pocket to consult a worn looking map and a compass. He unfolded it and laid it on the ground. Kent came up behind him panting as he knelt and trained the light on its creased squares.

'I've been trailing you two for ages,' he grunted, clasping his hips for moral support. 'What's the matter now? Why have we stopped?'

Usually stopping wouldn't have been a problem, but it was pitch black and there was nothing around but trees. He didn't want to spend the night in the woods.

'Haven't been here for years,' he said.

Kent looked down at the map. In the darkness it felt like a cosmonaut's view of the world but was no more comprehensible for it.

'Great,' he said, throwing his hands up in the air like an Indian chief invoking rain. 'You've driven around for hours on end to a clump of trees in the middle of nowhere with the self-assurance of a salmon on his way to the breeding grounds and now all of a sudden you're uncertain.'

'The metal cover is here somewhere,' he replied testily, scanning the area around him with his torch.

'What does it look like?'

'Like a big metal cover.'

'I'm sorry,' Kent said, 'but I'm not at my sharpest when routing around a dogging hotspot for someone else's delusion.' He looked over at his mother for support and was irritated to see her examining a group of ferns a few feet away.

'Keep looking.'

'How can I find what's in your head?'

'That's it, I've had enough of you.'

'The feeling is mutual. At least we have that in common.'

'I'm going to hurt you,' Trimble said, standing up.

'That's discrimination. I can't help being sane.'

His brother smiled coldly. 'I could kill you easily. No one saw me pick you up. If I buried you out here nobody would find you. I'm having trouble seeing the argument against doing that.'

'Mother,' Kent called, backing off in alarm.

'Yes, George,' she said distractedly.

'Mother,' he squeaked, his stare pinned on Trimble like a rabbit staring into the headlamps of a car.

He staggered backwards and hit the ground hard. His rectum exploded like a grenade.

'Please, I made a mistake. I'm a confused waterbrained buffoon, a simpleton -' He wanted to fart again but was terrified it might inflame the situation further.

'You're one lucky bitch is what you are.'

'What?'

'Come here, Mrs Kent.' Trimble said, beckoning her over.'

Now she can hear,' Kent muttered, feeling utterly miserable as the wet soil seeped through his trousers. She seemed to be doing everything she could to put him in harm's way. When was she going to realise it was too late to play favourites?

'Oh, well done dear,' she said, looking down at the sprawled figure of her son. 'You found it.'

'Huh?'

Trimble pointed down at Kent's scrotum. In the tiny gap between his thighs he saw a glint of metal.

'Just trying to be part of the team,' he said with as much aplomb as he could muster. It wasn't very much.

He rolled over with a grunt and crawled on his knees to a tree in front of him. After several minutes of grasping, panting, grunting and a little crying he found himself standing again.

'Oldest trick in the book,' he explained to his brother's unreadable expression. Someone better at reading expressions might have defined it as one part disgust and one part pity. 'Using the inertia of the tree as a lever. Physics 101,' he said, swiping futilely at the wet muddy patches on his elbows.

Trimble took out some keys from his pocket and selected a small worn one nestled amongst the others. It was a memento of times past, migrating from every set he owned to the next. He never thought he would ever use it again. He squatted down and inserted the key into a rusty padlock. The lock opened with a click. He was surprised by the lack of resistance before he remembered Richard had already been. He signalled for Kent to take the torch and grasped the handle that lay in an inclined space in the cover and pulled it open.

Hauling it to one side, he snatched the light and shone it inside, revealing a ladder leading vertically down into the darkness.

'This is it.'

'This is what?' Kent echoed, peering down into the hole nervously.

'This is where we are going to stay, George,' Mrs Kent said.

'Mother, I think it's best if you don't speak,' he said, annoyed at the ease at which she was adapting to the vagaries of their situation.

'What is this place?'

'Not sure. An old bomb shelter maybe. There's electricity and running water.'

'How's that possible? It's not exactly a standard billing address.'

'I don't know how, but it's on the grid.'

'So it's still in use?'

'No, it's been abandoned a long time.'

'Tell me, David, how does one learn about a thing like this? Are you sure there's no one out there on a computer somewhere, credit card in hand and himself in the other, waiting to watch me being endlessly tortured on www.secretdungeontorturefetish.com?'

'That's hilarious.'

'Thank you, but seriously, how did you find it?'

'Hiking with a friend. It was years ago and the story is not particularly interesting.'

'A lack of interesting things to say didn't stop you jabbering on in the car for the last God knows how many hours. Why stop now?'

'You'd better start realising how precarious your position is Kent or you're not going to get through this. Screwing with me can only hamper your chances.'

He considered the statement. It was hard to be sure what it really meant.

'How long do you expect me to stay down there?' he asked, changing the subject.

'I don't know...wait and see.'

'Wait for what? Deep Throat? You think that's the best guy to place our trust in?'

'We've been over this. What's to trust? We're safe. Nobody will find us. We wait for the call and then decide what to do. Hopefully, he'll help us make sense of this.'

'And if he doesn't call?'

'We wait for a few days and leave.'

'And then what?'

'I don't know?'

'Well, that's a great plan, David.'

'Fuck off, Kent.'

'I was just saying-'

'Well don't. Because of me you are still alive. Remember that. It's because I killed a man you can go on eating burgers or whatever it is you do every day.'

He let the insult go. There were more pressing matters at hand.

'Can your phone get a signal down there?' He asked, hoping a potential problem might precipitate a change in plan that didn't involve the bunker he was staring down into.

'I'll leave it up top. It has a loud ring. I should hear it if the cover's left opened a crack.' Trimble took it from his pocket and lit up the keys. 'And there's a good signal. I'll check every hour to make sure.'

Kent was disappointed but consoled himself with the knowledge he wouldn't be the one tackling those precipitous steps every sixty minutes.

'What do we do when the battery runs out?'

'I've got a charger.'

Kent was beaten. What kind of person was that prepared, he thought?

'I know its extreme, but we're in extreme circumstances.'

To Kent he sounded mad.

'Is there food down there?' he asked, more in the hope of delaying his descent than wanting anything in particular.

'Some. If we need to we'll get more supplies tomorrow.' That was untrue. No one was leaving until they worked out their next move. But honesty was a migraine waiting to happen.

'Tell me the truth, how much food do we have? Is there a chance we won't have enough?'

'None whatsoever,' he lied. 'There's ice-cream, steak, beer, plenty of cheese and bread...tonnes of stuff.' Kent regarded him suspiciously.

'A man should never joke about food. It's dangerous.'

'Just get in.'

'Strawberry?' he queried.

'What?'

'The ice-cream, is it strawberry?'

'Now.'

Trimble had never felt so shattered.

Chapter Twenty-Three

German sausage and a rapprochement

Trimble flicked a switch to reveal a large square concrete area. In each corner was a camp bed. On one of them lay three green sleeping bags and a stack of foam pillows. The unpainted grey walls were adorned with a few worn looking posters of the Beatles and Pink Floyd, which in the absence of youth no longer had the power to lighten their oppressiveness. Against the far wall was a simple gas ring on a rickety wooden table connected to a fuel canister underneath. Beside it sat a white fridge freezer with a purple logo that read Zanussi. High above was a network of pipes that clung to the ceiling like Ivy.

'What's in there?' Mrs Kent asked, walking towards a green door half way along the right wall. It was scarred with long brown jagged lines where the paint had started to peel.

'A loo and shower. Basic, I'm afraid.'

Kent pushed past impatiently, his footsteps reverberating around them. In a matter of seconds he had reached the fridge and was hastily inventorying its contents.

'Hey, where's the ice-cream?'

Mrs Kent opened the door and Trimble followed. The room was long and narrow, adjoining the main area like a wing on an aeroplane. The toilet had a dusty black broken seat with an old style cistern perched above. Trailing down one side was a metal chain, which ended in a cracked white handle. A simple sink with one faucet sat to the left. On the opposite wall was a small pipe attached to a corroded shower head. An orange smear connected the drain in the centre of the concrete floor to the rusty water that dripped from it.

'They didn't build these things for comfort,' Trimble said.

'I don't suppose it's heated?' she asked hopefully.

'Sorry.' He shrugged apologetically. 'But we shouldn't be here long enough to need it.'

'Don't worry, David.' She laid a sympathetic hand on his forearm. 'I'm not complaining. I appreciate everything you've done for me and George.'

He shook her off gently, feeling embarrassed by his half-hearted attempt to hurt her son a few moments ago.

'He appreciates it deep down,' she said, reading his thoughts.

'And I thought he was shallow.'

She was laughing as Kent waddled into the room clutching an assortment of Heinz soup cans.

'Is this it?' He snorted derisively at his haul. 'Soup, some hot dogs and beans?'

Trimble wondered how much effort it would take to beat the fat man unconscious.

'Although, I suppose the hot dogs are not altogether useless,' he said, 'providing we have the all-important condiment. Please tell me you have Ketchup.'

As Kent wittered on Trimble's thoughts turned to his old friend. He'd not seen him in three years and was sorry their first chat had been so hurried and strange. He wasn't sure Richard believed the story he'd concocted, but he had come through for him nevertheless.

They'd discovered the site together on a camping trip when they were sixteen. It was sheer luck they pitched their tent over the hatch and disturbed the layer of mulch that obscured it from the outside world. When they climbed inside and realised what they had, they were stunned. It was obvious from the dust and the cobwebs that the place hadn't been used in some time. Whatever its intended purpose was had been lost to the past. But somebody had gone to great pains to build it. The two of them had almost keeled over in fright when Richard hit the switch and the lights came on. It seemed incredible such a thing had been forgotten. Packing up their tents they marked it on their maps to return.

The home touches were added over two amazing summers, but when university arrived it was abandoned once again. They hadn't been back since. He was astonished Richard still had his key.

'Shall we see how George is getting on,' Mrs Kent said.

'Hmm?' he replied, tearing his gaze away from the dripping water. Trimble hadn't noticed the fat man leave the room.

'Are you okay?'

'Sorry, I was miles away. What did you say?'

'Your brother, he's-,'

'Don't call him that,' he said crossly.

Trimble saw from her expression that his reaction had hurt her. Perhaps it had been unnecessary, he thought. If she wanted to believe the fantasy in her head then let her. It changed nothing.

'I'm sorry,' he said. 'I'd better go check the phone.'

\#

Outside Trimble paced restlessly. Nobody had called. He knelt and checked the signal again. There were four solid bars. He could hear Kent's hushed voice below. What the hell was he doing here, he thought? Not long ago he had parents who loved him, a best friend, a wife and a soul mate. He had everything a person could ask for and the people beneath him didn't exist. How had it come to this? How had he killed someone? Let someone be killed?

Trimble allowed the tears to come. He wanted his family back and the Kents to be a secret again. Metres below his feet Kent also paced restlessly, although considerably slower than his counterpart above. His mother sat on a corner bed knitting contentedly.

'I mean the man is not the full loaf,' he said, dribbling slightly at the thought of toast and jam.

'Why, because he stopped a man trying to kill us?' she said, the steady rhythm of her knitting uninterrupted.

She was right. He needed to come up with an explanation for that. He flopped down beside her, wondering vaguely where she'd got the needles and wool.

'If you ask me he's the dangerous one. Look where we are. We didn't just stumble upon it?'

'I don't understand what you mean, George?'

'What does this look like to you?'

'Like a cave?' she ventured.

'Obviously, it's a lair. The man's a predator.'

She inhaled sharply and put down her knitting.

'George, he saved our lives!'

'Fine' he conceded, pausing long enough for her to return to her craft work. 'But he seemed remarkably comfortable playing matchmaker with a piece of metal and a man's chest.'

'Would you rather he did nothing? Why are you having such a hard time with this?'

'I'm just saying, how much do we know about him?'

'What's the matter with you?'

'With me? You're a lamb being led to the slaughter and instead of trying to clear the fence you've jumped in the oven and added your own seasoning.'

'You're being silly. I don't want to talk about this anymore.'

'Fine,' he said, 'we'll just hang around and wait for the Grim Reaper to show up.'

He watched her for a moment. 'He's been gone a long time. What's he up to?'

'He's checking the phone.'

'There probably is no phone.'

'You saw it, George!'

'Okay, I'll give you that, but he's probably switched it off or he's putting in a call to the hired help.'

'What hired help?'

'The one who does all the torturing.'

'What torturing?'

'How am I supposed to know?'

'George, you're free to leave any time.'

'Yeah, free to be killed the moment I poke my head outside.'

'And why would he do that?'

'I don't know. He's probably pissed off with you and by association me. Or maybe he's some sick weirdo who wants to remove my skin to make a lampshade.'

'I'm not listening anymore, George,' she said.

'Are you honestly telling me the vault of sanity hasn't been breached here?'

'Who's fault?'

He sighed in exasperation. 'Let me tell you a story.'

'If you like.'

'The place is Germany, 1929. A respectable looking gentleman, much like our David, is walking in a park.'

'That's nice,' she said.

'Suddenly he spots a woman being harassed by a rather unsavoury character and so he intervenes...as any good citizen would.'

'Like David did with us.'

'Nice to see you're spotting the parallels. Of course his assistance is gratefully received, much like David's yesterday.'

'I didn't see very much gratitude from you.'

'Ah yes, well, that's because I know the rest of the tale.'

'No one knows the future, George.'

'They can if they learn from the past.'

He paused to give Mrs Kent a chance to say something.

'...common sense suggests he saved the day, right?' he continued.

'Why don't you make me a nice cup of tea?' she said.

'Let me finish,' he said irritably. 'What the woman could not know...did not know...was that she'd exchanged a worm for a cobra. The man who offered to escort her safely home was none other than Peter Kurten, the Düsseldorf monster. And she,' he raised an eyebrow for dramatic effect, 'was never seen alive again. Now, does anything about this strike you as familiar?'

'George, be serious.'

'I am,' he said.

'You're being stupid.'

'Oh, I'm sorry,' he mocked. 'I wouldn't want to undermine the intellectual rigour applied so far.'

'You're not helping.'

'Who said I wanted to?'

'We all need faith sometimes.'

'What does that mean?'

'You're familiar with the story of Doubting Thomas, aren't you?'

'What are you on about?'

'You work it out,' she said.

'That he's one of Jesus' apostles? You've lost me.'

'Okay, George, tell me who that man was? Are you suggesting some stranger was walking around with nothing better to do?'

'No.'

'Or perhaps you believe that David organised it all, only to rescue us in order to kill us a few hours later?'

'Not necessarily.'

'Then you agree something is happening, something planned, and David is in as much danger as we are? And if that's true then you must believe he acted earlier and endangered himself to help you.'

'When did you suddenly become so lucid?'

'I'm not senile, George.'

Kent gave up and shuffled toward the toilet.

Trimble descended the ladder and greeted Mrs Kent's smile with a nod. He sensed she was the happiest in all of this. The seriousness of the situation had hit him full force up top. It threw everything into doubt and he realised he didn't know what he was doing.

'Where is Kent?' he asked.

'I'm in here,' a voice echoed from the toilet.

'We need to sit down and talk about what we're going to do.'

'I'm on the dumpster, but go ahead I'm listening.' The sentence was followed by a groan of what might have been pain or pleasure.

'I'll wait.'

Trimble and Mrs Kent exchanged uncomfortable glances as a series of grunts punctuated their reflective silence. It was half an hour before her son progressed beyond the sitting part of the exercise and graduated to a standing finale. The two-litre bottle of coke he downed earlier came out in uneven jolts leaving him with a feeling of pending relief. His hands fell away in defeat and he allowed it to hang unmolested under the considerable mound of flesh which hid it from view. Lamenting his lack of satisfaction he pulled up his pants.

'We need to talk,' Trimble said as he strolled in chewing on an obscenely large German sausage. Damn, he thought, watching his chubby digits work the shaft. He ate crap even when he was taking one.

Kent went to the fridge and picked up a can of cola from the top. He turned around and leant against it.

'What about?' he asked, popping the ring pull and taking a sip.

'We need to agree what we're going to do?'

'About what?' He gulped noisily.

'About our situation.'

'What about it?'

'That's just it, I don't know,' he said, trying to decide whether the fat man was being deliberately dumb.

'Well, David,' he said, scratching at the folds of skin under his neck, 'that particular phrase is getting rather stale. Why don't you try something else?'

'Shut up, Kent. I'm being serious. Two men are dead. I can't simply walk into a police station and explain this. I need some fucking help.'

The fridge let out an almost animate squeal as it gave under the pressure of Kent's weight. He stopped chewing. David looked pale. He envisaged him back in the bosom of his clinic suckling greedily from its narcotic breasts. Putting down the drink he pulled the plastic wrapping over the half-eaten sausage and laid it behind him.

'Settle down my troubled friend,' he said, revolving on his heels to launch another attack on the dwindling food supply.

Trimble stared at him, filled with loathing. 'We need to decide,' he said icily.

'Decide what?' came a muffled voice from the interior of the fridge.

'You know perfectly well what, you insufferable cunt.'

'David!' Mrs Kent said, surprised by his use of *that* word.

'I'm sorry, but he really is.'

Kent looked cautiously over his shoulder and opened a can of beef soup.

'Since we're handing out apologies you might want to bowl one in this direction,' he said to his mother, sniffing at the tin like a connoisseur.

'What is your fucking problem?' Trimble said.

'You mean apart from being in a cold war bunker with Private Slow and Captain Creepy?'

'Aren't you going to cook that?' Mrs Kent asked, pointing to the soup in his hand.

'On a diet like this I can't afford to waste the energy.'

Trimble felt an angry certainty galloping towards him and the fat man was giving it directions. He watched him slurp at the soup, oblivious to a pencil thin strip of sludge on his top lip, which had quickly warmed in the incandescence of his churning jaws. Mrs Kent was small comfort. She seemed to slip effortlessly between remarkable clarity to practical senility at the sight of her overgrown son.

'Either you answer me or you're on your own.'

Kent rooted around for any fragment of beef which might have gone amiss in the cracks of his teeth before draining the rest and discarding the empty tin beside him.

'Well,' he said finally. 'I recommend we go to the police and tell them what we know. They can't argue with the truth. Our stories will tally regardless of how much they try to trip us up. After that, we go to the papers, shine a spotlight on ourselves and hope it makes chasing us an unwise proposition. Sound good?'

Trimble was speechless. That almost sounded reasonable.

'And David, believe it or not, I am sorry about your family and your friend.' Kent swaggered off to the loo with the panache of a duck on a country road. The cold soup had not been a good idea.

'He's not so bad when you get to know him,' Mrs Kent said, after he'd gone. 'He's grumpy and he likes to test people. And he can make you feel like killing him sometimes, but if you get past that there are bits to like. Not many people do. Look what it's taken to keep you two together.'

Trimble shook his head in amazement. Maybe he wasn't so alone after all. 'May I offer you some tea or coffee, Mrs Kent?' He asked with mock formality, gesturing to a box of tea bags.

'A cup of tea would be wonderful dear.'

Chapter Twenty-Four
Under Control

Vatican City

Congregation for the Causes of the Saints

Giovanni slid his tongue frantically over the sludge that coated his teeth and gums. He snatched a jug of water from the credenza behind him, shaking violently as he gulped from the narrowed spout. He allowed it to spill over his chin and spot the front of his robe. The goop came away in congealed chunks like mud from a hill in heavy rain. They floated uneasily in his mouth before he forced them down his throat with a shudder. It hadn't been necessary to use quite so much, he thought, but then it wasn't everyday he killed a man with a few spoonfuls of peanut butter.

Crouching down beside his wheezing brother Giovanni took his wrist between his thumb and two forefingers and listened. His pulse was weak. In a few minutes the heart would stop pumping and the supply of oxygen to the tissues and organs would cease altogether. He got up, his forehead beaded with moisture. A few minutes more and he would make the call.

\#

The cardinal had spent most of the night turning the planned meeting with his brother over in his mind, but as dawn broke he had all but given up on finding a way out. He rested his head on his desk and tried to accept what was happening. The timing of this proved to be serendipitous for at that moment the embroidered gold leaf lettering on the bible decorating his desk reflected the winking rays of morning sun straight into his eyes. He realised the solution had been there all along. He pressed the book against his lips. Just as Judas betrayed Christ with a kiss, he would end his brother's betrayal with his.

Francesco had been diagnosed with nut anaphylaxis as a younger man. The proximity of the hospital to his collapse and the incisiveness of the doctor that treated him had conspired to save his life. The severity of his reaction implied many milder precursors and a prolonged period of sensitisation, which had been ignored.

Ever since the attack he had dedicated himself to his own protection and never touched anything he'd not personally prepared. He was hyper vigilant and perpetually ready to outline his circumstances wherever he went. On his wrist he wore a silver Medic Alert bracelet and in a pouch around his waist he carried two shots of epinephrine, a synthetic version of the naturally occurring hormone adrenaline. In the event of an attack it acted to constrict the blood vessels, increase blood pressure and stimulate the heart. In the few minutes he would have to respond he had to remove the safety cap from the automatic injector and push the tip against his thigh until the unit activated.

Francesco's natural caution had paid off and he'd not had cause to use it. The only necessity had been to replace the ampoules of epinephrine as they passed their expiration date.

\#

They embraced as they always did when they met. It was an action performed more out of malice than affection, a stubborn adherence to custom in the hope it would cause discomfort to the other. The meeting was distasteful to both of them, but they understood the importance of appearance. Their estrangement was acutely embarrassing and their bi-annual meetings, however ridiculous, allayed this shared fear of discovery.

This time the greeting was different for as Giovanni moved from the left cheek to the right he brought a sticky lump of peanut butter he'd secreted in the trench between his gums and pushed it forcefully into his brother's mouth. He clung on hard, his tongue thrashing about like a severed electric cable, as Francesco writhed and twisted against his grip. As he wriggled free his incomprehension turned to revulsion. He clawed at his face, smacking his lips in disbelief as he reeled and whirled towards the door. Giovanni jumped on him, grabbing him around the chest and pinning down his arms to prevent him reaching the pouch hidden beneath his clothes. The reaction had begun quickly and as they tussled the exertion increased the flow of poison. With his throat swollen Francesco buckled to the ground.

His eyes clicked slowly open and shut like the lens of a camera as he appealed in an endless soundless loop for the epinephrine at his waist. Giovanni tore the belt from him and deposited it in a drawer in his desk.

\#

Giovanni listened for movement outside the door. The paramedics would arrive any minute. He'd wanted to wait longer to phone, but any further delay would require an explanation. He stood trying to decide where best to situate himself. By the body seemed the most appropriate place. He looked at Francesco lying on his side. Was that the correct position? He squatted down and tilted the head back, appraising the finished work. He thought it appeared rather murderous and so adjusted it a few more times until he was satisfied. As an afterthought he forced a finger through his closed lips and felt around for any residue of the peanut butter. The sight of some visible streaks sent him scrabbling for the jug. He plunged in his hand, scooped up some water and shoved it into his brother's mouth, rubbing at the fleshy walls until he was sure no trace remained. An unexpected exhalation of breath made him quickly withdraw his fingers. He was still breathing.

Why couldn't Francesco have left things where they were, he thought? In dragging up the past, like some forgotten body, he had given him no choice. The Church might have forgiven a child, perhaps even allowed him to stay within the fold, but that was not enough. His destiny lay in the primacy of Peter. He had foreseen it. He would climb that platform, take his words and fill them with his message. But it would not be easy for those who slumbered so deeply would not awaken readily.

Religion in all its forms was a symptom of the human sickness. Christianity was a child's wish for immortality embodied in the worship of man made perfect; A deity of his own better reflection to comfort him at his end. The resurrection was a talisman to ward off the spectre of death, conceived in the same rich vein of ideas as transcendent love, enduring art and countless causes deemed worth dying for. Mankind's gift was also his burden for as he developed the tools to probe the boundaries of his existence he acquired an insatiable need to give his life meaning in a future without him. Strands of memories hung like parasites on the mind of human kind.

He understood and recognised this hunger in him too, but accepting his truth was a path to the absolute present. His road was not nihilism but liberation. Mankind had enslaved itself in fear and been impoverished by it. In the fleeting seconds of life a man could be all things. He could live without contradiction, compromise or regret. And in this speck of time he would be a god.

Giovanni's startled gaze met the noise of the door swinging open.

'Antonio!'

Antonio Piacente crossed the room quickly and with a cursory nod of acknowledgement knelt down beside Francesco.

'What happened?' he asked, as he examined him.

'Thank God you're here,' the cardinal said.

Piacente plopped a case like a toolbox in front of him and another the size of a briefcase slid off his shoulder. Giovanni watched him assess the scene. He was the Pope's private physician, a position complimented only by his reputation. He should have been away at the retreat. What was he doing here?

'Francesco, can you hear me? I need you to talk to me.' The doctor slapped the side of his face, but there was no response. He frowned. 'You're going to have to move,

Your Eminence,' he instructed. Piacente had mistaken his panic for shock. In medicine that was a useless emotion.

'Yes of course,' he muttered. A pale hand offered its assistance behind him.

He took it and found himself staring at a bush of red hair and a swarm of orange freckles, a stark contrast to the dark olive skin of the other man. He nodded and fell to the floor beside the doctor. The space he occupied gave way to the ashen stare of his secretary, Sister Brigitte. He took a shallow breath and gave her a reassuring smile. His knees were aching and he hoped his position on the hard wooden floor had made the right impression as they entered. What better image to illustrate his concern? Kneeling was a posture of prayer and faith.

'What happened, Your Eminence?' Piacente asked.

'I don't know. I think-' The sentence died.

Speaking was a lot harder than Giovanni imagined and his discomposure seemed to increase with each word he uttered. He was terrified of saying something that would reveal his guilt. He brushed his sweaty palms together. Was this what McCarthy experienced when he sent him to do the things he did? The outcome had always seemed more like something which might have happened. He never considered such a powerful sense of anxiety might accompany them. At any moment it seemed the doctor would look up and see what he'd done. He had to say something. He should mention the anaphylaxis. They would wonder why he hadn't later. His brother was as good as dead. Even Piacente couldn't stop that now.

'I don't know if you're aware, but my brother has a condition.'

Piacente had discovered the bracelet and was fingering it thoughtfully. The action was an unnecessary gesture. News of Francesco's arrival seldom failed to reach him. His need to alert the Vatican medical staff had come to feel almost hypochondriacal over the years. It had been something he found amusing in private, but now as he lay by his knees it was strangely disquieting.

'Hand me that jug,' he said, addressing Sister Brigitte as he pointed to the sideboard. She obliged, scurrying over and rushing it back to him.

'When did he last eat?' he asked, running his wet fingers around the inside of Francesco's mouth. He saw a glimmer of unease cross the doctor's face.

'I don't know,' Giovanni said. 'He just collapsed. You don't think it was that, do you?'

'Maybe,' he said tersely. Family always wanted to talk at the most inconvenient times. He wanted answers not questions.

'Urticaria..Laryngeal oedema,' the doctor murmured to himself.

He felt for the pulse in his neck.

'Give me 0.5mg epinephrine intra muscular, oxygen one hundred, 10 LPM,' he said.

The red head nodded and consulted his bag.

'Quickly,' he added.

His assistant filled up the hypodermic and handed it to him. Piacente squeezed gently and allowed a jet of liquid to shoot out of the top before lifting the robe and jabbing the point into his thigh. The paramedic followed with a ventilating mask. It fogged up straight away. He was still breathing. He slid a defibrillation machine from the soft bag Giovanni had seen earlier and placed some monitoring leads on his brother's chest. It began to emit a frantic beep.

'And 20mg of Chlorophenamine intra muscular,' the doctor called out. 'Respiration doesn't look good. Heartbeat is running away from us...pulse is bottoming out. We need a line. Give me an IV, five millilitres of one ten thousand epinephrine in a five percent dex solution.' Reaching for a tourniquet Piacente tapped Francesco's right arm and waited. A bright blue-green vein rose to the surface.

Giovanni saw the assistant inject something into a small pipe connected to a clear bag of solution. He slapped it into Piacente's waiting hand.

'Got a line,' he said, smoothly slipping in the IV.

'Blood pressure?' The doctor glanced up.

'It's falling.'

He turned back to Sister Brigitte. 'Call the Gimelli hospital. We're bringing him in. You need to tell them some things okay?' He stopped talking as he waited for a sign she understood.' She nodded meekly. 'The patient is elderly, suffering from anaphylactic shock. He's unconscious. Possible coma. Do you have all that?' She nodded again. 'Okay. Go,' he commanded.

'Stay with us Francesco,' he urged. He felt his throat as he peered expectantly inside. 'It's no good, severe upper airway obstruction, oxygen's not working. Give me 2 ml nebulised adrenaline.' His assistant tore the oxygen mask off and lifting Francesco's head roughly he pulled on another. It was connected by a tube to a small chamber half-filled with liquid. A pump on the other side turned the liquid into a fine mist.

Piacente stole a glance at the monitor and put his head to Francesco's chest. The action was redundant, but it gave him a few seconds to think. 'We're going to have to intubate,' he said.

The doctor grabbed a Victorian looking instrument from his assistant, ripped off the mask and inserted it into Francesco's throat.

'Damn, I'm not going to get in there. Nebuliser's taking too long.'

The beep of the heart monitor had sped up and was showing jagged lines.

'He's going into fib,' he said, snapping on a pair of latex gloves.

He picked up a gleaming surgical knife from the box beside him and made a half-inch horizontal cut between the Adam's apple and cricoid cartilage, slicing through two of the rings that made up the trachea. Giovanni thought the cut looked deep and he was surprised there was so little blood. The doctor pinched the skin surrounding the incision until an opening appeared and jammed his index finger into the slit. He wiggled it around before sliding in the tube with his other hand. The tips of his gloves were bright red.

The heart monitor sounded one long continuous beep.

'Flat line,' Piacente called out.

He snatched the resuscitation bag and attached it to the tube in Francesco's throat. He gave a couple of puffs of oxygen and observed his chest rise and then fall. As he did so the paramedic slid to the opposite side. He waited a moment and squeezed again before nodding to him to begin chest compressions. He counted five and repeated the procedure.

'Stop bagging, we need to shock him. Two hundred joules.' The assistant leant over and adjusted the machine. He grabbed a tube of lubricant and handed it to Piacente. He squeezed some onto the left paddle and rubbed it against the other before pushing the paddles hard against Francesco's chest. The current hit the body with the force of a hammer, pulling the chest skyward. The two men looked at the machine in anticipation. There was a brief flutter before it settled back to a continuous beep.

'Charging. Okay, clear.' The body arched again and the monitor sprung into life. Another brief flutter and the line settled down again.

Giovanni was giddy. Now it was happening, he couldn't believe it. In his early years as a priest he'd seen death many times and observed others as they went through the grieving process. He believed, in spite of everything, he would feel more for this one. In a way he did. He felt exhilaration.

'Charging again,' Piacente said.

This time the line settled into a slow rhythmic beat. He froze, waiting to see if it would hold.

'Blood pressure?'

'Ninety over sixty and climbing...one hundred over seventy.' The ginger haired man couldn't suppress a smile. It was holding.

'Beautiful,' Piacente sang triumphantly. The other man grinned.

'Looks like the adrenaline is kicking in, but we're not out of the woods yet. Let's get him back to the Polli. Prepare a ringer lactate IV 0.9 percent sodium chloride. We need to get that blood pressure under control. And give me 400mg hydrocortisone IM.'

The two men stood up together and reached behind Giovanni for the medical gurney. They collapsed the trolley and slid the body on. He watched in a daze as they pulled it upward to waist height and snapped it into place.

'Okay, Your Eminence, we need to get going,' he said, gesturing politely with the IV he was holding for him to move. The cardinal nodded slowly. He was thinking of the morgue next to St Anne's gate.

'He hasn't regained consciousness, is that normal?' he asked, afraid his voice would betray him.

'That is a concern, Your Eminence, but we'll know more when we get to the hospital. It wouldn't hurt to ask for some help.' The doctor motioned upwards.

'Yes, yes,' he said, bowing his head solemnly.

Talk of divine intervention made no sense to him. What made people think their God would be moved to intervene? Preference? A whim? A cog of action in an inscrutable blueprint? The former made him an ogre and the latter rendered any petition pointless. Praying to the heavens for intercession was a loss either way.

'I'm sorry, Your Eminence, but we really must go.' The doctor signalled for the other man to get going.

He looked on as the trolley moved away.

'Thank you doctor,' he said, sensing he should say something. 'If you weren't here I-'

Piacente dismissed his gratitude.

The cardinal couldn't say any more. For some reason he had a desperate desire to laugh.

Chapter Twenty-Five

Breakfast at Tiffanies

Lechlade, Wiltshire

Tomorrow the conclave will begin deliberations to elect the next pope. The last incumbent was known for his uncompromising brand of evangelical diplomacy, often engendering as much controversy as he did support. The former pontiff will be remembered with greatest affection in his native land for his tireless efforts in improving the lives of its people. In the aftermath of his death, one thing is certain, it is a papacy that will not be forgotten. Speculation has...'

Trimble hadn't heard a word the reporter on the television said. His rich mellifluous tones, like almost everything in the last few days, slipped in and out of his mind unnoticed. Only the interactions with the fat man and his mother seemed to capture his attention. For almost a week he'd listened to nothing else.

Kent had been the engineer of the decision to leave the bunker. Trimble couldn't work out how he'd managed it without his input. He'd not foreseen in his long periods of introspection the seeds of mild insurrection would be sown. For most of the second night the fat man whispered in the old woman's ear and by the beginning of the third morning she was ready to go. He'd made a token objection, but looking back the move was the right one. After nearly two days of silence staying no longer served any purpose. It had been almost a week now and there had been no contact from his caller.

Returning down an empty motorway in the early hours of the morning Trimble had contemplated the grim prospect of returning to his flat and the body of his friend. He knew the police would have to be called and Jim's parents told. He'd wrestled with telling them the truth, as Kent had suggested, but decided in the end it would only cause greater distress.

Mrs Kent had eagerly agreed to supply him with an alibi for the night of Jim's murder. Kent had taken more convincing. With a rehearsed version of events he returned to London. He found the body where he had left it. The blood had dried, but the grim tableau was unchanged. He wasn't sure what he'd been expecting, but the sudden rush of guilt at leaving Jim like that caused him to question the virtue of what he was about to do. But he stuck to the plan they'd worked out, taking valuables, cash and credit cards and dumping them in a waste bin a few miles from the flat.

At the station a sympathetic inspector appeared to accept his account of events, that he'd returned from a short stay with the Kents and discovered his friend dead. Trimble's hermitic lifestyle made the deception easier than it should have been. No one had come to his home in months and even Jim's friends, as he'd insisted from the beginning, stayed away. CID had canvassed the area and nobody had seen him in the days leading up to the murder. People in London rarely paid attention to their neighbours. With no reason to disbelieve him a theory of a burglary gone wrong was posited and tentatively accepted. The inspector had been kind, attempting in a perfunctory way to absolve him of responsibility for what happened.

After he was released Trimble hailed a cab and reluctantly made his way to the worst meeting of his life. Jim's parents had already been informed, but he owed it to him to go and answer their questions. The interrogation had left him drained and consumed with shame. Even in the grip of their grief they'd sought no blame, foregoing that last merciful distraction out of love for him. They offered only concern and he repaid their kindness with deception. It was the early hours before he was able to leave them. As they parted their fear for his well-being had all but broken him. He found himself a while later on the motorway en route to Clotilde Manor. He didn't know where else to go.

In the following days his alibi held. No one could say for sure whether he had been in London or not. Residents at Clotilde, with the exception of Mrs Kent and her son, had been for the most part unreliable or confused. The police had not connected Jim's death to the other killings and without witnesses and motives beyond robbery they had no choice but to leave him alone. He had been there ever since. He'd read in the papers the man he killed was a priest. The news had floored him. Why would a man of the church want him dead?

'It's so exciting,' Mrs Kent said merrily from the armchair next to him.

Trimble stared at her blankly as Kent grunted from somewhere on the other side of her.

The reporter on the television talked animatedly into the camera as he pointed to a long stretch of exposed walkway behind him.

'Yes,' he said, unsure what he had agreed to. It struck him as odd how the two of them were able to continue as though nothing had happened.

'I've been reading all about it,' she said. 'Behind him is the Sistine Chapel. That's where the voting takes place. After each round they return to their sleeping quarters along there.' She shifted forward and pointed to some spot in the middle of the screen. 'They're not allowed out until they make up their minds.'

The cardinals made a daily trip of three hundred and fifty metres between the Chapel and the Domus Sanctae Marthae. Before its construction they were bivouacked in cubicles in the apostolic palace. The advanced age of many of the conclave however and the progressive times they lived in had meant that such conditions were deemed unacceptable. Vatican commentators satisfied themselves with the glimpse these trips afforded, scrutinising every wrinkle and gesture as they tried to divine the outcome.

The rules of secrecy laid down in the Universi Dominici Gregis were overseen by the Marshal of the Conclave who was responsible for policing the cardinals. He enforced tough security measures, including a ban on all forms of communication, which might result in a leak. Any disclosure regarding the voting or deliberations was done so under the threat of excommunication.

'If you examine them you can get an idea of what's going on. Why don't we make it interesting and have a flutter? I've studied them quite carefully and I think the odds on favourite is-'

'Oh, for Christ sake, it's not the Grand National,' Kent said.

He had been quiet for the last few days, still troubled by his mother's ultimatum of obedience or poverty. It was infuriating because it had been so unnecessary. He'd fully intended to help Trimble with his alibi and was procrastinating only to ensure his decision was properly appreciated. He wanted David to know he had agonised over sacrificing the principles involved in accommodating him. His mother had ruined all of that in a crude act of blackmail and made him feel like a twenty-dollar hooker.

'But it's like a horse race, isn't it?' she said. 'I placed a bet on the Belgian to win.'

'I placed a bet,' he mimicked. 'I can place a bloody bet on whether it will snow on Christmas day, but that doesn't mean Christmas day is a horse race.'

'I didn't mean the election *was* a horse race, George. I said it was *like* a horse race.'

'Yes, I know about the literal and the figurative. My point simply is that you have an annoying habit of using analogy when it's not warranted. So don't.'

'George, I'm your mother. You should show me some respect.'

'We'll have to see about that. I have a different father than I had last week. Next week, who knows?'

'Don't be cruel.'

'*To a heart that's true,*' he crooned, breaking into a fit of giggles.

'Will you bloody stop,' Trimble said.

They fell into an uneasy silence. Mrs Kent gazed guiltily at the television, wondering whether his admonition had been meant for her too. She concentrated on the blurry shot of three robed figures gliding above the reporter. There was something about the middle man which looked awfully familiar.

Chapter Twenty-Six

Silence is Golden

Policlinico Gemelli Hospital, Rome

The hospital was an austere building, composed of a series of seemingly indiscriminate right angles. It had settled for the time being in the shape of a cross that had begun on its horizontal axis to double back on itself. From above it looked like a crudely drawn trident lain down by some half imagined god in the heart of the city.

Inside, on the tenth floor Giovanni struggled to hear his brother's breathing over the beep of the cardiac monitor. He'd been waiting fifteen minutes and desperately wanted to leave. His presence in the hospital felt dangerous, but he had to be certain. Tomorrow the conclave began and today he was a superstitious man. Although it had been six days since his brother's collapse he took no reassurance from it. He couldn't take his eyes from the machine. Each illusory change in pitch conjured every dark fancy and each twitch of his body became a precursor to speech.

The doctor entered the room with a loud crash. An empty metal tray rattled on the ground by his feet.

'Sorry,' he muttered, glancing upwards as he stooped to pick it up. 'I apologise for keeping you so long... Your Eminence, what's wrong?' he asked, catching sight of the alarm on the cardinal's face.

'He moved,' Giovanni replied, shaking his head in contradiction.

'Really?'

'...in the direction of the sound.'

The doctor got up and placed the tray gently on the table next to him.

'Let's take a look, shall we?'

He took out a torch pen and lifted Francesco's right eyelid. He examined it and then bent over to inspect the other.

'What is it?' Giovanni asked, frightened his brother might suddenly awaken and whisper what he'd done in his ear.

'I'm sorry.' The doctor smiled apologetically. 'I'm afraid it's not what you think. These things are often taken for more than they are.'

Giovanni glanced nervously in Francesco's direction, half expecting to see him staring back at him. 'I don't understand,' he said.

'Patients in a coma often exhibit behaviour which mimics conscious action.'

'But I saw him, he turned his head towards the noise.'

'What may seem like purposeful movement is often unconscious...reflexive.'

Giovanni took a deep breath and expelled it in anxious uneven bursts. 'I see.'

'I'm sorry,' the doctor said, taking his relief for disappointment.

'Will he wake up?'

'That's difficult to say.'

'Difficult, or you're unsure about giving an old man bad news?'

'No sir, I mean, Your Eminence,' he replied, disconcerted by his directness. 'It's just with this type of injury the variables involved are often more difficult to quantify, which makes the prognosis less... definitive.'

'What variables?' Giovanni asked gruffly, annoyed by the evasiveness of the reply.

'Injuries occurring within the skull...like those sustained as the result of impact trauma, for example, are often easier to diagnose and treat than those which originate outside it...which is the case with a stroke or cardiac arrest. In these instances the damage arises not from blunt force but anoxia or periods of hypoxia and therefore tends to be more diffuse. This makes it difficult to measure and treat.'

'Anoxia?'

'After an arrest oxygen levels in the brain drop rapidly, which I'm sure you understand is not good. The team that arrived at the scene to treat your brother did everything right. They were able to restore cardiac function very quickly.'

'That's good, isn't it?'

'Normally this would be very good news, but in your brother's case any optimism must be moderated by his age and the degree of hypoxia.'

'Hypoxia?'

'I'm afraid that although his heart was restarted the attack triggered a prolonged drop in blood pressure, which severely impeded its ability to pump oxygen. Whilst there was not a complete cessation in supply, the reduction he suffered before the medical team's arrival has most likely caused considerable damage. Ultimately the extent will depend at what level it was deprived and for how long. If he does wake up we have to be realistic about his degree of recovery.'

'And what is that?'

'I don't know....we've given him an MRI scan, but unfortunately this seldom finds any recent damage, acute or otherwise. It may take weeks, perhaps even months, for any indications to show up. We followed the initial EEG with another one earlier today and while it shows positive levels of cortical activity we should be cautious in our expectations. It's a waiting game now.

This was like getting blood from a stone, Giovanni thought. He needed more than maybes.

'So there is a chance he might recover?'

'Anything is possible, Your Eminence. No two injuries are the same, but you have to be aware that people of your brother's age often have a poorer rate of recovery than younger patients.'

'But he could wake up tomorrow and be fine?'

'I don't think you appreciate how unlikely that is.'

'But possible?'

'We don't know enough about the brain to make infallible predictions and the truth is we don't know why some people cope better than others. Some patients awake with little or no loss of functioning while others lapse into a vegetative state. They breathe, swallow unaided, even startle to stimuli, but they've lost the higher functions which allow consciousness and personality. As I said his EEG shows some cortical activity and he clearly lacks the prominent abnormal reflexes, such as stiffening or jerking of the arms and legs, which is characteristic of such states. He also has good pupillary activity. That being said...' The doctor swallowed uneasily. 'If he does regain consciousness you should prepare yourself for the fact he may be severely impaired.'

'What impairments are we talking about?'

The doctor frowned. 'Are you sure you want to do this now? I think-'

'Quite sure,' he interrupted.

'They may be mild or-'

'I want you to be honest with me,' he cautioned.

'The areas sensitive to a lack of oxygen include the hippocampus, which is a region critical for identity and essential for the retention and formation of new memories. Cognitive effects may involve problems in reasoning and judgement. There may well be disturbances in processing visual information.' Giovanni ran an arm over his brow. The doctor paused, his pessimism felt almost blasphemous in the presence of the cardinal.

'Are you okay?' he asked.

'I'm fine, please go on.'

'Any degradation to the border zone areas of the cerebral cortex, the cerebellum, basal ganglia and the thoracic region of the spinal cord could have a wide range of effects...ataxia, apraxia, spasticity-'

'Will he be able to speak? Understand?' Giovanni said, trying to shake the image of his brother advancing on him in jerky accusatory steps.

'I think it may have been irresponsible of me to lay all of this out so bluntly.'

'I asked for honesty,' he said ,wishing the doctor would forgo the unnecessary sentiment. It was only the dread of discovery that gave his vigil any meaning.

'I see from my notes you agreed to the hypothermic treatment. The effects may not have shown themselves yet.'

'Hypothermic treatment?' Giovanni looked puzzled.

'When your brother was admitted?'

He remembered now. He'd been railroaded into that.

'It's standard for patients with your brother's complications.'

'What does it do?'

'They didn't explain this to you?' The doctor frowned again.

'I was pre-occupied.'

'Of course,' he said. 'A cool saline solution is circulated through the vena cava to achieve a hypothermic state. The body temperature is lowered to thirty-three degrees.'

'And, this is good because..?'

'A lack of oxygen sets in motion a destructive sequence of biochemical events. Resuscitation and rapidly restored blood flow, however, begins another chain reaction and this wreaks comparable destruction on the cells. The cooled state slows this down, retarding these negative processes and protecting the brain so that the healing process can proceed occur unhampered. After twenty-four hours the temperature is slowly brought back to normal...I'm surprised you were not made aware of any of this.'

'So it didn't work?' he asked, ignoring the doctor's question. 'He's still unconscious.'

'It's too early to tell, but some of the signs are encouraging.' The doctor paused, aware that he appeared to be contradicting his earlier prognosis. 'Waking up is a slow process. If it does happen it could be weeks or months. And even then it would be some time before the extent of his injuries are clear.'

He hadn't answered the question, Giovanni thought.

'So you think he will come out of this?' he asked, pushing him for an answer.

The doctor concealed his frustration with a smile. 'The duration of coma is often a significant factor in determining whether a patient will wake up and what type of recovery he will make. Most people who make a full recovery are unconscious only briefly. With straightforward head trauma a longer period is tolerated, but in cases of oxygen deprivation the outer limit is generally breached a lot sooner. Your brother has been unresponsive for a week and as you are aware the onset was rapid. I want to give you hope, Your Eminence, but...'

The two men looked at each other without speaking. The conversation was over, but the doctor hesitated in ending it.

'I'm sorry, Your Eminence,' he said, 'but I have to complete my rounds. If there is anything else I can do.'

'Of course, I understand. Thank you for being direct,' he said, allowing him to leave.

For Giovanni, it was a largely unsatisfactory meeting. He didn't want ambiguities or uncertainties, not when he was so close. He gazed out at the dome of St Peter and thought about a day two years ago when he'd looked out at the same view down the hall.

His Holiness had begun his papacy as a relatively young man, but old age had treated him with as much contempt as anyone else. With each stay in the hospital there were renewed rumblings of dissent, suggesting an infirm mind to accompany his weakened body. But as the Holy Father had confided in him once, Kings abdicated not popes. Giovanni had been in no position to mount a claim then and an election would in all probability have seen off his ambitions for good. There were papacies of months of course, but these were the exceptions. He'd needed a little more time to convince them of his suitability. The old man had given him that.

He looked back at his brother. 'You're dead, Francesco,' he said, 'and you're going to stay that way.'

Chapter Twenty-Seven
An Old Flame

Clotilde Manor

Mrs Kent had been in the bathroom for most of the afternoon. The occupation had begun peacefully enough. A rapid succession of deep fried chicken legs had had a stuporous effect on Kent's bat senses and the sound of gushing water passed him by. The porcelain playpen had beckoned to him during lunch, like a ghost trapped in limbo, sometime between the shepherd's pie and spotted dick. His stubborn refusal to listen until he swallowed his dick led him to where he was now, banging like a double crossed pimp on his mother's bathroom door. He could have gone in search of another of course but was disinclined to take any course of action which placed exertion and compromise over inertia and petulance.

His hammering had not caused its inhabitant any significant discomfort, bar the occasional need to reread a line of the book clutched in her wet wrinkled hands. *Love in the Antarctic* was a satisfying read with all the required components of a first rate romantic novel. The juxtaposition of the character's steamy and fertile love in such a barren and frigidly hostile environment was a clever motif. She particularly liked the use of sci-fi to reinvigorate the genre. The male protagonist had unusually dug up his female lead from the ice, where she had lain for the last one hundred thousand years. He'd used his scientist skills to revive her and soon discovered, despite obvious difficulties in language, that they shared a profound physical and spiritual attraction.

'Mother, for God's sake,' he yelled at a flowery ceramic sign, which read *mamma's house.*

Mrs Kent rolled her shoulders with a contented sigh. Ronaldo had proposed to Christine in the Jacuzzi inside the laboratory. The thawed out female had chosen the name after she had mastered the rudiments of the English language and a working knowledge of human history. She had made surprisingly good progress after just a week. He'd confided in her his contempt for his world and the media furore he feared would follow the exposure of their relationship. It had been hard to explain the last concept to her, but it seemed to Mrs Kent she understood. Between lovemaking they'd decided to remain in their glacial paradise for as long as possible.

'Mother, this is intolerable. If you want to give me bowel cancer you're going the right way about it.'

Mrs Kent's silence was finally broken. 'George, go away!' The movement of her body was like a shifting of tectonic plates, sending a wall of water hurtling to the other end of the bath, splashing up against the taps and spilling over the sides.

'Can't I have a moment's peace to read my book?'

'Don't tell me you're reading that light porn in there?'

'George, why don't you use the bathroom in your room?'

'You don't give a damn, do you? ' he said, clouting the door for added emphasis.

'Oh don't be so melodramatic, George,' She said, quivering as Ronaldo placed his hairy palms on the inside of Christine's thigh. She loved shaggy men too.

'What kind of fiend are you?' Kent said, stealing a glance at the television flickering behind him. If he went slowly and clenched he might be able to make it to the chair.

'How long are you going to be?' he asked.

'I'll be as long as I will be.'

'And you call yourself a mother? Your only son and this is how you treat him.'

'Two sons, George,' came a muffled correction.

'I think it's better if you don't mention him. He's more likely to appear as a witness for the prosecution rather than the defence. Why do you think he went home?'

'Because he killed a man and you didn't thank him for it.'

'He went home because of you, because of this.' Kent held his hands out in illustration.

'You mean, because I wouldn't let him in the bathroom?'

He could hear her chuckling to herself. She had become considerably more impish since David had entered her life, he thought. It was as though some previous constraint had been removed.

'No, because you put your own carnal needs first.'

'How is lying in a bath carnal, George?'

'Look at the filth you're reading. It was your relentless debauchery that got us into this situation in the first place.'

There was another violent splash of water. 'I keep telling you, George, you can leave any time you want to.

It's been weeks since anything happened. It's over. So if you want to go, then go.'

'Oh really, well thank you very much. I'll be happy to do that as soon as you explain exactly what you called me back here for.'

'Honestly, George, you would try the patience of a saint. You know perfectly well why.'

'What, to put my childhood memories to death? To tell me my father is in fact a shadowy character who may well want me dead? To learn I have a brother who may or may not be Jack the Ripper 2.0 and that my mother's morals are not so much loose but likely to slip off?'

'What do you want, George?'

He gritted his teeth. 'Are you coming out or not?'

'Oh, don't go on,' she sighed. 'Why can't you try and be more like David.'

'What slightly taller and more insane?'

'You might try thinking about other people for a change. David doesn't act like this and he's just lost his best friend.'

'Yes, I seem to remember you were the one who gave the killer directions with that little love note of yours? It is sort of why I tactfully stay off the subject. I don't spout that cow shit about him remaining alive in here.' Kent placed a hand mockingly on his heart.

'Memories keep people alive, George.'

'Why don't we nip down to the cemetery and pop up the lid. Let's test the theory shall we?'

'That's not what I meant.'

'What you meant is not worth mentioning.'

'It's time for you to go back to China, George.'

'Are you running more hot water?' he cried in disbelief.

'Go away.'

'Believe me, I'm already there, but perhaps as a parting gift you might relieve me of at least one burden. God knows you've given me enough.'

'I'm not listening to you anymore.'

'It's like a baby elephant trapped in here,' he wailed.

'If you want to lose weight, you'll have to exercise like everybody else. I'm not paying for liposuction.'

'Why are you being like this?' he said.

'I'll be out when I'm out, George.'

Kent hobbled in the direction of the armchair. There was clearly no reasoning with her.

\#

The television was failing in its duty to distract Kent from the commotion in his pants. The onset of stomach pains had placed him in a serious dilemma. Should he risk the journey upstairs or hold his position and try and breach the wooden barricade once more? He was rapidly approaching the point of no return and the exertion necessary for either course of action left a high probability of collateral damage. Damn her, he thought, letting out a dangerous whoosh of air.

The click of the bathroom lock coincided with a loud cheer from the television and the combined shock nearly resolved the matter for him. His mother appeared out of a fog dressed in a white bathrobe. Her hair was slicked back in thick healthy strands. The blue rinse had disappeared and she looked even younger. The devil only knew how she did it.

'You have no idea how much suffering you have put me through,' he said, scowling at her cheerful visage.

'Must you be so argumentative?'

'I'm not going to dignify that with a response.'

He shuffled forward in precarious pigeon steps, swaying markedly at the effort of keeping his balance and his two feet together.

'This is your fault,' he snapped, edging his way toward her. The muscles in his behind were tiring.

A chant of *Viva il Papa* started as a camera panned across a sea of people. It was getting dark and soon the huge lamps of the Vatican Palace and the Propaganda College would flood their jubilant faces. Thousands of small excited gesture gave the illusion of larger movement as the crowd seemed to swirl like a storm around the giant obelisk in its centre. The week had been long, but tiredness was forgotten now. The atmosphere was charged and anything seemed possible. They were a part of this day and the joy they felt in being there spilled out to the man standing next to them.

'They've done it,' Mrs Kent cried excitedly.

'I don't know why you're so excited. The nearest you've come to a church is driving by it on the way to the off-licence.'

'I don't care what you say, George, it's an important day.'

'Yes, I suppose now you can see whether your horse won.'

Kent groaned at another stab of pain from his gut as Mrs Kent pushed hurriedly past him. 'It can't be,' she said, pressing her nose up to the television.

'What can't?' Kent said to the back of her head.

She leant back and looked askance at the picture. 'It can't be.'

'What?'

'That's him,' she screeched.

'Who?' he asked reluctantly, concerned she might screech again. It made no difference to him which old man came to the balcony.

'That's him!' she said, pointing to the figure in white. 'That's your father!'

'No dear, that's the Pope. I know it's easy to get the box mixed up with real life but try.'

Mrs Kent turned around to face him, her mouth open.

'No, you're not starting any more of that nonsense,' he said.

'You're the son of a pope,' she gasped.

Kent swore he heard pride in those words.

Chapter Twenty-Eight
While you were Sleeping

Gemelli Hospital, Rome

The glow from the strip bulbs on the corridor filtered into the room through the wire mesh glass. In the gloom a shape stirred into life. Francesco blinked blearily as he tried to clear the fog from his mind. He was lying down. When had he gone to bed, he wondered? Straining his neck he struggled to make sense of the hard alien shapes that loomed out of the smoky light. Where was he?

He pulled back the covers in confusion and revealed a white hospital smock. The sight of it brought the present back with the speed of an injection. He saw Giovanni's bulging eyes and his skin flushed with hateful exertion. He felt a terrible embrace and a tongue zigzagging an angry trail of gritty slime into his mouth. He watched himself jerking in helpless terror on a dusty wooden floor as the future unfolded in front of him like a map. He had been condemned to die and his life reduced to a footnote in his brother's story. But history had not given up on him so easily. There were more pages to be written.

Instinct told him to get up, but he was afraid. In the darkness there lurked a power to twist his thoughts against him. How long had he been gone? Where had he disappeared to? Where was he now? Francesco shivered as he imagined his body lying in some sun lit room while he roamed this twilight world of his own making. He chastised himself for yielding to such foolishness. He was awake. He'd come back from the dead.

He accepted the needle's appearance in the back of his hand without surprise and calmly followed the attached tube to an intravenous drip hanging from a stand above him. He would deal with that later. He checked himself over thoroughly, wiggling each finger and every toe, marking every nuance and subtlety of movement until he was happy everything operated as it should. His excitement was growing. He was stiff in places but no worse than when he came in. He couldn't stifle his laughter anymore. It was loud and full-bellied.

'Initial comments, doctor?' he asked himself aloud.

'Good,' he answered with a chuckle. And no cognitive difficulties, he thought. A good sign. He said the word a few more times. His speech was good. His brain was making all the right connections.

'You can't beat me, you bastard,' he said.

He pulled back the blanket in a decisive sweep and his bare feet met the floor with a pleasant thwack. His toes curled at the coldness of its touch. Sensitivity to cold, another good sign.

He carefully extracted the needle from his hand and readied himself to stand. As he did so he spotted another tube running from a transparent bag strapped to his side with surgical tape. He prodded it curiously and recoiled in disgust as he heard a swash of liquid hit the sides. He fought the impulse to rip it off, tracking its course as it disappeared beneath thick padding to a dull ache below his waist. He had a feeling that would be unwise.

Francesco tore off the nappy with a crackle and ejected it across the room, unveiling the catheter which snaked out from the end of his penis. He retched as a wave of nausea hit him. A flurry of fingers pulled down the smock as he tried to cover himself and banish the image from his mind. He'd been right not to pull it out. Medical personnel would have to remove that humiliation.

He tried to stand but fell back, his head spinning. He'd expected that. Who knew how long he had been out? When he got up again the dizziness returned, but this time it wasn't strong enough to knock him down. After a few minutes the wooziness had subsided enough for him to move. He stayed close to the bed, pacing up and down its length as he got used to his body again. With each repetition his confidence grew. Movement was pushing back his anxiety, giving space for his reason to return. It wasn't long before he was ready to venture further.

He crossed the room and gazed down at the city lights which stretched and arced in long dazzling lines away from him. Where better to be resurrected, he thought, than Rome? He popped the window open with a click and the sound of distant traffic came rushing in like a forgotten melody. The night air bombarded him with smells and old sensations that suddenly felt new and intoxicating. The nothingness of his sleep had dulled the memory of them and imbued the world with renewed wonder. His senses were heightened and he felt fully in the present. The craving for a cigarette took him by surprise. He had given up years before, shortly after his attack. He wanted a drink too. He suddenly yearned for a hundred things and the vigour of these competing desires made him giddy. He thought of Giovanni and his reaction when he saw him. A ball of excitement burst inside him and rippled outwards. He needed to be out there.

He strode back toward the wardrobe and swung it open. Inside it was empty except for his shoes, which lay neatly in one corner. Closing the doors he caught sight of his reflection and was surprised to see he was clean-shaven. They had seen to everything. He looked himself over. In the semi-darkness the figure in the mirror could have been a stranger. The white smock was unflattering and foreign on his wrinkled body. When did he get so old, he wondered?

Francesco spied a chunky rectangular box attached to a thick rubber hose dangling on a hook next to his bed. He took it in his hand and squinted at it. His glasses were with his things, but he could make out a keypad with numbers and other symbols on it. The most prominent buttons featured a picture of a bell and a stick figure in a dress. He hesitated a moment before pushing the latter.

Almost five minutes elapsed before a middle-aged nurse with bobbed hair appeared in the doorway.

'Hello, nurse,' he said, surprised a coma patient calling for assistance had not warranted more urgency. He wondered whether he should have pressed the button with the bell instead.

'The alarm is really for patients, sir,' she said ill-temperedly, taking Francesco for a visitor as he sat calmly in the murk. 'You shouldn't be here. Visiting hours are over.'

He looked down puzzled. 'I would like you to remove this and fetch me my clothes.' He tapped the bag of liquid at his side.

The nurse's stern expression turned to shock as she took in the empty bed. He gave a wry grin.

'You're awake,' she said, transferring her startled attention to his bare feet.

'Yes, I'm aware of that.'

'But you're not supposed to be.'

The nurse was having trouble comprehending the turn of events. His chart had ruled out such a dialogue taking place.

'Well, I apologise for that, but I'd like something to put on.'

'I'll call the doctor,' she said, flustered. 'Please get back into bed.'

'No,' he said, sounding out the word slowly and deliberately. He was in no mood to negotiate. His immodest attire and the growing discomfort of the catheter removed whatever joy he might have had in their exchange. 'I've spent long enough there.'

'But I must call the doctor,' she said.

'As you wish, but do what I've asked or I'll find somebody who will.'

'Yes, of course,' she said.

He waited for her to go, but she dithered on the spot, unsure what to do first.

'Nurse,' he said. 'My clothes?'

'Yes, of course,' she replied, giggling nervously before departing down the hall.

'Nurse,' he called after her.

He heard the sound of squeaking shoes as she revolved on her heels and the soft echo of their patter as they made their way back to him.

'Yes,' she said, her poking in her head around the doorframe.

'How long have I been away?'

'Away?'

'Asleep?'

'Oh, I see...ten days I think.'

Francesco's brow creased. 'Really that long?'

'You know, you're very lucky.'

He said nothing.

'It might be less,' she added, aware her answer had not been the one he wanted. 'This is my first shift back. I've been away.'

The nurse glanced awkwardly into the corridor as he looked passed her.

'Are the elections concluded?' he asked.

She let out a gasp of recognition. 'Oh my God,' she said excitedly. 'I'm sorry I didn't realise.'

'Then Giovanni is Pope,' he sighed, filling in the blanks. 'Could you get my clothes?' he asked, closing his eyes.

When Francesco opened them again she was gone. What did he do now, he thought? Before his brother's accession a whiff of scandal under the right nose would have been sufficient to end his ascent, but things were different now. Giovanni was enthroned. He had become the institution and the institution would protect itself at all costs. A wagging tongue no longer had the power to hurt him and back channel whispers of an illegitimate child would be buried beneath subterfuge and counter attack.

A public allegation on the other hand posed a risk for both of them. It would lead to bodies and he couldn't hazard that, not yet. But without the threat of the media he didn't have enough juice to get an appointment at the kingmakers' table. To make an approach he needed evidence that couldn't be covered up and a bluff they couldn't call. The question was, where did he get proof like that?

The nurse reappeared in the doorway clutching a bag with his clothes folded neatly inside. They'd been cleaned and pressed.

'The doctor is on his way,' she announced.

He stared at a man with a pronounced limp passing behind her. His lopsided gait made him look like he was riding an invisible bicycle.

'Are you okay?' she asked.
'I'm fine.'
'Can I get you anything?'
'I need a phone.'

#

Francesco dialled the number and waited.

'Hello,' he began in English. 'May I please speak to Mrs Kent?'

Chapter Twenty-Nine

A Roman Holiday

Four Weeks Later

Sala Nervi Hall, Vatican

Beneath the thick travertine slabs that covered the ribbed barrel roof of the papal audience hall Kent fought the desire to sleep. The tiredness had worsened since he'd woken, pulling at the delicate edges of his sanity like a beggar at a businessman's sleeve. Things were taking an age to get going and the noise of its occupants had succeeded in making a bad situation worse.

He'd imagined a General Audience with the Pope would be a sombre affair. Instead a carnival atmosphere prevailed. The Sala Nervi hall was filled to breaking point, far beyond the six thousand three hundred seated capacity, and everywhere there were banners, flags and declarations of group affiliation. Behind him the prattle of a group of American school children clothed homogeneously in blue pants and white T-shirts bearing the name *St Joseph's Miami* in bold black lettering seeped into his head like chemical waste into ground water. It was complimented by a French howler monkey attempting to communicate with a mate several rows away and a troop of Germans smacking him about the skull with an endless succession of guttural consonants. His brain felt like a sponge swimming in a bucket of puke.

The blame for his malaise and his ill-temper lay with two bottles of Velletri Rosso Riserva he'd drained the night before. The lingering effects of the alcohol and the natural slump of his shoulders combined to make him look like a bald and haggard Richard Nixon frozen in a half-finished victory salute. Kent was disinclined to take responsibility for his condition and placed it squarely on the comfort of the wheelchair in which he sat. From the moment it welcomed his buttocks into its soundless embrace he was convinced there was something preternatural about its construction. The reading matter boasted it to be a model nine design, marrying practical mobility with chiropractic ingenuity. That didn't mean a lot to him, but something had been created far greater than a mere conglomeration of nuts and bolts.

The chair had been Francesco's idea, believing a disability would help to facilitate and divert attention from the request he'd made to the prefecture of the papal household the previous week. Four reserved seats and a place in the meet and greet afterwards had felt conspicuous in the circumstances. Trimble and Mrs Kent agreed her son would make the better invalid, a decision he'd accepted like an award. In the speech that followed he used the word authenticity quite liberally and talked at length about the actor's method, which seemed to involve a lot of being wheeled around.

Kent had hoped yesterday's gathering at the hotel would make the grand plan clearer, but after five minutes he'd lost interest. He spent much of the meeting struggling to open a packet of cheese. Later, as he finished it off in solitude with a plate of spring onion crackers he blamed the bad packaging and Francesco's reluctance to repeat himself for being in the dark. In his present state even the vaguest memory of what was discussed proved elusive. His eyelids felt heavier than a ten-pound dumbbell so he did the only thing he could. He settled down like a cow in a thunder-storm and let them close.

\#

Kent awoke with a start and treated the room to a sleepy glare. He cursed its occupants in Chinese for disturbing him and rested the implied weight of his over-sized head on his watch. He'd only been dozing a few minutes. The banging in his head confirmed it. Whoever advanced the theory of power naps as a solution to sleep deprivation had obviously spent their childhood in a CIA interrogation suite. He had no business being here, he thought, gazing at the vast strange bronze sculpture set against the back wall.

Fazzini's masterpiece dominated the stage and beckoned like some abstract nightmare to the large high-backed papal chair which sat at the centre edge on a tiny square platform. It was lit by a pair of giant spotlights and flanked by two simple wooden chairs. Either side was a statuesque Swiss guard, clothed in the striped yellow, blue and red knickerbockers, white ruffs and striking crimson plumes that sent tourists into a clucking frenzy. The ensemble was completed with a towering halberd.

He stretched restlessly, scowling at the vacant stare of his mother. It was ten thirty-two. Popes were obviously no more punctual than anybody else outside Japan. He squirmed at an unpleasant stab of pain below. The breakfast had brutalised his insides and his gut had bloated like a four-day old corpse. The need to vent was unavoidable. He caressed his stomach and allowed the distension in his rectum to build before emptying it to the left. A lady with toothpaste white hair bore the brunt of his ill wind. Her nose twitched in the manner of a condemned man in a gas chamber as she battled to make sense of it. Kent felt his spirits lift and yawned with momentary contentment.

'It's almost time.' The words swept past him in a low whisper. He turned to see his mother patting an empty chair beside him for Francesco.

He had been big news since he walked out of the hospital. It wasn't quite a tomb, but it had lit up the blogosphere and the social media networks. Many followers had used his relationship to the pontiff and his surprising recovery as proof that a spiritual interpretation was needed. Some had even gone as far as to proclaim it the first miracle of the new papacy. Science, they reasoned, merely peeled back the boundaries of the concealed universe until it revealed God's greater mysteries. The more secular minded had spun the flat narrative of the miraculous with an eye to the ironic; A parable on the science of belief and the politics of religion.

When they entered the hall it didn't take long for the cameras to find them. From the safety of the chair

Kent basked in the jostling of lenses and clicking of shutters like a seal on a rock in summer. Trimble's comparative discomfort was spared by Mrs Kent's decisive action as she punched her way through the throng with a protesting fat man at the prow. He followed gratefully in her wake as a mob closed around *The Resurrection Man*.

'Everything all right, Frannie?' Mrs Kent asked.

'Yes,' he said quietly, nodding discreetly at Trimble as he took his seat. 'We need to be careful Bee. Eyes are on us.'

'Don't worry, I can be a real Mata Hari when I want to be,' she whispered back.

Kent exploded with laughter, causing heads to turn in his direction. Francesco shot him a nervous glare.

'Mi Scusi,' he said, stifling the rest of the outburst with the back of his hand.

The silent hostility that greeted his apology found its mark. Kent had noted his circumspect nod to David as he sat and the pang of jealousy it elicited was unexpected. Where was his nod of respect? Gripped by a desire to end his censure he was compelled to say something clever.

'It's all in his reaction, right?' he offered lamely.

'What?' Francesco replied, examining him with barely contained irritation.

'The old boat race will betray him,' he said, unsure why he'd dropped into cockney rhyming slang. Did Italians even know about that?'

'What are you talking about?'

Kent thought about this before he realised he wasn't sure what he had meant. He probably should have listened to the plan last night.

'Don't worry, we're gonna get him,' he said, hoping his endorsement of the general goal would be enough to earn him some points.

'Enough talking,' Francesco said bluntly. He wished he'd gone with his instincts and left the fat man out of the day's events. For reasons lost on him he'd relented.

The response was not the one Kent had been hoping for.

'I think,' he persisted, prodding him until he turned around, 'that the day will be won with a cool head and a willingness to see the job through.'

That sounded good, he thought. Vague but rousing. He waited for the nod of approval and an indication they were back on an equal footing.

Francesco's eyes ran frenetically over the round face in bewilderment. What was the fat man up to? Was he trying to sabotage him?

'What?'

Anticipating the brush off Kent leant over and attempted to clarify his point. The hillock of flesh around his midriff squashed uncomfortably against the sides of the chair and prevented him from getting too close.

'I suppose it's a question of Mon frère or Mon amis,' he said, with a smile of suave reassurance, which resembled a female monkey proffering its behind to an alpha male.

'What?'

'Just a little bit of La filosofia,' he said, exaggerating the word with a flourish of fingers and some unnecessary aerial punctuation. He had to confess even he didn't understand why he said that.

'What?'

Kent gave up.

'Just trying to help my simian friend,' he said, flashing his hands at him like a croupier leaving a black jack table.

'What?'

Francesco's pitch had climbed enough decibels to raise a few eyebrows behind him. He looked around self-consciously, appalled and unnerved by his lack of control. Sensing the danger he turned around. The fat man was unpredictable and volatile. He couldn't risk engaging him now.

'I'm sorry, non-parlo tutti frutti,' Kent tittered, following up on his previous witticism with the grace of an overweight jaguar with one leg missing. Damn him, he thought. He was the one doing him the favour. Whatever the hell that was.

Chapter Thirty

Stairway to Heaven

Sala Nervi Hall,

Vatican

The ripple of applause became a roaring wall of sound.

'What's happening?' Kent shouted, tugging on Francesco's limp arm as his question disappeared into the noise. Seated he was virtually blind, snatching only glimpses of what was going on like shafts of sunlight through the branches of a tree. The applause had started somewhere behind, triggered by a sign not immediately obvious to him that things were about to get underway. For many this was not their first time.

Giovanni emerged from stage left in a robe of brilliant white followed by a string of bishops in bright red sashes. The noise rose another octave and everywhere people were standing and clapping wildly. When Francesco saw him it was as if someone had punched him in the stomach. He hadn't prepared himself for how he would feel. He held on to the back of the chair in front of him, propping up his legs. His brother looked radiant and in that instance he was transfigured. He'd become a construct of pure desire, superheating and condensing in a supercharged air around him. His presence was alchemy, turning a wave to bliss and a gaze into love. And it sickened him. How could anyone begin to guess the putridity that lay beneath?

Mrs Kent squeezed Trimble's hand tightly. The man up on stage had so much to answer for. She'd spent three decades living half an existence and even now, after she'd found David again, it broke her heart to know she'd lost more of him than she could ever get back. But she wasn't afraid anymore and she wouldn't allow him to take what little she had left. He'd shown he would kill to protect what was his and she knew at that moment she was capable of matching his resolve. She stared at him intently, willing him to look at her.

Trimble stared at the white figure and dug his nails into the back of his hands. He drew blood, but the pain could not distract him from the rage he felt. He trembled as it bubbled up inside him. He wanted to wrap his fingers around that windpipe and choke the smug placid expression from his face. This maggot of a man had ordered the slaughter of innocents as though it were nothing. He had taken a woman and infected her with his malignancy of mind, diverting the flow of her life, his life, before it had even begun. He stole a sideways look at Mrs Kent. Like a river he had rejoined his source and perhaps the symmetry of that meant something, but his waters had already nourished and been nourished by others. His affections would be forever fixed to three boxes in the ground and he would sacrifice the remainder of his life for five minutes more with them. He could not harbour resentment for the days he'd lived, but good fortune and good people did not absolve Giovanni. His intentions came from the same wellspring that killed Jim. To have such a monster dictate the hearts of billions would be the worst sin of all.

Trimble wanted to ignore Francesco's involvement in all of it, but questions continued to trouble him. He'd walked away from his responsibilities, from him, and left a vulnerable woman to fend for herself. After thirty years he'd returned not with contrition but with more destruction. What kind of man did that make him? He'd claimed his silence had been for her protection and yet in one moment of advantage he'd exposed the truth? Had he been ignorant of what might happen? Trimble couldn't say for sure, but he was certain that Francesco had thrown them into this with little consideration of where it might lead. How could he expect them to overlook these things? He thought of the aloof stranger he'd spoken to that night on the phone in his flat. He seemed so different now. Was it an act? He should have pushed harder for answers and perhaps he would have done if they hadn't needed him now.

'He puts on quite a show, doesn't he? Really knows how to work the room,' Kent boomed in Francesco's ear. 'It's all a bit presidential, isn't it?'

He spun around and fixed him with a stare of disbelief. 'Sit down, you idiot,' he said through thinly parted lips. He glanced around to see if anyone had noticed.

Kent frowned, puzzled by the sudden display of enmity. 'Oh cripes, that's right the chair,' he said, feeling for one of the arms behind him. 'Totally forgot in all the excitement.'

'Now,' he said, his features flushed with the effort of not shouting.

'Okay Mussolini, jeez, calm down,' he muttered.

As Giovanni took up his position on his platform Francesco stood tall, readying himself for the moment he would see him. He was certain his face would not be lost in the crowd.

Their eyes met and a flicker of dark recognition passed between them.

'My venerable brother,' Giovanni said into the microphone, his arms reaching out toward him.

A murmur went through the crowd as necks craned to trace the inspiration for his words. Some of the people nearby seemed to have guessed the connection and had already started applauding.

Giovanni descended the steps and made his way to the barrier at the front, eliciting an audible gasp from the audience. The crowd parted around Francesco and opened a path as three men in black suits a few feet away scanned the place nervously. No-one had seen anything like this before.

'Your Holiness.' Francesco took his outstretched hand and bent to kiss the papal ring. He thought of Mrs Kent revealed behind him, which gave the act a perverse pleasure.

'It's good to see you well,' he responded, clasping his hand between his. 'Praise be to God.' He smiled, as though entertained by the duplicity of their encounter.

'Praise be to God.'

Giovanni's attention darted to the seated figure of Kent in the wheelchair and the older woman who stood by him. She looked familiar, he thought.

'May Christ keep you safe and protect you,' he said, turning to leave.

He disappeared back up the steps to rapturous applause and took his seat in the high-backed papal chair.

'Welcome,' he said to the hall as one of the bishops in a wooden chair to his left adjusted the height of the microphone.

Kent had expected most of the proceedings to be in English and was bored to discover during the next hour he might as well have been listening to a Serbian dance station. Other groups had made better preparations, employing the services of translators who filled the pauses in scriptural meditation with French, Spanish and a number of languages he couldn't identify. He had caught snippets from a heavily accented English translation floating from the back of the room. It confirmed his suspicions. He wasn't missing very much. An instruction to fight against sin in his daily life was simply not feasible when he considered how much of his routine it constituted.

#

Consciousness came back to Kent in uneven bursts like a learner driver trying to negotiate a three-point turn. He had resisted it, but his efforts were futile. Ten minutes of cheering as various groups responded to a microphone on the far left of the stage had begun the assault, bombarding the infrastructure of his dream world with auditory artillery shells. The singing, which had begun in the last-minute or so, had proven too much and his kingdom collapsed on top of him. He stepped out of the rubble with a snarl to a choir of children serenading a group of men and women in wedding gowns and suits.

'Who are they?' he asked Francesco.

'They are the *Sposi Novelli*.' The way he said it gave him a start as it suddenly transformed from lightly accented English to full fruity Italian.

'Steady on there champ.'

'New Spouses,' he translated irritably. 'They've come to receive a blessing on their marriage.'

He shrugged at the explanation. He didn't understand why the children had to sing as well.

When they were finished a photographer took some final pictures as papal messengers were sent out to gather up those selected for the meet and greet.

Francesco addressed the three of them quietly. 'Okay, this is it. Bee, don't do anything crazy, yes? We just need him to recognise you.'

Mrs Kent nodded solemnly.

'This means you too,' he said to Kent. 'Now is not the time, yes?'

'Look they're off,' he grinned, pointing at a man in crutches slowly mounting the first step.

'There will be an opportunity to say what you want later,' he added.

'Yeah, whatever,' Kent said.

'I mean it,' he warned.

'Yeah, I got it, nothing reckless. You know, I resent the implication-'

'It's not an implication,' he interrupted. 'Your behaviour is often stupid and irresponsible.'

'I'm not sure you want to open that particular box, sunshine.'

'Okay,' Francesco said, 'but please, be calm, yes?'

Kent huffed a few times, annoyed by the attempt to placate him.

'David, are you ready?'

He nodded.

'Let's go then.'

'What do you mean, let's go? Where's his pep talk? Why am I always singled out?'

'I'm sorry, same goes for David, all right?'

'Yeah, but you don't really mean that, do you?' he sulked.

'Please, let's go.'

Trimble pushed past him.

'Get up,' he said from the centre aisle. Kent saw that he was holding a pair of crutches. He'd not noticed them before.

'What do you mean get up? I'm crippled, remember? He looked at Francesco. 'And I seem to recall you telling me to get back in the chair.'

'There is no way we can lift you up those steps,' Trimble said. 'Atlas would struggle.'

'I don't deal well with insults and I'm not comfortable changing the play at the eleventh hour. Perhaps if you had confided in me before we might have worked something out but-'

'You have three seconds to take those crutches or I'm walking out of here,' Mrs Kent said.

'Uh, okay,' he said, unsure why her absence should be a cause for concern.

'And if I do you'll never get a penny from this day on, George.' He scrutinised her with one pirate like eye. How many times had she blackmailed him in the last few days? As soon as he won the lottery he was going to tell her what she could do with her money. The Kenster wasn't for sale.

He snatched them from Trimble with a puff of air. After several different pouts a la Victoria Beckham, he wobbled to his feet. Francesco and Trimble held his upper arm as a show of solidarity as Mrs Kent fussed about nervously in front of them. Every now and again she stole a glance over her shoulder as if frightened someone might realise what they were up to.

The four of them fell into line behind a wheelchair occupied by a diminutive woman of considerable age. Her heavily wrinkled skin and the hunch on her back gave her the look of a tortoise that had lost its carapace. Two burly looking men with biceps like small hills accompanied her.

'She still has hers,' Kent grumbled.

'That's because she weighs four pounds,' Trimble said. 'And they,' he indicated the two men, 'look like the offspring of Hercules and Sampson. You on the other hand weigh a gargantuan amount and she,' he pointed to Mrs Kent, 'looks like she might struggle to carry a bag of light groceries.'

'My, My, aren't we garrulous,' he said. Trimble gripped his arm tighter causing a gentle yelp of protest as he witnessed the chair in front sail effortlessly upwards.

Kent began his ascent slowly, but the situation deteriorated rapidly. As he reached the third step his breathing had become laboured and by the fifth it had evolved into great stertorous snorts. On the sixth he made a miscalculation that proved fatal. He'd reasoned in his deleterious state that distributing more of his weight on to Trimble would take the pressure off his legs, which were in imminent danger of buckling. The decision to displace the entire four hundred and twenty five pounds in one limp application was a combination of greed, criminal slothfulness and incredibly poor judgement.

Kent's tumble to the bottom of the steps hurt almost as much as the knowledge he'd have to climb up them again. Lying in a confused, defeated, sweaty and quite unattractive heap he experienced something he rarely, if ever, felt. Embarrassment.

'I'm fine, I'm fine, really, couldn't be better,' he cried out, clambering to his feet. Those who had formed a circle of concern around him didn't look convinced. One of them reminded Kent of a pretty air stewardess who had spurned his advances shortly after take-off from Beijing, somewhere between dispensing orange juice and handing him a moist towel.

'Grazie, Grazie,' he continued, flapping his arms around in the hope they might waft away.

As the crowd began to dissipate he realised he'd dismissed their offers of assistance too rashly. Employing a series of crude gestures, which looked like a dwarf giving birth to an ostrich egg, he enlisted the help of the few remaining stragglers and began a second ascent. On the seventh step they handed him off to the waiting figures of Francesco and Trimble who had gawped motionlessly during the entire debacle. A sea of hands followed him for the rest of his journey to the top, ready should he waver again. Mrs Kent in a fit of maternal pride scurried around to join the throng behind. Francesco turned to look at them and thought he saw one or two tears of admiration.

The four them quickly caught up with the tail end of the line inching its way ahead. Six attendees, including the small woman in the wheelchair lay between them and Giovanni.

'Where are you from?'

The question came from an usher who had appeared beside them.

'England. London,' Trimble said tonelessly, taking over the task from a startled Kent.

'What group?' he asked perfunctorily.

Francesco coughed to make his presence known. The usher looked at him and nodded with a smile before disappearing. He re-emerged a moment later next to the papal throne.

'Remember, when you approach, bow, don't kneel,' he said to the three of them, 'that's the preferred way. You may kiss his ring if you choose. He is addressed as his Holiness, Your Holiness or Most Holy Father.'

Francesco was becoming anxious. They'd not seen each other in private since the hospital. He'd started to believe they never would again.

'Kneel?' Kent said derisorily. 'Christ, I couldn't do that if God himself came down. And as for kissing his ring, you can forget that...never going to happen.'

'Do what's expected,' he said. 'Now is not the time for other matters.'

'But-' Francesco raised a hand and silenced the protest.

The tortoise woman leant forward and kissed Giovanni's right hand. She said something low in Italian and after a few words in return she moved on. As they approached, the aide whispered the information he'd gathered into his ear. Looking up in surprise he immediately caught sight of his brother's wry expression.

He recovered quickly, taking in a wider view of the bald fat man whose arm he was clutching.

Kent was transfixed. This was the guy who tried to have him killed, he thought. This smiling kindly face had ordered his death. Francesco pinched the tender skin on the back of his arm.

'Il Padre,' he crooned, bowing with a grossly exaggerated gesture like a courtier at the palace of Versailles.

The assistant froze, aghast at the bizarre and unexpected nature of the display. Giovanni stared at him in astonishment.

'I am your most obedient servant. I prostrate myself before your Holiness. May I kiss your ring?' he bellowed, chuckling loudly with a mocking circular motion of his hands.

The usher moved forward, his mind scrabbling to deal with such a colossal break in protocol. He looked apprehensively at Giovanni trying to gauge his feelings and then at the Swiss Guard, unable to decide whether they constituted a threat. At that moment Mrs Kent stepped out from behind them.

'Your Majesty,' she cooed, following her son's lead with a curtsey. 'I bet you didn't think you'd see me again, huh Vinnie,' she said, treating him to a haunting cackle.

Giovanni stood up in fright. He opened his mouth to speak but was overwhelmed. He knew who the old woman was. What was she doing here? The assistant had recovered and recognising his master's disquiet shielded him from view as they conferred in whispers. He accepted an inaudible instruction with a nod and signalled for him to be whisked away. He waited until he was half way across the stage before he turned back to the line. Eyeing Francesco and the others suspiciously he explained to those waiting that his Holiness had been called away. The news was taken with a groan of charitable disappointment. He hovered a little longer, watching the queue as it dispersed, before giving them a final once over and scurrying off.

'Well, thanks for doing exactly what I asked you not to,' Francesco said to Kent. 'What were you thinking? And you,' he said looking at Mrs Kent, 'I'm really disappointed.'

'Hey, hey, hey' Kent said, holding his hands up in mock surrender. 'Why you be getting all up in my grill. If you don't like the way I roll then why you bring me for? This shit is ma biznez.' He had no idea why he'd opted to speak like he was from a Bronx housing project.

'You couldn't do one thing I asked?'

He abandoned the attempt at gangsta. 'Why on earth should I do anything for you? You're not my father. That was my father,' he giggled, pointing at the side of the stage with his thumb. His expression suddenly became serious. 'The bastard tried to kill me. What did you think I would do? I'm fed up listening to your crap. Who do you think you are anyway? We wouldn't be here if it wasn't for your deep throat routine.'

'This is not the time,' he said stonily.

'Well it was for me,' he said. 'So deal with it.'

'What happens next?' Trimble asked.

'We go back to the hotel and hope he calls,' Francesco said, balling his fists in frustration.

'Why would he do that?'

He shrugged, staring at Kent. 'Reassurance. He wants to know what I'm up to.'

Chapter Thirty-One

An Audience with the Pope

Francesco had spent most of the night lying fully clothed on his bed propped up by two pillows watching a muted television throw flickering shadows on the walls. He'd dozed off for barely an hour when the shrill ring of the telephone woke him. A meeting had been set up for 10:30 a.m. As he paced impatiently outside the hotel he looked down towards St Anne's gate and silently berated the fat man for making him wait. He had not been in his room and the others had gone to find him.

He suspected this morning had been arranged out of curiosity rather than fear. Giovanni had reacted in the hall because he had not anticipated their encounter. He would not be caught off guard again. This was his last chance and he hated to admit it, but he needed Kent. Bee and David had been channelling the persistence of Sisyphus to keep the fat one on track and he needed them to do it one last time. Regardless of what happened he was grateful to them. He'd exploited them and put them in harm's way and they had given him more assistance than he had any right to expect. It was because of David hope flickered on. He had been the one who had put the plan together and if it worked he owed him everything.

\#

Trimble and the old woman found Kent alone in the frescoed breakfast cellar reclining in a white plastic chair with a glass waiting at his lips. It appeared as though he was sleeping, but the firm grasp of its stem hinted at a level of wakefulness above that. The indiscriminate consumption of most of the menu, including fried calamari, butta alla matriaciana, lamb alla cacciatore, a slice of pangiallo, a cheese tray of several ricottas and one or two mozzarellas, two espressos and a bottle of mineral water had brought on a severe attack of meal fatigue. This had nothing in common with battle fatigue as it was precipitated by an intense bout of gorging rather than any act of self-sacrifice.

'Kent,' Trimble called.

The lump stirred, recognising at some level it was being addressed, but dismissed the intrusion and fell still.

'Kent,' he called again, his voice echoing loudly against the thick stone walls as he moved.

He opened an eye in acknowledgment and saw Trimble standing over him, supported by the smaller form of his mother who peeked out from his rear. He followed reluctantly with the other.

'What is it?' he asked tiredly.

'We have to go.'

'My God, what is that excrescence?' he said, pointing disparagingly at a large flower brooch sitting on the right breast of Mrs Kent's red cardigan.

'Oh this old thing?' she said, touching it lightly. 'Have you not seen it before? It was my mother's. It's been in the family generations.'

'So has dementia, but that doesn't mean we should pass it on. Get rid of it.'

'Just get the fudge up, George,' she said.

He was barely able to believe the transformation which had taken place in her during the last few weeks.

'And if I refuse?'

'Then you'll be paying for everything you've just stuffed into your mouth.'

Kent grudgingly held out his hands and signalled for them to help him up. 'Don't expect a postcard when I get back to China,' he said. 'We're going to be seeing a lot less of each other when this thing is done.'

\#

Outside, Francesco's pacing had intensified. When he finally caught sight of David and Mrs Kent he was relieved to see the fat one looming behind them like a giant blimp.

'Come on, we need to hurry,' he called.

'What time are we meeting Pot Pourri?' Kent hollered back.

Francesco waited until the distance between them had closed before he answered.

'You should show some respect,' he said testily.

'What are you talking about, you mad bastard?' he panted. 'What do you think we're doing here? It's certainly not to endorse his liberal interpretation of the Ten Commandments.'

'It's not about Giovanni. The position represents more than any one person. You can understand that, yes?'

'Christ, throw a stone anywhere in the Emerald City and you'd hit five sex offenders. And if you think I'm going to drop my knickers because a bunch of geriatric virgins gave some bloke a pointy hat then you're deluded.'

'So because one man has been ensnared by sin you would damn an entire religion followed by millions? What would you champion instead, Mr Kent? Atheism? Empiricism? Would you have people eschew a road of spiritual wonder for a path of vitriol and doubt?'

'I don't think there's much spiritual wonder in an inappropriately dressed man droning on about birth control and transubstantiation? I think I'll use my own grey matter as council rather than defer to a pensioner in a cape.'

'The Church has stood for centuries as an edifice of goodness and a beacon of light for those in darkness. I suppose one who does not value such things is able to dismiss them easily,' he said haughtily.

'That must be why you were trying to blackmail the murderous bastard in charge of your nice beacon.'

'Let's go, shall we?' Trimble said, interposing himself between the two of them.

'Fine by me bro,' Kent sang.

'Don't call me that,' he said.

#

A line of people stretched back towards them as they waited to be fed into an airport style metal detector. It was flanked by two guards equipped with detecting wands. Touching the concealed pocket below his hip Francesco glanced nervously at Trimble.

'We're not going to have any problems here, right?' Kent asked, spotting the exchange.

He shook his head.

'Because if there's any illegality, I'm not going down with the good ship Crazy. Miss Senility and Travis Bickle are on their own,' he said, pointing at his mother and David.

'There's no problem,' he replied curtly.

Francesco placed Mrs Kent's bag on the x-ray machine's conveyor belt and stepped through the detector. The sharp beep brought a practised expression to his face. He tapped his pocket and fished out a set of keys, dangling them in the air by way of explanation. He shrugged good-humouredly at the guard in front of him as a bad-tempered colleague with latex gloves looked on. He waved him on with a polite smile.

They headed past the Swiss barracks to the Bronze doors, the entrance through which all those attending a private meeting with the pontiff passed. As they came into view Trimble suddenly stopped. It was another step or two before Francesco registered it and turned around.

'What's the matter?' he asked.

'I'm not going in.'

'What's wrong?'

'I can't do it.'

Francesco didn't need him to explain any further. If David needed to step away he wouldn't try to stop him. He'd done enough. And he didn't really need him for this part.

'We'll see you on the way out,' he replied without further discussion.

Trimble patted him on the shoulder. 'Good luck.'

Francesco didn't say anything but was moved by the generosity of the gesture.

'Whoa, Whoa, Whoa, back the truck up.' Kent said, appearing beside them. 'Why the hell is he getting a time out?'

Francesco started to walk away but was obstructed by a surprisingly long arm.

'I asked you what's going on?' he said icily.

'It's all right,' Trimble answered.

'For you maybe,' he glared. 'Are you listening to this?' he asked his mother.

She nodded merrily and took a bite of an apple that had appeared from her pocket. Why did he look to her for support, he thought? These days, she was as helpful as a hernia in a tractor pulling contest.

'If you think,' he said to Francesco, 'I'm leaving Dave out here searching for a grassy knoll, you can think again.'

'I know you're concerned, but nothing has changed,' Trimble said.

'So why are you bailing out then?'

'I don't trust myself in there...not after what he did to Jim. I would kill him.'

Kent crossed his arms. 'I don't believe you.'

'Come on, George,' Mrs Kent cajoled, joining the conversation. 'I won't let anything happen to you.'

'No.'

'Fine, go home then,' she said mercurially.

'Fine then, I will then.'

It was Mrs Kent's turn to cross her arms. 'Good, that's settled then. Frannie, let's go,' she commanded, winking at David as she walked away.

Francesco turned to look at him, his eyes wide in dismay. What was she doing?

'Don't worry,' Trimble mouthed.

'So what now?' Kent asked, watching his mother and Francesco navigate their way around the streams of tourists.

'Piss off.'

'Well, that's not very nice.'

'I have nothing to say to you.'

Kent considered his expression. The last time he looked like that somebody ended up dead.

'Good luck,' he said, before pursuing his mother as briskly as he could manage.

\#

The bronze doors sat between two massive columns atop a flight of steps beyond the right arm of Bernini's Colonnade. A solitary Swiss guard with a spear protected them.

'What an outfit,' Kent mocked.

'That uniform takes thirty hours to make,' Francesco said, irritated by his flippancy.

'It takes that long to look like a clown?' he smirked. 'Do they juggle?'

'They're very well trained, I can assure you. They're responsible for the security of the pontiff and they'll give their lives if necessary to defend him.'

'They still look like clowns.'

Francesco gave up. The fat man was an uncultured moron.

At the doors a guard performed a cursory sweep before directing them onwards. They were led immediately to the Scalia Regia, Bernini's ornate staircase, which led into the Apostolic Palace. Kent greeted the steps with a sharp accusatory breath. He was less hung-over than when he'd last attempted such a feat, but they were still going to chafe.

At the top they entered a courtyard and crossed to a hallway on the other side where there were two elevators waiting to take them to their floor. They exited through a marble hall to the papal apartments where they were seated in an antechamber adjacent to the library. A striking portrait of St John the Evangelist by El Greco and two oil paintings, one of St Peter holding the keys to the Kingdom and the other of St Paul Clutching a sword, hung on the walls.

Moments later a small man in his sixties appeared to escort them.

'Hello,' he said in English for the benefit of Kent and his mother, 'I am His Holiness' personal secretary, Monsignor Roberto Ballarmino. I will take you through to His Holiness Pope Giovanni I.'

Every time Francesco heard the name spoken aloud a cluster of dark emotions swirled like a cyclone inside his head. No pope had used his baptismal name in over four hundred years. What vanity to ignore centuries of tradition.

The library was enormous with large windows sweeping across St Peter's Square. Contemporary art adorned the walls and in its centre was a large conference table hinting at the power of his position. Giovanni sat at a smaller walnut desk beneath a rendering of the resurrected Jesus emerging from the tomb.

'One moment,' he said, marooning them in the middle of the room as he pretended to finish off some paper work. A smile played at the edges of his lips. He was toying with him, demonstrating his power.

When he rose to embrace him he dismissed the monsignor with a faux beam of contentment. He waited until he had closed the door before speaking again.

The conversation began in low rumbling Italian. It had the dark resonance of a monastic prayer and sounded utterly different to anything Kent had heard over the last few days.

'Um, Hello?' he interrupted, waving his arms to get their attention.

The two men were nose to nose and made no indication they'd heard him.

'Hello,' he repeated loudly.

'Who is this?' Giovanni said impatiently. He spoke in English but addressed the question purposefully to Francesco.

'You are joking?' Kent answered.

He disregarded the outburst and waited for his brother to respond.

'You had better start looking at me when I'm speaking to you otherwise I'm going to do something you'll regret,' he said.

He had his brother's attention. This was exactly what he needed him for, Francesco thought.

'And what is that?' he replied calmly in heavily accented English.

'Is this guy stupid?' Kent asked Francesco. 'Are you stupid?' he said to him. 'Do you think you're untouchable, is that it?'

'I'm not going to quarrel with you, Mr -'

'The name is Kent, you irredeemable bottom feeding sewer scum. Remember it.'

'I would imagine it's preferable not to know names given the circumstances.' Giovanni laughed and walked back towards his desk, falling into his chair with exaggerated nonchalance.

Francesco sat down in a green backed leather chair in front of him. He fumbled in his pocket and pulled out a pack of cigarettes.

'You're smoking again?' he said, ignoring Kent for the second time. 'You always were weak willed. You never had what it took to see things through.'

Out of the corner of his eye he could see the fat man's features had started to bulge.

'Call it a new lease of life. Coming back from the dead does that to you,' Francesco said, placing one to his lips.

'You can't smoke in here,' he said gesturing at the paintings.

'You can always call a guard,' he replied, lighting up and placing the pack defiantly down on the desk.

'What do you want Francesco?'

'Say my name,' Kent cut in menacingly. The rage he felt inside equalled nothing he'd experienced before and although he was a coward by nature he could feel the lifelong restraint slipping away. He was ready to kill this prick.

Giovanni considered the demand carefully. 'Okay, Mr Kent,' he sighed. 'What is it you want?'

'I want to know what kind of man orders the death of his own children?' he said, his tone rolling thunder.

'Is this really why you came to see me? For an explanation?' He feigned a look of amazement. 'Look around you, isn't it obvious?'

'You inbred son of a jackal.'

Francesco twisted in his seat, sensing the situation was starting to slip from his control.

'Stop,' he commanded.

Kent halted in front of the desk, glowering a deep dark red.

'Be still,' he said reassuringly. 'We expected this, yes?'

His mother's eyes flitted anxiously between them.

Giovanni smirked. 'Impressive. What other tricks does it do?'

'Why did you agree to see us?' Francesco asked.

He studied the fat man warily. He had taken a number of steps closer.

'To put an end to this nonsense.'

#

Outside Trimble was fixed on the window above him. Was it unfolding as he hoped, he wondered? It wasn't much of a plan, but at least it was better than the hole ridden scheme Francesco had come to him with. With so little time to prepare he'd had to improvise. He'd made a number of assumptions and there were a hundred ways it could go wrong, but if the old man's incredulity at what he proposed was an indication of his brother's ignorance then they might have a chance.

#

Giovanni regarded the indignant group wearily. It was not as much fun as he'd imagined it would be. 'I'm becoming bored of this. If you have something to say then do so and leave.'

'Don't worry,' Kent said. 'I'm going to enjoy telling it to every paper I can find.'

'You think such threats intimidate me?' he laughed.

'You won't get away with this.'

'But I already have. The world will never believe you. It can't. I am a conduit to God, all but worshipped in his place. You think my people will allow you to take a wrecking ball to that?'

Mrs Kent approached them and sat down on the arm of the chair Francesco was sitting in.

'Vinnie, you tried to kill our sons and you murdered someone else's child instead. What was David's crime?'

'The name is Giovanni, you imbecile.'

'Call me whatever you want Vinnie, but tell me, what was David's crime?'

'David ?'

'Our son.'

She looked at Kent. 'And this is George. He's your son too,' she said, taking hold of his hand. Kent's instinct was to withdraw, but he let her have her moment.

'That's my son?' He raised his eyebrows in amusement. 'Now, that is hard to believe. Please, just take your pet and leave.'

Kent pulled away from her. Francesco, spotting the danger, stopped him with his arm.

'How can you not care about the things you've done, Vinnie?' she said.

'The name is Giovanni and I don't, truly I don't. I am driven by forces and currents beyond your feeble morality. Lives are expendable, Mrs Kent. Mr McCarthy's demise was regrettable, but he was a means to an end. His function was the extent of his worth and the man he killed was of no consequence. You equally are of no importance and if it's expedient for you to die then you will die and I will not lose a second sleep over it. I gathered you here today for my entertainment and I'm afraid I no longer find you entertaining. If you wish to preserve what remains of your family, Mrs Kent, I suggest you leave and never come back.'

'You're a monster,' she said.

'No, you destroyed my monster and now I have to find another.'

'You will pay for what you've done,' Kent said. The man was unaffected by his anger and without reciprocation it felt pointless. Satisfaction would not come from words.

'As you keep informing me.'

'Regardless of what you think you have, in the end you'll see everything you've done means nothing. You are as banal and unimportant as all the other evil little men who thought they had a unique perspective on the world. You'll end up where they all do.'

'And where's that?'

'Crying out in the dark.'

'That's very poetic, Mr Kent. I'm only sorry others have had to perish in your place.'

Kent lunged across the desk, his fist raised to strike him, but was stopped by his mother's voice wafting up gently behind him.

'Don't, George,' she said, touching him on the back. He turned around to see tears rolling down her cheeks.

'Mum, are you alright?' he asked.

'I've done what I came to do. I have two wonderful sons. This man can't hurt us anymore. Let's go, George. Please?'

Francesco stubbed out his cigarette on the desk and picked up his lighter.

'I agree. This is over,' he said to the two of them. Mrs Kent pulled gently at her son's elbow and guided him away.

'Goodbye Giovanni,' Francesco said. 'We won't meet like this again.'

'What, that's it?' he teased as they headed for the door. 'You came for that? That was pathetic.'

Mrs Kent twirled around. 'You know what, Vinnie?'

'What?' he said coolly. 'And the name is Giovanni.'

'You think you've won, but you haven't. When death comes for you, and it will, you'll be more frightened than you can possibly realise. Your achievements will be counted as the lives you hurt. I believe in God and justice. My pain will last a few more years but yours will endure for an eternity.'

She grabbed Kent and hauled him out the door.

'What was that?' he asked, once they were out in the hall.

'What?'

'It was well said.'

'Thank you, George.'

'Now, why can't you be like that more often?' he said as they made their way out.

'It takes too much out of me, George,' she said breathlessly. 'Too much.'

'Mother, this is not a bad movie. I was being absolutely serious.'

'I know, George. I know.'

They exited the papal apartments by a different staircase and walked outside into the bright sunshine of St Peter's square where Trimble was waiting for them.

'Did you get it?' he asked.
'Crystal clear,' Francesco answered.
'Get what?' Kent said.
He put his arm around him. 'Let's have a drink.'

Chapter Thirty-Two
Infallibility and the Mediocre Trinity

Papal Apartments, Apostolic Palace

Giovanni looked down at the candles bobbing on the square. Those were his people, he thought, hanging about in the cold for a handful of muttered words. In a little while he would step out on the balcony and give them what they came for. He wished it would come quickly. He was tired. The day had been long and the wine from the late supper had intensified its grip. He gave his head a retaliatory shake, longing for the darkness to swallow him up and spit him out sometime tomorrow.

He peeked behind him at a pile of documentation on his desk, annoyed Roberto hadn't waited until the morning to present him with it. His secretary considered each piece of paper ,regardless of content, vital and conveyed it through his door with ungainly urgency. He rubbed his arm irritably where he'd knocked into him. He would have to do something about that.

Giovanni barely noticed the tingling at first, but as it slithered downwards from his neck and wrapped itself around his chest he shifted uneasily. Something didn't feel right. As he tried to shake it off the sudden heaviness in his arms startled him. The tingling had turned to numbness and it was spreading.

He stumbled forward in panic and felt his feet disappear in a quicksand of carpet. He looked down and saw them bent at grotesque angles. What was happening? Frightened of falling to the floor he propelled himself across the space between the window and bed and collapsed through the curtain, landing with a heavy bounce. He lay on his back gulping at the air.

With a wild uncertain thrash he rolled over to his side and swung a blind fearful arm at the table beside him. A glass of water hit the marble floor with a clink and scutter. He tried to cry out, but the sound emerged as a hoarse and frightened mew. His eyes locked on to the alarm above. He'd forgotten about that. He'd never really believed in his own frailty. He began to claw vigorously at the sheets jerking and cursing until he hauled his reluctant body upright. With sweat running down his cheeks he tilted backwards and searched the wall again. He spotted it a few inches up and fell back. His hands continued the search, scrabbling sightlessly above him, as his heart pounded in his ears like a tribal drum. His arms were lead weights. They wouldn't last much longer.

His fingers finally touched upon the button and he experienced a relief that bordered on delirium. One more push and help would come. Suddenly, an unseen hand penetrated the curtain and snapped like a handcuff around his wrist.

'I'm afraid that's not going to do you any good,' said a voice he recognised. Giovanni blinked in astonishment and the world was locked shut behind them. He had no more fight left.

\#

The light came flooding back and the room around him took on blurry and then solid edges until it resolved itself into a face peering down at him.

'I thought you'd like to see your final moments. I'm afraid it was necessary to force them open. With a bit of luck they should stay that way,' Francesco said, disappearing from view.

Giovanni tried to track his movements, but his gaze remained resolutely fixed on the canopy above. He heard the clunk of a door shutting and the sound of footsteps tracking back to him. Francesco took a seat gently beside him.

'You must have a hundred questions,' he said, 'but unfortunately time is limited. I hope you'll forgive me if I leave anything out.'

His brother stared upwards. He'd become a ghost in the machine of his body.

'Oh, I'm sorry,' Francesco said, propping his head up with some pillows and angling it so he was looking at him. 'I forgot about that.'

He stopped and listened. Giovanni's lungs had settled into a slow rhythmic wheeze.

'Where should we begin?' He took a deep breath. 'I suppose you're probably wondering how I knew about you and her? The answer is not as complicated as you might think. I'm ashamed to say she was a shared sin.'

He let the revelation hang for a second. His brother was in there, he thought; A raging beast contained in a submerging cage.

'Appalling, yes, but at least I was discrete. You on the other hand...How did you expect to keep it from me? He shrugged. 'Maybe you didn't give a damn, but you should have.'

Giovanni twitched imperceptibly. He was listening.

'The truth is I enjoyed the deception and I took pleasure in knowing the secret you thought you'd hidden away like some dog with a bone. Pathetic as it is I was proud that she preferred me to you. I knew from the start there was no future in it and I'm ashamed to say I led her on. More than that I broke her heart and I abandoned her when she was vulnerable and needed me most. I never understood how badly I had behaved until I came back. That's pretty shocking, isn't it? I guess saying you care is not enough.'

Giovanni's thoughts whirred inside his head? Was there doubt in his brother, he wondered? Was there enough uncertainty for a change of heart?

'You probably won't believe me, but I never intended to use her against you. I was inclined to leave the squalidness of what you and I had done in the past, but when I saw where you were heading the memory of her came back to me like an answered prayer. I was convinced it would be enough to stop you but...I guess I got that wrong. Had I known what you were capable of....' Francesco frowned.

'She knew more than I gave her credit for. It didn't take her long to see what you were. She was frightened of you back then and she was right to fear you.

I don't know how, but Bee saw all of this and she's spent thirty years running from it.'

He looked down at the floor and traced the swirling patterns of marble.

'I persuaded myself the baby couldn't be mine, but I knew our indiscretions overlapped.' He laughed hollowly. 'Does that surprise you?' His features suddenly hardened. He was thinking about the boy who had been killed. That was an evil they would both pay for.

'Look where you've brought us to. You had to know I wouldn't just walk away. This is the ending you made for yourself.'

He paused and stared at him for a moment. 'Did you feel nothing when you tried to kill those boys?' He looked for a flicker of understanding, but his brother remained unmoved.

'I think you would have liked David. He's a smart kid...man. He guessed what I'd done and why you'd come after him. I wouldn't be here now without him.' He smiled sadly. 'Like I said, he's smart. Maybe he'll forgive me one day.'

Giovanni's respiration had grown shallow. Each intake of breath was heavier than the last. His complexion was bone white.

'I suppose you want to know why I'm here...how this happened?'

He reached for something inside his pocket and held it up in front of his brother so that he could see it. Between his thumb and index finger Francesco waggled a gold Zippo lighter.

'A movie camera and recorder reduced to the size of a few postage stamps,' he said in awe. 'You never kept up with the world Giovanni. Things that belonged in the spy comics of our youth are realities now.' He pointed to the bottom of the lighter. 'A lens smaller than a pinhead. It's truly wondrous what technology is capable of today.'

Francesco contemplated the object reverently, still finding it hard to accept it was responsible for the remarkable turnaround in his fortunes. Justice for a few hundred Euros, he thought.

'You wouldn't think an old man like me could operate such a thing. Truthfully, I have David to thank for that,' he said, putting it away. 'Killing his friend was a costly mistake for you.'

Picking up the glass by his feet he poured himself some water from a porcelain pitcher on the table.

'You can imagine what kind of bargaining position this has put me in. Video and audio, its irrefutable...undeniable. They saw it was no use trying to extract it from me. We're in a digital age, Giovanni. Information can be multiplied and transferred across continents in seconds. It can be held anywhere and released in an instant...and there are so many with so much to lose. This recording is more than just one man. It is an unfathomable ripple that begins here and reverberates through everything. It's a flap of a butterfly's wing and a storm that could reshape the world.'

Francesco swallowed noisily. His throat was dry from talking so long.

'My demands were not so unreasonable all things considered. But it left a problem. What were we to do with you? A cardinal or bishop is easily sent away...sacrificed...forgotten.... I'm afraid your victory is also your undoing Giovanni. The Church can no longer allow the law to treat you as it does other men. The importance of your position prohibits it.'

He ran his finger around the rim of the glass nestling between his thighs.

'I looked for a way out, I really did. Things are different today. Dante's scorn of Celestine V...the Western Schism...it belongs to another age. Paternity can be resigned, Giovanni, but only if you will it freely. I'm afraid your refusal to go gently has led us to this impasse. What avenue did you leave us? There are no canonically acceptable procedures for removing a pope that doesn't want to go. It is not as if we can pick up the phone and divulge to the world what you've done.' He inhaled deeply and let out a long continuous breath.

'If this were the old days we might have locked you away, but we live in a shrinking world and every day the space gets a little smaller...I'm afraid this administration favours the more pragmatic solutions of the Borgias when it comes to such matters. And these walls have always been adept at burying their secrets.'

'You're not convinced?' he asked, imagining his brother's objection. 'Surely you haven't forgotten John Paul I? I suppose people don't want to believe such things are possible and it's because of this they are possible.'

Francesco took another sip of water. He was feeling drained. He hadn't planned to say this much.

'Only a spattering of malcontents are ever left to give voice to suspicion, squabbling amongst themselves as though dissent were a hallmark of integrity until the truth is no more discernible than the lie. Nervous freemasons? Shady financial dealings within the Vatican bank? Money laundering? Links to the Mafia? Arms dealers? Credibility lost in a blizzard of speculation. Come tomorrow your time will end and your narrative will be a humble man forced into ill health under the burden of office. It will be accepted because the real one is unthinkable.'

Francesco bent down and placed his ear to Giovanni's chest. It was no longer rising. He could feel the air against his cheek coming in weak irregular puffs. He envisioned his heart slowing with each beat like the unwinding of a clock.

'I think we've digressed,' he said, resisting the impulse toward pity. He pictured himself on the floor of his brother's office. This was the way it had to be.

'You want to know the how, don't you?' he said, pausing as he organised his final words. 'It is in our nature to want and to be afraid. Everyone has a desire they wish to fill... a secret they need to keep. Perhaps you felt a sting or a tap? I'm afraid the toxin has to be administered directly into the blood stream, otherwise a simple cup of tea might have sufficed.' He wagged an accusatory finger at him. 'You should have been more careful.'

Roberto's clumsy elbow when he delivered the papers, Giovanni thought dreamily, slipping further away from the sound of Francesco above him.

'You are experiencing the effects of Curare. Tribes in the Amazon Basin have been using it on the wildlife for millennia. It's a rather potent muscle relaxant, which, I'm sure you appreciate by now, is bad news for the diaphragm and lungs. By the time its worn off...well, you don't need me to spell it out. Fortunately, the stuff doesn't cross the blood brain barrier, which is why you can hear me now. I insisted on being here and having this moment. Do you remember Mrs Kent's promise?'

Was he still in there, Francesco wondered? He thought about the hills of Santa Brigada. How had the two of them sailed a course from there to here?

'You have no right to feel sorry for yourself,' he said, angry at himself for yielding to sentiment. 'This is the pact you made.'

He got up. It was time to leave.

'I'm sorry,' he said patting the bed awkwardly. 'But it's over Giovanni and no-one is coming for you.'

\#

Sister Sodano hesitated outside the main chamber and listened. His Holiness was due to give his blessing in ten minutes, but she could hear no sound of movement or preparation within. With a loud rap of her knuckles the moment of indecision passed and she waited for the familiar noises that preceded her entry. When nothing came she pushed the door open.

The room was dark. He was lying down, she thought. He had looked tired after dinner. But there wasn't much time before the address. She would have to wake him. Crossing reluctantly she parted the curtains with a tentative sweep and saw Giovanni staring lifelessly ahead. She started to scream.

Chapter Thirty-Three
Yellow Brick Road

In a surprising turn of events today Cardinal Francesco Militello, the former Archbishop of Milan and brother of the last pontiff, has become the two hundred and sixty-sixth pope of the Roman Catholic Church. He was elected on the first ballot on the first day of deliberations in one of the quickest conclaves on record. The news was welcomed with cheers of approval from the crowds gathered in the square and is already being hailed as a fitting end to the papacy of his predecessor.

The new pontiff's star has been steadily on the rise since his almost miraculous recovery from an anaphylactic coma earlier this year and many believe it has been bolstered by the widespread sympathy following the death of his brother, Pope Giovanni I. The candidate was a favourite amongst conservative liberals during the run up to the last conclave, but some have viewed the outcome of the election as having little to do with internal politics and more to do with preventing any unseemly parallels to the short reign of John Paul I. The Vatican has adamantly denied such speculation.

Whatever the view, one thing is certain, history is being made today and the coming years may prove to be interesting. I'm Dermot O'Callaghan for...'

Kent pressed the off button on his iPhone. He was in on the biggest inside joke in the world and that made him feel six-foot tall. A short strut later he took up position behind a Chinese couple at the Tarom Romanian Airways check-in desk. Another cheap flight and another stopover in Bucharest. It felt as if the last few months had never happened. Everything was still the same. Terminal two was still as shitty as ever and his mother was still as mad as a dung beetle with an allergy to faeces.

After Trimble had come back into her life she had been reinvigorated. The most recent sign of her reawakening had been a sexual attachment to a trolley gatherer at a moderately sized Tesco on the outskirts of the nearby town of Swindon. Darren Bunn was almost thirty years her junior, but he had assured Kent he would look after her and provide for any of the children their union might result in. He didn't have the heart to point out the unlikelihood of that, despite her assertion that she was contemplating aggressive fertilisation therapy at a dubious European clinic. She was excited about life again and full of affected naivety for the future. She had said to him on numerous occasions since Rome that nothing was impossible anymore. She was a single sensual woman liberated from guilt and free from prison. He didn't rise to the provocation, not much anyway. He simply brushed the spittle from his lips with the back of his sleeve, forced to conclude discretion was the better part of understanding.

For George Kent things would go on as they always had. He would eat and be given to occasional bouts of flatulence, he would drink and become inebriated and he would visit his mother from time to time and dance the eternal dance of mad mother and overweight son.

'Sorry I'm late,' came a breathless voice behind him.

'I thought you had gotten lost,' he replied suspiciously. Trimble grinned uneasily and scratched his neck. Kent could guess pretty well what that meant. He knew David a little better each day. He couldn't blame him for having doubts. If he were travelling with another version of himself he'd probably give it more consideration too.

'We'll you're here now. Shall we go?' Trimble nodded. He decided to give things a shot. Mrs Kent and her son were all he had now. They could never replace what he had, but maybe they'd give him a reason to hang around a bit longer.

The couple in front of them disappeared and the woman at the desk grabbed the passport in his hand and in one fluid movement slammed the checked ticket on the counter, dispatched his rucksack into the crematory like opening behind her and motioned for the next in line to come forward with her head. He stepped aside and let Trimble through.

The woman's harassed features melted into unhurried pleasure. She asked David a lot of questions she had not asked him and then a bunch more that didn't have much to do with baggage or seats.

Kent walked off slowly toward the gate. He was happy he was coming with him. He had a brother now. That beat the daylights out of a dog that crapped under his bed. David would have the women and the fortune, but just maybe the Kenster would get a taste once in a while.

He continued a little longer before he turned around again. When he did he spotted David a few yards away looking at his feet in consternation as busy holidaymakers jostled past him. He didn't trust that look.

'Are you coming?' he said, fearing he already knew the answer.

After a moment that seemed interminable Trimble looked up.

'Yes, I'm coming,' he said.

Kent grinned. The two of them would take China by storm.

The End